Her hands were bloody.

Cathy flinched as he inspected them. Looking down, she saw the bloodied scratches, the flakes of rust embedded in her skin.

"I guess I'm a mess," she murmured.

Victor smiled and stroked her face. "You could use some washing up. Go ahead. I'll get us something to eat."

She retreated into the bathroom. Through the door she could hear the drone of the TV, Victor's voice ordering a pizza over the phone. She ran hot water over her cold, numb hands. In the mirror over the sink she caught an unflattering glimpse of herself, her hair a tangled mess, her chin smudged with dirt. Glancing down, she noticed Victor's razor on the counter. The sight of that blade cast her situation into a new focus—a frightening one. She picked up the razor, thinking how lethal that blade looked, how vulnerable she would be tonight....

TESS GERRITSEN

WHISTLEBLOWER

MIRA®

ISBN 1-55166-468-2

WHISTLEBLOWER

Copyright © 1992 by Terry Gerritsen.

Printed in U.S.A.

To Fien and Frans

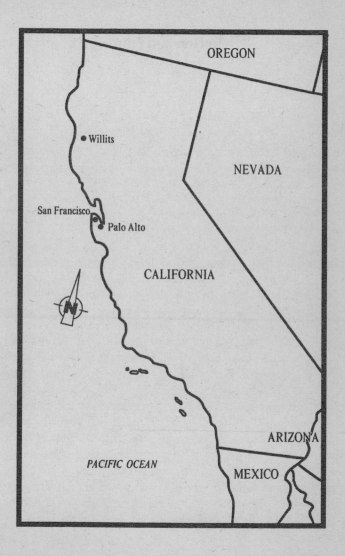

Prologue

Branches whipped his face, and his heart was pounding so hard he thought his chest would explode, but he couldn't stop running. Already, he could hear the man gaining on him, could almost imagine the bullet slicing through the night and slamming into his back. Maybe it already had. Maybe he was trailing a river of blood; he was too numb with terror to feel anything now, except the desperate hunger to live. The rain was pouring down his face, icy, blinding sheets of it, rattling on the dead leaves of winter. He stumbled through a pool of darkness and found himself sprawled flat on his belly in the mud. The sound of his fall was deafening. His pursuer, alerted by the sharp crack of branches, altered course and was now headed straight for him. The thud of a silencer, the zing of a bullet past his cheek, told him he'd been spotted. He forced himself to his feet and made a sharp right, zigzagging back toward the highway. Here in the woods, he was a dead man. But if he could flag down a car, if he could draw someone's attention, he might have a chance.

A crash of branches, a coarse oath, told him his pursuer had stumbled. He'd gained a few precious seconds. He kept running, moving only by an instinctive sense of direction. There was no light to guide his way, nothing except the dim glow of the clouds in the night sky. The road had to be just ahead. Any second now, his feet would hit pavement.

And then what? What if there's no car to flag down, no one to help me?

Then, through the trees ahead, he saw a faint flickering, two watery beams of light.

With a desperate burst of speed, he sprinted toward the car. His lungs were on fire, his eyes blinded by the lash of branches and rain. Another bullet whipped past him and thudded into a tree trunk, but the gunman behind him had suddenly lost all importance. All that mattered was those lights, beckoning him through the darkness, taunting him with the promise of salvation.

When his feet suddenly hit the pavement, he was shocked. The lights were still ahead, bobbing somewhere beyond the trees. Had he missed the car? Was it already moving away, around a curve? No, there it was, brighter now. It was coming this way. He ran to meet it, following the bend of the road and knowing all the time that here in the open, he was an easy target. The sound of his shoes slapping the wet road filled his ears. The lights twisted toward him. At that instant, he heard the gun fire a third time. The force of the impact made him stumble to his knees, and he was vaguely aware of the bullet tearing through his shoulder, of the warmth of his own blood dribbling down his arm, but he was oblivious to pain. He could focus only on staying alive. He struggled back to his feet, took a stumbling step forward...

And was blinded by the onrush of headlights. There was no time to throw himself out of the way, no time even to register panic. Tires screamed across the pavement, throwing up a spray of water.

He didn't feel the impact. All he knew was that he was suddenly lying on the ground and the rain was pouring into his mouth and he was very, very cold.

And that he had something to do, something important. Feebly, he reached into the pocket of his windbreaker, and his fingers curled around the small plastic cylinder. He couldn't quite remember why it mattered so much, but it was still there and he was relieved. He clutched it tightly in his palm.

Someone was calling to him. A woman. He couldn't see her face through the rain, but he could hear her voice, hoarse with panic, floating through the buzz in his head. He tried to speak, tried to warn her that they had to get away, that death was waiting in the woods. But all that came out was a groan.

1

Three miles out of Redwood Valley, a tree had fallen across the road, and with the heavy rains and backed-up cars, it took Catherine Weaver nearly three hours to get past the town of Willits. By then it was already ten o'clock and she knew she wouldn't reach Garberville till midnight. She hoped Sarah wouldn't sit up all night waiting for her. But knowing Sarah, there'd be a supper still warm in the oven and a fire blazing in the hearth. She wondered how pregnancy suited her friend. Wonderfully, of course. Sarah had talked about this baby for years, had chosen its name— Sam or Emma—long before it was conceived. The fact she no longer had a husband was a minor point. "You can only wait around so long for the right father," Sarah had said. "Then you have to take matters into your own hands."

And she had. With her biological clock furiously ticking its last years away, Sarah had driven down to visit Cathy in San Francisco and had calmly selected a fertility clinic from the yellow pages. A liberal-minded one, of course. One that would understand the desperate longings of a thirty-nine-year-old single woman. The insemination itself had been a coolly clinical affair, she'd said later. Hop on the table, slip your feet into the stirrups, and five minutes later, you were pregnant. Well, almost. But it was a simple procedure, the donors were certifiably healthy, and best of all, a woman could fulfill her maternal instincts without all that foolishness about marriage.

Yes, the old marriage game. They'd both suffered

through it. And after their divorces, they'd both carried on, albeit with battle scars.

Brave Sarah, thought Cathy. *At least she has the courage to go through with this on her own.*

The old anger washed through her, still potent enough to make her mouth tighten. She could forgive her ex-husband Jack for a lot of things. For his selfishness. His demands. His infidelity. But she could never forgive him for denying her the chance to have a child. Oh, she could have gone against his wishes and had a baby anyway, but she'd wanted him to want one as well. So she'd waited for the time to be right. But during their ten years of marriage, he'd never been "ready," never felt it was the "right time."

What he should have told her was the truth: that he was too self-centered to be bothered with a baby.

I'm thirty-seven years old, she thought. *I no longer have a husband. I don't even have a steady boyfriend. But I could be content, if only I could hold my own child in my arms.*

At least Sarah would soon be blessed.

Four months to go and then the baby was due. Sarah's baby. Cathy had to smile at that thought, despite the rain now pouring over her windshield. It was coming down harder now; even with the wipers thrashing at full speed, she could barely make out the road. She glanced at her watch and saw it was already eleven-thirty; there were no other cars in sight. If she had engine trouble out here, she'd probably have to spend the night huddled in the backseat, waiting for help to arrive.

Peering ahead, she tried to make out the road's dividing line and saw nothing but a solid wall of rain. This was ridiculous. She really should have stopped at that motel in Willits, but she hated the thought of being only fifty miles from her goal, especially when she'd already driven so far.

She spotted a sign ahead: Garberville, 10 Miles. So she was closer than she'd thought. Twenty-five miles more, then there'd be a turnoff and a five-mile drive through dense woods to Sarah's cedar house. The thought of being so close fueled her impatience. She fed the old Datsun some gas and sped up to forty-five miles an hour. It was a reckless thing to do, especially in these conditions, but the thought of a warm house and hot chocolate was just too tempting.

The road curved unexpectedly; startled, she jerked the wheel to the right and the car slid sideways, tobogganing wildly across the rain-slicked pavement. She knew enough not to slam on the brakes. Instead, she clutched the wheel, fighting to regain control. The tires skidded a few feet, a heart-stopping ride that took her to the very edge of the road. Just as she thought she'd clip the trees, the tires gripped the pavement. The car was still moving twenty miles an hour, but at least it was headed in a straight line. With clammy hands, she managed to negotiate the rest of the curve.

What happened next caught her completely by surprise. One instant she was congratulating herself for averting disaster, the next, she was staring ahead in disbelief.

The man had appeared out of nowhere. He was crouched in the road, captured like a wild animal in the glare of her headlights. Reflexes took over. She slammed on the brakes, but it was already too late. The screech of her tires was punctuated by the thud of the man's body against the hood of her car.

For what seemed like eternity, she sat frozen and unable to do anything but clutch the steering wheel and stare at the windshield wipers skating back and forth. Then, as the reality of what she'd just done sank in, she shoved the door open and dashed out into the rain.

At first she could see nothing through the downpour,

only a glistening strip of blacktop lit by the dim glow of her taillights. *Where is he?* she thought frantically. With water streaming past her eyes, she traced the road backward, struggling to see in the darkness. Then, through the pounding rain, she heard a low moan. It came from somewhere off to the side, near the trees.

Shifting direction, she plunged into the shadows and sank ankle-deep in mud and pine needles. Again she heard the moan, closer now, almost within reach.

"Where are you?" she screamed. "Help me find you!"

"Here..." The answer was so weak she barely heard it, but it was all she needed. Turning, she took a few steps and practically stumbled over his crumpled body in the darkness. At first, he seemed to be only a confusing jumble of soaked clothes, then she managed to locate his hand and feel for his pulse. It was fast but steady, probably steadier than her own pulse, which was skipping wildly. His fingers suddenly closed over hers in a desperate grip. He rolled against her and struggled to sit up.

"Please! Don't move!" she said.

"Can't—can't stay here—"

"Where are you hurt?"

"No time. Help me. Hurry—"

"Not till you tell me where you're hurt!"

He reached out and grabbed her shoulder in a clumsy attempt to rise to his feet. To her amazement, he managed to pull himself halfway up. For an instant they wobbled against each other, then his strength seemed to collapse and they both slid to their knees in the mud. His breathing had turned harsh and irregular and she wondered about his injuries. If he was bleeding internally he could die within minutes. She had to get him to a hospital now, even if it meant dragging him back to the car.

"Okay. Let's try again," she said, grabbing his left arm and draping it around her neck. She was startled by his gasp of agony. Immediately she released him. His arm left a sticky trail of warmth around her neck. *Blood.*

"My other side's okay," he grunted. "Try again."

She shifted to his right side and pulled his arm over her neck. If she weren't so frantic, it would have struck her as a comical scene, the two of them struggling like drunkards to stand up. When at last he was on his feet and they stood swaying together in the mud, she wondered if he even had the strength to put one foot in front of the other. She certainly couldn't move them both. Though he was slender, he was also a great deal taller than she'd expected, and much more than her five-foot-five frame could support.

But something seemed to compel him forward, a kindling of some hidden reserves. Even through their soaked clothes, she could feel the heat of his body and could sense the urgency driving him onward. A dozen questions formed in her head, but she was breathing too hard to voice them. Her every effort had to be concentrated on getting him to the car, and then to a hospital.

Gripping him around the waist, she latched her fingers through his belt. Painfully they made their way to the road, struggling step by step. His arm felt taut as wire over her neck. It seemed everything about him was wound up tight. There was something desperate about the way his muscles strained to move forward. His urgency penetrated right through to her skin. It was a panic as palpable as the warmth of his body, and she was suddenly infected with his need to flee, a need made more desperate by the fact they could move no faster than they already were. Every few feet she had to stop and shove back her dripping hair just to see where she was going. And all around them, the rain and darkness closed off all view of whatever danger pursued.

The taillights of her car glowed ahead like ruby eyes winking in the night. With every step the man grew heavier and her legs felt so rubbery she thought they'd both topple in the road. If they did, she wouldn't have the strength to haul him back up again. Already, his head was sagging against her cheek and water trickled from his rain-matted hair down her neck. The simple act of putting one foot in front of the other was so automatic that she never even considered dropping him on the road and backing the car to him instead. And the taillights were already so close, just beyond the next veil of rain.

By the time she'd guided him to the passenger side, her arm felt ready to fall off. With the man on the verge of sliding from her grasp, she barely managed to wrench the door open. She had no strength left to be gentle; she simply shoved him inside.

He flopped onto the front seat with his legs still hanging out. She bent down, grabbed his ankles, and heaved them one by one into the car, noting with a sense of detachment that no man with feet this big could possibly be graceful.

As she slid into the driver's seat, he made a feeble attempt to raise his head, then let it sink back again. "Hurry," he whispered.

At the first turn of the key in the ignition, the engine sputtered and died. Dear God, she pleaded. Start. *Start!* She switched the key off, counted slowly to three, and tried again. This time the engine caught. Almost shouting with relief, she jammed it into gear and made a tire-screeching takeoff toward Garberville. Even a town that small must have a hospital or, at the very least, an emergency clinic. The question was: could she find it in this downpour? And what if she was wrong? What if the nearest medical help was in Willits, the other direction? She might be wasting precious minutes on the road while the man bled to death.

Suddenly panicked by that thought, she glanced at her passenger. By the glow of the dashboard, she saw that his head was still flopped back against the seat. He wasn't moving.

"Hey! Are you all right?" she cried.

The answer came back in a whisper. "I'm still here."

"Dear God. For a minute I thought..." She looked back at the road, her heart pounding. "There's got to be a clinic somewhere—"

"Near Garberville—there's a hospital—"

"Do you know how to find it?"

"I drove past it—fifteen miles..."

If he drove here, where's his car? she thought. "What happened?" she asked. "Did you have an accident?"

He started to speak but his answer was cut off by a sudden flicker of light. Struggling to sit up, he turned and stared at the headlights of another car far behind them. His whispered oath made her look sideways in alarm.

"What is it?"

"That car."

She glanced in the rearview mirror. "What about it?"

"How long's it been following us?"

"I don't know. A few miles. Why?"

The effort of keeping his head up suddenly seemed too much for him, and he let it sink back down with a groan. "Can't think," he whispered. "Christ, I can't think..."

He's lost too much blood, she thought. In a panic, she shoved hard on the gas pedal. The car seemed to leap through the rain, the steering wheel vibrating wildly as sheets of spray flew up from the tires. Darkness flew at dizzying speed against their windshield. *Slow down, slow down! Or I'll get us both killed.*

Easing back on the gas, she let the speedometer fall to a more manageable forty-five miles per hour. The man was struggling to sit up again.

"Please, keep your head down!" she pleaded.

"That car—"

"It's not there anymore."

"Are you sure?"

She looked at the rearview mirror. Through the rain, she saw only a faint twinkling of light, but nothing as definite as headlights. "I'm sure," she lied and was relieved to see him slowly settle back again. *How much farther?* she thought. *Five miles? Ten?* And then the next thought forced its way into her mind: *He might die before we get there.*

His silence terrified her. She needed to hear his voice, needed to be reassured that he hadn't slipped into oblivion. "Talk to me," she urged. "Please."

"I'm tired...."

"Don't stop. Keep talking. What—what's your name?"

The answer was a mere whisper: "Victor."

"Victor. That's a great name. I like that name. What do you do, Victor?"

His silence told her he was too weak to carry on any conversation. She couldn't let him lose consciousness! For some reason it suddenly seemed crucial to keep him awake, to keep him in touch with a living voice. If that fragile connection was broken, she feared he might slip away entirely.

"All right," she said, forcing her voice to remain low and steady. "Then *I'll* talk. You don't have to say a thing. Just listen. Keep listening. My name is Catherine. Cathy Weaver. I live in San Francisco, the Richmond district. Do you know the city?" There was no answer, but she sensed some movement in his head, a silent acknowledgement of her words. "Okay," she went on, mindlessly filling the silence. "Maybe you don't know the city. It really doesn't matter. I work with an independent film company. Actually, it's Jack's company. My ex-husband. We make horror films. Grade B, really, but they turn a profit. Our last one was *Reptilian*. I did the special-effects makeup. Really gruesome stuff. Lots of green scales and slime..." She laughed—it was a strange, panicked sound. It had an un-mistakable note of hysteria.

She had to fight to regain control.

A wink of light made her glance up sharply at the rear-view mirror. A pair of headlights was barely discernible through the rain. For a few seconds she watched them, de-bating whether to say anything to Victor. Then, like phan-toms, the lights flickered off and vanished.

"Victor?" she called softly. He responded with an un-intelligible grunt, but it was all she needed to be reassured that he was still alive. That he was listening. *I've got to keep him awake,* she thought, her mind scrambling for some new topic of conversation. She'd never been good at the glib sort of chitchat so highly valued at filmmakers' cock-tail parties. What she needed was a joke, however stupid, as long as it was vaguely funny. *Laughter heals.* Hadn't she read it somewhere? That a steady barrage of comedy could shrink tumors? *Oh sure,* she chided herself. *Just make him laugh and the bleeding will miraculously stop....*

But she couldn't think of a joke, anyway, not a single damn one. So she returned to the topic that had first come to mind: her work.

"Our next project's slated for January. *Ghouls.* We'll be filming in Mexico, which I hate, because the damn heat always melts the makeup...."

She looked at Victor but saw no response, not even a flicker of movement. Terrified that she was losing him, she reached out to feel for his pulse and discovered that his hand was buried deep in the pocket of his windbreaker. She tried to tug it free, and to her amazement he reacted to her invasion with immediate and savage resistance. Lurching awake, he blindly lashed at her, trying to force her away.

"Victor, it's all right!" she cried, fighting to steer the car and protect herself at the same time. "It's all right! It's me, Cathy. I'm only trying to help!"

At the sound of her voice, his struggles weakened. As the tension eased from his body, she felt his head settle slowly against her shoulder. "Cathy," he whispered. It was a sound of wonder, of relief. "Cathy..."

"That's right. It's only me." Gently, she reached up and brushed back the tendrils of his wet hair. She wondered what color it was, a concern that struck her as totally irrelevant but nonetheless compelling. He reached for her hand. His fingers closed around hers in a grip that was surprisingly strong and steadying. *I'm still here,* it said. *I'm warm and alive and breathing.* He pressed her palm to his lips. So tender was the gesture, she was startled by the roughness of his unshaven jaw against her skin. It was a caress between strangers, and it left her shaken and trembling.

She returned her grip to the steering wheel and shifted her full attention back to the road. He had fallen silent again, but she couldn't ignore the weight of his head on her shoulder or the heat of his breath in her hair.

The torrent eased to a slow but steady rain, and she coaxed the car to fifty. The Sunnyside Up cafe whipped past, a drab little box beneath a single streetlight, and she caught a glimpse of Victor's face in the brief glow of light. She saw him only in profile: a high forehead, sharp nose, a jutting chin, and then the light was gone and he was only a shadow breathing softly against her. But she'd seen enough to know she'd never forget that face. Even as she peered through the darkness, his profile floated before her like an image burned into her memory.

"We have to be getting close," she said, as much to reassure herself as him. "Where a cafe appears, a town is sure to follow." There was no response. "Victor?" Still no response. Swallowing her panic, she sped up to fifty-five.

Though they'd passed the Sunnyside Up over a mile ago,

she could still make out the streetlight winking on and off
in her mirror. It took her a few seconds to realize it wasn't
just one light she was watching but two, and that they were
moving—a pair of headlights, winding along the highway.
Was it the same car she'd spotted earlier?

Mesmerized, she watched the lights dance like twin
wraiths among the trees, then, suddenly, they vanished and
she saw only darkness. A ghost? she wondered irrationally.
Any instant she expected the lights to rematerialize, to re-
sume their phantom twinkling in the woods. She was
watching the mirror so intently that she almost missed the
road sign:

Garberville, Pop, 5,750
Gas—Food—Lodging

A half mile later streetlights appeared, glowing a hazy
yellow in the drizzle; a flatbed truck splashed by, headed
in the other direction. Though the speed limit had dropped
to thirty-five, she kept her foot firmly on the gas pedal and
for once in her life prayed for a police car to give chase.

The *Hospital* road sign seemed to leap out at her from
nowhere. She braked and swerved onto the turnoff. A quar-
ter mile away, a red *Emergency* sign directed her up a
driveway to a side entrance. Leaving Victor in the front
seat, she ran inside, through a deserted waiting room, and
cried to a nurse sitting at her desk: "Please, help me! I've
got a man in my car...."

The nurse responded instantly. She followed Cathy outside, took one look at the man slumped in the front seat,
and yelled for assistance.

Even with the help of a burly ER physician, they had
difficulty pulling Victor out of the car. He had slid sideways, and his arm was wedged under the emergency hand
brake.

"Hey, Miss!" the doctor barked at Cathy. "Climb in the other side and free up his arm!"

Cathy scrambled to the driver's seat. There she hesitated. She would have to manipulate his injured arm. She took his elbow and tried to unhook it from around the brake, but discovered his wristwatch was snagged in the pocket of his windbreaker. After unsnapping the watchband, she took hold of his arm and lifted it over the brake. He responded with a groan of pure agony. The arm slid limply toward the floor.

"Okay!" said the doctor. "Arm's free! Now, just ease him toward me and we'll take it from there."

Gingerly, she guided Victor's head and shoulders safely past the emergency brake. Then she scrambled back outside to help load him onto the wheeled stretcher. Three straps were buckled into place. Everything became a blur of noise and motion as the stretcher was wheeled through the open double doors into the building.

"What happened?" the doctor barked over his shoulder at Cathy.

"I hit him—on the road—"

"When?"

"Fifteen—twenty minutes ago."

"How fast were you driving?"

"About thirty-five."

"Was he conscious when you found him?"

"For about ten minutes—then he sort of faded—"

A nurse said: "Shirt's soaked with blood. He's got broken glass in his shoulder."

In that mad dash beneath harsh fluorescent lights, Cathy had her first clear look at Victor, and she saw a lean, mud-streaked face, a jaw tightly squared in pain, a broad forehead matted damply with light brown hair. He reached out to her, grasping for her hand.

"Cathy—"

"I'm here, Victor."

He held on tightly, refusing to break contact. The pressure of his fingers in her flesh was almost painful. Squinting through the pain, he focused on her face. "I have to—have to tell you—"

"Later!" snapped the doctor.

"No, wait!" Victor was fighting to keep her in view, to hold her beside him. He struggled to speak, agony etching lines on his face.

Cathy bent close, drawn by the desperation of his gaze. "Yes, Victor," she whispered, stroking his hair, longing to ease his pain. This link between their hands, their gazes, felt forged in timeless steel. "Tell me."

"We can't delay!" barked the doctor. "Get him in the room."

All at once, Victor's hand was wrenched away from her as they whisked him into the trauma suite, a nightmarish room of stainless steel and blindingly bright lights. He was lifted onto the surgical table.

"Pulse 110," said a nurse. "Blood pressure eight-five over fifty!"

The doctor ordered, "Let's get two IVs in. Type and cross six units of blood. And get hold of a surgeon. We're going to need help...."

The machine-gun fire of voices, the metallic clang of cabinets and IV poles and instruments was deafening. No one seemed to notice Cathy standing in the doorway, watching in horrified fascination as a nurse pulled out a knife and began to tear off Victor's bloody clothing. With each rip, more and more flesh was exposed, until the shirt and windbreaker were shredded off, revealing a broad chest thickly matted with tawny hair. To the doctors and nurses, this was just another body to labor over, another patient to be saved. To Cathy, this was a living, breathing man, a man she cared about, if only because they had shared those last harrowing moments. The nurse shifted her attention to his belt, which she quickly unbuckled. With a few firm tugs, she peeled off his trousers and shorts and threw them into a pile with the other soiled clothing. Cathy scarcely noticed the man's nakedness, or the nurses and technicians shoving past her into the room. Her shocked gaze had focused on Victor's left shoulder, which was oozing fresh blood onto the table. She remembered how his whole body had resonated with pain when she'd grabbed that shoulder; only now did she understand how much he must have suffered.

A sour taste flooded her throat. She was going to be sick.

Struggling against the nausea, she somehow managed to stumble away and sink into a nearby chair. There she sat for a few minutes, oblivious to the chaos whirling around her. Looking down, she noted with instinctive horror the blood on her hands.

"There you are," someone said. A nurse had just emerged from the trauma room, carrying a bundle of the patient's belongings. She motioned Cathy over to a desk. "We'll need your name and address in case the doctors have any more questions. And the police will have to be notified. Have you called them?"

Cathy shook her head numbly. "I—I guess I should..."

"You can use this phone."

"Thank you."

It rang eight times before anyone answered. The voice that greeted her was raspy with sleep. Obviously, Garberville provided little late-night stimulation, even for the local police. The desk officer took down Cathy's report and told her he'd be in touch with her later, after they'd checked the accident scene.

The nurse had opened Victor's wallet and was flipping through the various ID cards for information. Cathy watched her fill in the blanks on a patient admission form: *Name: Victor Holland. Age: 41. Occupation: Biochemist. Next of kin: Unknown.*

So that was his full name. Victor Holland. Cathy stared down at the stack of ID cards and focused on what appeared to be a security pass for some company called Viratek. A color photograph showed Victor's quietly sober face, its green eyes gazing straight into the camera. Even if she had never seen his face, this was exactly how she would have pictured him, his expression unyielding, his gaze unflinchingly direct. She touched her palm, where he had kissed her. She could still recall how his beard had stung her flesh.

Softly, she asked, "Is he going to be all right?"

The nurse continued writing. "He's lost a lot of blood. But he looks like a pretty tough guy...."

Cathy nodded, remembering how, even in his agony, Victor had somehow dredged up the strength to keep moving through the rain. Yes, she knew just how tough a man he was.

The nurse handed her a pen and the information sheet. "If you could write your name and address at the bottom. In case the doctor has any more questions."

Cathy fished out Sarah's address and phone number from her purse and copied them onto the form. "My name's Cathy Weaver. You can get hold of me at this number."

"You're staying in Garberville?"

"For three weeks. I'm just visiting."

"Oh. Terrific way to start a vacation, huh?"

Cathy sighed as she rose to leave. "Yeah. Terrific."

She paused outside the trauma room, wondering what was happening inside, knowing that Victor was fighting for his life. She wondered if he was still conscious, if he would remember her. It seemed important that he *did* remember her.

Cathy turned to the nurse. "You will call me, won't you? I mean, you'll let me know if he..."

The nurse nodded. "We'll keep you informed."

Outside, the rain had finally stopped and a belt of stars twinkled through a parting in the clouds. To Cathy's weary eyes, it was an exhilarating sight, that first glimpse of the storm's end. As she drove out of the hospital parking lot, she was shaking from fatigue. She never noticed the car parked across the street or the brief glow of the cigarette before it was snuffed out.

2

Barely a minute after Cathy left the hospital, a man walked into the emergency room, sweeping the smells of a stormy night in with him through the double doors. The nurse on duty was busy with the new patient's admission papers. At the sudden rush of cold air, she looked up to see a man approach her desk. He was about thirty-five, gaunt-faced, silent, his dark hair lightly feathered by gray. Droplets of water sparkled on his tan Burberry raincoat.

"Can I help you, sir?" she asked, focusing on his eyes, which were as black and polished as pebbles in a pond.

Nodding, he said quietly, "Was there a man brought in a short time ago? Victor Holland?"

The nurse glanced down at the papers on her desk. That was the name. Victor Holland. "Yes," she said. "Are you a relative?"

"I'm his brother. How is he?"

"He just arrived, sir. They're working on him now. If you'll wait, I can check on how he's doing—" She stopped to answer the ringing telephone. It was a technician calling with the new patient's laboratory results. As she jotted down the numbers, she noticed out of the corner of her eye that the man had turned and was gazing at the closed door to the trauma room. It suddenly swung open as an orderly emerged carrying a bulging plastic bag streaked with blood. The clamor of voices spilled from the room:

"Pressure up to 110 over 70!"

"OR says they're ready to go."

"Where's that surgeon?"

"On his way. He had car trouble."

"Ready for X rays! Everyone back!"

Slowly the door closed, muffling the voices. The nurse hung up just as the orderly deposited the plastic bag on her desk. "What's this?" she asked.

"Patient's clothes. They're a mess. Should I just toss 'em?"

"I'll take them home," the man in the raincoat cut in. "Is everything here?"

The orderly flashed the nurse an uncomfortable glance. "I'm not sure he'd want to…I mean, they're kind of…uh, dirty.…"

The nurse said quickly, "Mr. Holland, why don't you let us dispose of the clothes for you? There's nothing worth keeping in there. I've already collected his valuables." She unlocked a drawer and pulled out a sealed manila envelope labeled: Holland, Victor. Contents: Wallet, Wristwatch. "You can take these home. Just sign this receipt."

The man nodded and signed his name: David Holland. "Tell me," he said, sliding the envelope in his pocket. "Is Victor awake? Has he said anything?"

"I'm afraid not. He was semiconscious when he arrived."

The man took this information in silence, a silence that the nurse found suddenly and profoundly disturbing. "Excuse me, Mr. Holland?" she asked. "How did you hear your brother was hurt? I didn't get a chance to contact any relatives.…"

"The police called me. Victor was driving my car. They found it smashed up at the side of the road."

"Oh. What an awful way to be notified."

"Yes. The stuff of nightmares."

"At least someone was able to get in touch with you." She sifted through the sheaf of papers on her desk. "Can we get your address and phone number? In case we need to reach you?''

"Of course." The man took the ER papers, which he quickly scanned before scrawling his name and phone number on the blank marked Next of Kin. "Who's this Catherine Weaver?" he asked, pointing to the name and address at the bottom of the page.

"She's the woman who brought him in."

"I'll have to thank her." He handed back the papers. "Nurse?"

She looked around and saw that the doctor was calling to her from the trauma room doorway. "Yes?"

"I want you to call the police. Tell them to get in here as soon as possible."

"They've been called, Doctor. They know about the accident—"

"Call them again. This is no accident."

"What?"

"We just got the X rays. The man's got a bullet in his shoulder."

"A *bullet?*" A chill went through the nurse's body, like a cold wind sweeping in from the night. Slowly, she turned toward the man in the raincoat, the man who'd claimed to be Victor Holland's brother. To her amazement, no one was there. She felt only a cold puff of night air, and then she saw the double doors quietly slide shut.

"Where the hell did he go?" the orderly whispered.

For a few seconds she could only stare at the closed doors. Then her gaze dropped and she focused on the empty spot on her desk. The bag containing Victor Holland's clothes had vanished.

"Why did the police call again?"

Cathy slowly replaced the telephone receiver. Even though she was bundled in a warm terry-cloth robe, she was shivering. She turned and stared across the kitchen at Sarah. "That man on the road—they found a bullet in his shoulder."

In the midst of pouring tea, Sarah glanced up in surprise. "You mean—someone *shot* him?"

Cathy sank down at the kitchen table and gazed numbly at the cup of cinnamon tea that Sarah had just slid in front of her. A hot bath and a soothing hour of sitting by the fireplace had made the night's events seem like nothing more than a bad dream. Here in Sarah's kitchen, with its chintz curtains and its cinnamon and spice smells, the violence of the real world seemed a million miles away.

Sarah leaned toward her. "Do they know what happened? Has he said anything?"

"He just got out of surgery." She turned and glanced at the telephone. "I should call the hospital again—"

"No. You shouldn't. You've done everything you possibly can." Sarah gently touched her arm. "And your tea's getting cold."

With a shaking hand, Cathy brushed back a strand of damp hair and settled uneasily in her chair. A bullet in his shoulder, she thought. Why? Had it been a random attack, a highway gunslinger blasting out the car window at a total stranger? She'd read about it in the newspapers, the stories of freeway arguments settled by the pulling of a trigger.

Or had it been a deliberate attack? Had Victor Holland been targeted for death?

Outside, something rattled and clanged against the house. Cathy sat up sharply. "What was that?"

"Believe me, it's not the bogeyman," said Sarah, laughing. She went to the kitchen door and reached for the bolt.

"Sarah!" Cathy called in panic as the bold slid open. "Wait!"

"Take a look for yourself." Sarah opened the door. The kitchen light swung across a cluster of trash cans sitting in the carport. A shadow slid to the ground and scurried away, trailing food wrappers across the driveway. "Raccoons," said Sarah. "If I don't tie the lids down, those pests'll scatter trash all over the yard." Another shadow popped its head out of a can and stared at her, its eyes glowing in the darkness. Sarah clapped her hands and yelled, "Go on, get lost!" The raccoon didn't budge. "Don't you have a home to go to?" At last, the raccoon dropped to the ground and ambled off into the trees. "They get bolder every year," Sarah sighed, closing the door. She turned and winked at Cathy. "So take it easy. This isn't the big city."

"Keep reminding me." Cathy took a slice of banana bread and began to spread it with sweet butter. "You know, Sarah, I think it'll be a lot nicer spending Christmas with you than it ever was with old Jack."

"Uh-oh. Since we're now speaking of ex-husbands—" Sarah shuffled over to a cabinet "—we might as well get in the right frame of mind. And tea just won't cut it." She grinned and waved a bottle of brandy.

"Sarah, you're not drinking alcohol, are you?"

"It's not for *me*." Sarah set the bottle and a single wine glass in front of Cathy. "But I think *you* could use a nip. After all, it's been a cold, traumatic night. And here we are, talking about turkeys of the male variety."

"Well, since you put it that way…" Cathy poured out a generous shot of brandy. "To the turkeys of the world," she declared and took a sip. It felt just right going down.

"So how *is* old Jack?" asked Sarah.

"Same as always."

"Blondes?"

"He's moved on to brunettes."

"It took him only a year to go through the world's supply of blondes?"

Cathy shrugged. "He might have missed a few."

They both laughed then, light and easy laughter that told

them their wounds were well on the way to healing, that men were now creatures to be discussed without pain, without sorrow.

Cathy regarded her glass of brandy. "Do you suppose there *are* any good men left in the world? I mean, shouldn't there be *one* floating around somewhere? Maybe a mutation or something? One measly decent guy?"

"Sure. Somewhere in Siberia. But he's a hundred-and-twenty years old."

"I've always liked older men."

They laughed again, but this time the sound wasn't as lighthearted. So many years had passed since their college days together, the days when they had *known*, had never doubted, that Prince Charmings abounded in the world.

Cathy drained her glass of brandy and set it down. "What a lousy friend I am. Keeping a pregnant lady up all night! What time is it, anyway?"

"Only two-thirty in the morning."

"Oh, Sarah! Go to bed!" Cathy went to the sink and began wetting a handful of paper towels.

"And what are you going to do?" Sarah asked.

"I just want to clean up the car. I didn't get all the blood off the seat."

"I already did it."

"What? When?"

"While you were taking a bath."

"Sarah, you idiot."

"Hey, I didn't have a miscarriage or anything. Oh, I almost forgot." Sarah pointed to a tiny film canister on the counter. "I found that on the floor of your car."

Cathy shook her head and sighed. "It's Hickey's."

"Hickey! Now *there's* a waste of a man."

'He's also a good friend of mine."

"That's all Hickey will ever be to a woman. A *friend*. So what's on the roll of film? Naked women, as usual?"

"I don't even want to know. When I dropped him off at the airport, he handed me a half-dozen rolls and told me he'd pick them up when he got back. Guess he didn't want to lug 'em all the way to Nairobi."

"Is that where he went? Nairobi?"

"He's shooting 'gorgeous ladies of Africa' or something." Cathy slipped the film canister into her bathrobe pocket. "This must've dropped out of the glove compartment. Gee. I hope it's not pornographic."

"Knowing Hickey, it probably is."

They both laughed at the irony of it all. Hickman Von Trapp, whose only job it was to photograph naked females in erotic poses, had absolutely no interest in the opposite sex, with the possible exception of his mother.

"A guy like Hickey only goes to prove my point," Sarah said over her shoulder as she headed up the hall to bed.

"What point is that?"

"There really *are* no good men left in the world!"

It was the light that dragged Victor up from the depths of unconsciousness, a light brighter than a dozen suns, beating against his closed eyelids. He didn't want to wake up; he knew, in some dim, scarcely functioning part of his brain, that if he continued to struggle against this blessed oblivion he would feel pain and nausea and something else, something much, much worse: terror. Of what, he couldn't remember. Of death? No, no, this was death, or as close as one could come to it, and it was warm and black and comfortable. But he had something important to do, something that he couldn't allow himself to forget. He tried to think, but all he could remember was a hand, gentle but somehow strong, brushing his forehead, and a voice, reaching to him softly in the darkness.

My name is Catherine....

As her touch, her voice, flooded his memory, so too did

the fear. Not for himself (he was dead, wasn't he?) but for her. Strong, gentle Catherine. He'd seen her face only briefly, could scarcely remember it, but somehow he knew she was beautiful, the way a blind man knows, without benefit of vision, that a rainbow or the sky or his own dear child's face is beautiful. And now he was afraid for her.

Where are you? he wanted to cry out.

"He's coming around," said a female voice (not Catherine's, it was too hard, too crisp) followed by a confusing rush of other voices.

"Watch that IV!"

"Mr. Holland, hold still. Everything's going to be all right—"

"I said, watch the IV!"

"Hand me that second unit of blood—"

"Don't move, Mr. Holland—"

Where are you, Catherine? The shout exploded in his head. Fighting the temptation to sink back into unconsciousness, he struggled to lift his eyelids. At first, there was only a blur of light and color, so harsh he felt it stab through his sockets straight to his brain. Gradually the blur took the shape of faces, strangers in blue, frowning down at him. He tried to focus but the effort made his stomach rebel.

"Mr. Holland, take it easy," said a quietly gruff voice. "You're in the hospital—the recovery room. They've just operated on your shoulder. You just rest and go back to sleep...."

No. No, I can't, he tried to say.

"Five milligrams of morphine going in," someone said, and Victor felt a warm flush creep up his arm and spread across his chest.

"That should help," he heard. "Now, sleep. Everything went just fine...."

You don't understand, he wanted to scream. *I have to*

warn her—It was the last conscious thought he had before the lights once again were swallowed by the gentle darkness.

Alone in her husbandless bed, Sarah lay smiling. No, laughing! Her whole body seemed filled with laughter tonight. She wanted to sing, to dance. To stand at the open window and shout out her joy! It was all hormonal, she'd been told, this chemical pandemonium of pregnancy, dragging her body on a roller coaster of emotions. She knew she should rest, she should work toward serenity, but tonight she wasn't tired at all. Poor exhausted Cathy had dragged herself up the attic steps to bed. But here was Sarah, still wide awake.

She closed her eyes and focused her thoughts on the child resting in her belly. *How are you, my love? Are you asleep? Or are you listening, hearing my thoughts even now?*

The baby wiggled in her belly, then fell silent. It was a reply, secret words shared only between them. Sarah was almost glad there was no husband to distract her from this silent conversation, to lie here in jealousy, an outsider. There was only mother and child, the ancient bond, the mystical link.

Poor Cathy, she thought, riding those roller coaster emotions from joy to sadness for her friend. She knew Cathy yearned just as deeply for a child, but eventually time would snatch the chance away from her. Cathy was too much of a romantic to realize that the man, the circumstances, might never be right. Hadn't it taken Cathy ten long years to finally acknowledge that her marriage was a miserable failure? Not that Cathy hadn't tried to make it work. She had tried to the point of developing a monumental blind spot to Jack's faults, primarily his selfishness. It was surprising how a woman so bright, so intuitive, could have let things drag on as long as she did. But that was Cathy. Even at thirty-seven she was open and trusting and loyal to the point of idiocy.

The clatter of gravel outside on the driveway pricked Sarah's awareness. Lying perfectly still, she listened and for a moment heard only the familiar creak of the trees, the rustle of branches against the shake roof. Then—there it was again. Stones skittering across the road, and then the faint squeal of metal. Those raccoons again. If she didn't shoo them off now, they'd litter garbage all over the driveway.

Sighing, she sat up and hunted in the darkness for her slippers. Shuffling quietly out of her bedroom, she navigated instinctively down the hallway and into the kitchen. Her eyes found the night too comfortable; she didn't want to assault them with light. Instead of flipping on the carport switch, she grabbed the flashlight from its usual spot on the kitchen shelf and unlocked the door.

Outside, moonlight glowed dimly through the clouds. She pointed the flashlight at the trash cans, but her beam caught no raccoon eyes, no telltale scattering of garbage, only the dull reflection of stainless steel. Puzzled, she crossed the carport and paused next to the Datsun that Cathy had parked in the driveway.

That was when she noticed the light glowing faintly inside the car. Glancing through the window, she saw that the glove compartment was open. Her first thought was that it had somehow fallen open by itself or that she or Cathy had forgotten to close it. Then she spotted the road maps strewn haphazardly across the front seat.

With fear suddenly hissing in her ear, she backed away, but terror made her legs slow and stiff. Only then did she sense that someone was nearby, waiting in the darkness; she could feel his presence, like a chill wind in the night.

She wheeled around for the house. As she turned, the

beam of her flashlight swung around in a wild arc, only to freeze on the face of a man. The eyes that stared down at her were as slick and as black as pebbles. She scarcely focused on the rest of his face: the hawk nose, the thin, bloodless lips. It was only the eyes she saw. They were the eyes of a man without a soul.

"Hello, Catherine," he whispered, and she heard, in his voice, the greeting of death.

Please, she wanted to cry out as she felt him wrench her hair backward, exposing her neck. *Let me live!*

But no sound escaped. The words, like his blade, were buried in her throat.

Cathy woke up to the quarreling of blue jays outside her window, a sound that brought a smile to her lips for it struck her as somehow whimsical, this flap and flutter of wings across the panes, this maniacal crackling of feathered enemies. So unlike the morning roar of buses and cars she was accustomed to. The blue jays' quarrel moved to the rooftop, and she heard their claws scratching across the shakes in a dance of combat. She trailed their progress across the ceiling, up one side of the roof and down the other. Then, tired of the battle, she focused on the window.

Morning sunlight cascaded in, bathing the attic room in a soft haze. Such a perfect room for a nursery! She could see all the changes Sarah had already made here—the Jack-and-Jill curtains, the watercolor animal portraits. The very prospect of a baby sleeping in this room filled her with such joy that she sat up, grinning, and hugged the covers to her knees. Then she glanced at her watch on the nightstand and saw it was already nine-thirty—half the morning gone!

Reluctantly, she left the warmth of her bed and poked around in her suitcase for a sweater and jeans. She dressed to the thrashing of blue jays in the branches, the battle having moved from the roof to the treetops. From the window, she watched them dart from twig to twig until one finally hoisted up the feathered version of a white flag and took off, defeated. The victor, his authority no longer in question, gave one last screech and settled back to preen his feathers.

Only then did Cathy notice the silence of the house, a stillness that magnified her every heartbeat, her every breath.

Leaving the room, she descended the attic steps and confronted the empty living room. Ashes from last night's fire mounded the grate. A silver garland drooped from the Christmas tree. A cardboard angel with glittery wings winked on the mantelpiece. She followed the hallway to Sarah's room and frowned at the rumpled bed, the coverlet flung aside. "Sarah?"

Her voice was swallowed up in the stillness. How could a cottage seem so immense? She wandered back through the living room and into the kitchen. Last night's teacups still sat in the sink. On the windowsill, an asparagus fern trembled, stirred by a breeze through the open door.

Cathy stepped out into the carport where Sarah's old Dodge was parked. "Sarah?" she called.

Something skittered across the roof. Startled, Cathy looked up and suddenly laughed as she heard the blue jay chattering in the tree above—a victory speech, no doubt. Even the animal kingdom had its conceits.

She started to head back into the house when her gaze swept past a stain on the gravel near the car's rear tire. For a few seconds she stared at the blot of rust-brown, unable to comprehend its meaning. Slowly, she moved alongside the car, her gaze tracing the stain backward along its meandering course.

As she rounded the rear of the car, the driveway came

into full view. The dried rivulet of brown became a crimson lake in which a single swimmer lay open-eyed and still.

The blue jay's chatter abruptly ceased as another sound rose up and filled the trees. It was Cathy, screaming.

"Hey, mister. Hey, mister."

Victor tried to brush off the sound but it kept buzzing in his ear, like a fly that can't be shooed away.

"Hey, mister. You awake?"

Victor opened his eyes and focused painfully on a wry little face stubbled with gray whiskers. The apparition grinned, and darkness gaped where teeth should have been. Victor stared into that foul black hole of a mouth and thought: *I've died and gone to hell.*

"Hey, mister, you got a cigarette?"

Victor shook his head and barely managed to whisper: "I don't think so."

"Well, you got a dollar I could borrow?"

"Go away," groaned Victor, shutting his eyes against the daylight. He tried to think, tried to remember where he was, but his head ached and the little man's voice kept distracting him.

"Can't get no cigarettes in this place. Like a jail in here. Don't know why I don't just get up and walk out. But y'know, streets are cold this time of year. Been rainin' all night long. Least in here it's warm...."

Raining all night long... Suddenly Victor remembered. The rain. Running and running through the rain.

Victor's eyes shot open. "Where am I?"

"Three East. Land o' the bitches."

He struggled to sit up and almost gasped from the pain. Dizzily, he focused on the metal pole with its bag of fluid dripping slowly into the plastic intravenous tube, then stared at the bandages on his left shoulder. Through the window, he saw that the day was already drenched in sunshine. "What time is it?"

"Dunno. Nine o'clock, I guess. You missed breakfast."

"I've got to get out of here." Victor swung his legs out of bed and discovered that, except for a flimsy hospital gown, he was stark naked. "Where's my clothes? My wallet?"

The old man shrugged. "Nurse'd know. Ask her."

Victor found the call button buried among the bed sheets. He stabbed it a few times, then turned his attention to peeling off the tape affixing the IV tube to his arm.

The door hissed open and a woman's voice barked, *"Mr. Holland! What do you think you're doing?"*

"I'm getting out of here, that's what I'm doing," said Victor as he stripped off the last piece of tape. Before he could pull the IV out, the nurse rushed across the room as fast as her stout legs could carry her and slapped a piece of gauze over the catheter.

"Don't blame me, Miss Redfern!" screeched the little man.

"Lenny, go back to your own bed this instant! And as for you, Mr. Holland," she said, turning her steel-blue eyes on Victor, "you've lost too much blood." Trapping his arm against her massive biceps, she began to retape the catheter firmly in place.

"Just get me my clothes."

"Don't argue, Mr. Holland. You have to stay."

"Why?"

"Because you've got an IV, that's why!" she snapped, as if the plastic tube itself was some sort of irreversible condition.

"I want my clothes."

"I'd have to check with the ER. Nothing of yours came up to the floor."

"Then call the ER, damn you!" At Miss Redfern's disapproving scowl, he added with strained politeness, "*If* you don't mind."

It was another half hour before a woman showed up from the business office to explain what had happened to Victor's belongings.

"I'm afraid we—well, we seem to have…lost your clothes, Mr. Holland," she said, fidgeting under his astonished gaze.

"What do you mean, *lost?*"

"They were—" she cleared her throat "—er, stolen. From the emergency room. Believe me, this has never happened before. We're really very sorry about this, Mr. Holland, and I'm sure we'll be able to arrange a purchase of replacement clothing.…"

She was too busy trying to make excuses to notice that Victor's face had frozen in alarm. That his mind was racing as he tried to remember, through the blur of last night's events, just what had happened to the film canister. He knew he'd had it in his pocket during the endless drive to the hospital. He remembered clutching it there, remembered flailing senselessly at the woman when she'd tried to pull his hand from his pocket. After that, nothing was clear, nothing was certain. *Have I lost it?* he thought. *Have I lost my only evidence?*

"…While the money's missing, your credit cards seem to be all there, so I guess that's something to be thankful for."

He looked at her blankly. "What?"

"Your valuables, Mr. Holland." She pointed to the wallet and watch she'd just placed on the bedside table. "The security guard found them in the trash bin outside the hospital. Looks like the thief only wanted your cash."

"And my clothes. Right."

The instant the woman left, Victor pressed the button for Miss Redfern. She walked in carrying a breakfast tray.

"Eat, Mr. Holland" she said. "Maybe your behavior's all due to hypoglycemia."

"A woman brought me to the ER," he said. "Her first name was Catherine. I have to get hold of her."

"Oh, look! Eggs and Rice Krispies! Here's your fork—"

"Miss Redfern, will you forget the damned Rice Krispies!"

Miss Redfern slapped down the cereal box. "There is no need for profanity!"

"I have to find that woman!"

Without a word, Miss Redfern spun around and marched out of the room. A few minutes later she returned and brusquely handed him a slip of paper. On it was written the name Catherine Weaver followed by a local address.

"You'd better eat fast," she said. "There's a policeman coming over to talk to you."

"Fine," he grunted, stuffing a forkful of cold, rubbery egg in his mouth.

"And some man from the FBI called. He's on his way, too."

Victor's head jerked up in alarm. "The FBI? What was his name?"

"Oh, for heaven's sake, how should I know? Something Polish, I think."

Staring at her, Victor slowly put down his fork. "Polowski," he said softly.

"That sounds like it. Polowski." She turned and headed out of the room. "The FBI indeed," she muttered. "Wonder what he did to get *their* attention...."

Before the door had even swung shut behind her, Victor was out of bed and tearing at his IV. He scarcely felt the sting of the tape wrenching the hair off his arm; he had to concentrate on getting the hell out of this hospital before Polowski showed up. He was certain the FBI agent had set him up for that ambush last night, and he wasn't about to wait around for another attack.

He turned and snapped at his roommate, "Lenny, where are your clothes?"

Lenny's gaze traveled reluctantly to a cabinet near the sink. "Don't got no other clothes. Besides, they wouldn't fit you, mister..."

Victor yanked open the cabinet door and pulled out a frayed cotton shirt and a pair of baggy polyester pants. The pants were too short and about six inches of Victor's hairy legs stuck out below the cuffs, but he had no trouble fastening the belt. The real trouble was going to be finding a pair of size twelve shoes. To his relief, he discovered that the cabinet also contained a pair of Lenny's thongs. His heels hung at least an inch over the back edge, but at least he wouldn't be barefoot.

"Those are mine!" protested Lenny.

"Here. You can have this." Victor tossed his wristwatch to the old man. "You should be able to hock that for a whole new outfit."

Suspicious, Lenny put the watch up against his ear. "Piece of junk. It's not ticking."

"It's quartz."

"Oh. Yeah. I knew that."

Victor pocketed his wallet and went to the door. Opening it just a crack, he peered down the hall toward the nurses' station. The coast was clear. He glanced back at Lenny. "So long, buddy. Give my regards to Miss Redfern."

Slipping out of the room, Victor headed quietly down the hall, away from the nurses' station. The emergency stairwell door was at the far end, marked by the warning painted in red: Alarm Will Sound If Opened. He walked steadily towards it, willing himself not to run, not to attract attention. But just as he neared the door, a familiar voice echoed in the hall.

"Mr. Holland! You come back here this instant!"

Victor lunged for the door, slammed against the closing bar, and dashed into the stairwell.

His footsteps echoed against the concrete as he pounded down the stairs. By the time he heard Miss Redfern scramble after him into the stairwell, he'd already reached the first floor and was pushing through the last door to freedom.

"Mr. Holland!" yelled Miss Redfern.

Even as he dashed across the parking lot, he could still hear Miss Redfern's outraged voice echoing in his ears.

Eight blocks away he turned into a K Mart, and within ten minutes had bought a shirt, blue jeans, underwear, socks and a pair of size-twelve tennis shoes, all of which he paid for with his credit card. He tossed Lenny's old clothes into a trash can.

Before emerging back outside, he peered through the store window at the street. It seemed like a perfectly normal mid-December morning in a small town, shoppers strolling beneath a tacky garland of Christmas decorations, a half-dozen cars waiting patiently at a red light. He was just about to step out the door when he spotted the police car creeping down the road. Immediately he ducked behind an undressed mannequin and watched through the nude plastic limbs as the police car made its way slowly past the K Mart and continued in the direction of the hospital. They were obviously searching for someone. Was he the one they wanted?

He couldn't afford to risk a stroll down Main Street. There was no way of knowing who else besides Polowski was involved in the double cross.

It took him at least an hour on foot to reach the outskirts of town, and by then he was so weak and wobbly he could barely stand. The surge of adrenaline that had sent him dashing from the hospital was at last petering out. Too tired to take another step, he sank onto a boulder at the side of the highway and halfheartedly held out his thumb. To his immense relief, the next vehicle to come along—a pickup truck loaded with firewood—pulled over. Victor climbed in and collapsed gratefully on the seat.

The driver spat out the window, then squinted at Victor from beneath an Agway Seeds cap. "Goin' far?"

"Just a few miles. Oak Hill Road."

"Yep. I go right past it." The driver pulled back onto the road. The truck spewed black exhaust as they roared down the highway, country music blaring from the radio.

Through the plucked strains of guitar music, Victor heard a sound that made him sit up sharply. A siren. Whipping his head around, he saw a patrol car zooming up fast behind them. *That's it,* thought Victor. *They've found me. They're going to stop this truck and arrest me....*

But for what? For walking away from the hospital? For insulting Miss Redfern? Or had Polowski fabricated some charge against him?

With a sense of impending doom, he waited for the patrol car to overtake them and start flashing its signal to pull over. In fact, he was so certain they *would* be pulled over that when the police car sped right past them and roared off down the highway, he could only stare ahead in amazement.

"Must be some kinda trouble," his companion said blandly, nodding at the rapidly vanishing police car.

Victor managed to clear his throat. "Trouble?"

"Yep. Don't get much of a chance to use that siren of theirs but when they do, boy oh boy, do they go to town with it."

With his heart hammering against his ribs, Victor sat back and forced himself to calm down. He had nothing to worry about. The police weren't after him, they were busy with some other concern. He wondered what sort of small-town catastrophe could warrant blaring sirens. Probably nothing more exciting than a few kids out on a joyride.

By the time they reached the turnoff to Oak Hill Road, Victor's pulse had settled back to normal. He thanked the driver, climbed out, and began the trek to Catherine Weaver's house. It was a long walk, and the road wound through a forest of pines. Every so often he'd pass a mailbox along the road and, peering through the trees, would spot a house. Catherine's address was coming up fast.

What on earth should he say to her? Up till now he'd concentrated only on reaching her house. Now that he was almost there, he had to come up with some reasonable explanation for why he'd dragged himself out of a hospital bed and trudged all this way to see her. A simple *thanks for saving my life* just wouldn't do it. He had to find out if she had the film canister. But she, of course, would want to know why the damn thing was so important.

You could tell her the truth.

No, forget that. He could imagine her reaction if he were to launch into his wild tale about viruses and dead scientists and double-crossing FBI agents. *The FBI is out to get you? I see. And who else is after you, Mr. Holland?* It was so absurdly paranoid he almost felt like laughing. No, he couldn't tell her any of it or he'd end up right back in a hospital, and this time in a ward that would make Miss Redfern's Three East look like paradise.

She didn't need to know any of it. In fact, she was better off ignorant. The woman had saved his life, and the last thing he wanted to do was put her in any danger. The film was all he wanted from her. After today, she'd never see him again.

He was so busy debating what to tell her that he didn't notice the police cars until well after he'd rounded the road's bend. Suddenly he froze, confronted by three squad cars—probably the entire police fleet of Garberville—

parked in front of a rustic cedar house. A half-dozen neighbors lingered in the gravel driveway, shaking their heads in disbelief. Good God, had something happened to Catherine?

Swallowing the urge to turn and flee, Victor propelled himself forward, past the squad cars and through the loose gathering of onlookers, only to be stopped by a uniformed officer.

"I'm sorry, sir. No one's allowed past this point."

Dazed, Victor stared down and saw that the police had strung out a perimeter of red tape. Slowly, his gaze moved beyond the tape, to the old Datsun parked near the carport. Was that Catherine's car? He tried desperately to remember if she'd driven a Datsun, but last night it had been so dark and he'd been in so much pain that he hadn't bothered to pay attention. All he could remember was that it was a compact model, with scarcely enough room for his legs. Then he noticed the faded parking sticker on the rear bumper: Parking Permit, Studio Lot A.

I work for an independent film company, she'd told him last night.

It was Catherine's car.

Unwillingly, he focused on the stained gravel just beside the Datsun, and even though the rational part of him knew that that peculiar brick red could only be dried blood, he wanted to deny it. He wanted to believe there was some other explanation for that stain, for this ominous gathering of police.

He tried to speak, but his voice sounded like something dragged up through gravel.

"What did you say, sir?" the police officer asked.

"What—what happened?"

The officer shook his head sadly. "Woman was killed here last night. Our first murder in ten years."

"Murder?" Victor's gaze was still fixed in horror on the bloodstained gravel. "But—*why?*"

The officer shrugged. "Don't know yet. Maybe robbery, though I don't think he got much." He nodded at the Datsun. "Car was the only thing broken into."

If Victor said anything at that point, he never remembered what it was. He was vaguely aware of his legs carrying him back through the onlookers, past the three police cars, toward the road. The sunshine was so brilliant it hurt his eyes and he could barely see where he was going.

I killed her, he thought. *She saved my life and I killed her....*

Guilt slashed its way to his throat and he could scarcely breathe, could barely take another step for the pain. For a long time he stood there at the side of the road, his head bent in the sunshine, his ears filled with the sound of blue jays, and mourned a woman he'd never known.

When at last he was able to raise his head again, rage fueled the rest of his walk back to the highway, rage against Catherine's murderer. Rage at himself for having put her in such danger. It was the film the killer had been searching for, and he'd probably found it in the Datsun. If he hadn't, the house would have been ransacked, as well.

Now what? thought Victor. He dismissed the possibility that his briefcase—with most of the evidence—might still be in his wrecked car. That was the first place the killer would have searched. Without the film, Victor was left with no evidence at all. It would all come down to his word against Viratek's. The newspapers would dismiss him as nothing more than a disgruntled ex-employee. And after Polowski's double cross, he couldn't trust the FBI.

At that last thought, he quickened his pace. The sooner he got out of Garberville, the better. When he got back to the highway, he'd hitch another ride. Once safely out of town, he could take the time to plan his next move.

He decided to head south, to San Francisco.

3

From the window of his office at Viratek, Archibald Black watched the limousine glide up the tree-lined driveway and pull to a stop at the front entrance. Black snorted derisively. The cowboy was back in town, damn him. And after all the man's fussing about the importance of secrecy, about keeping his little visit discreet, the idiot had the gall to show up in a limousine—with a uniformed driver, no less.

Black turned from the window and paced over to his desk. Despite his contempt for the visitor, he had to acknowledge the man made him uneasy, the way all so-called men of action made him uneasy. Not enough brains behind all that muscle. Too much power in the hands of imbeciles, he thought. Is this an example of who we have running the country?

The intercom buzzed. "Mr. Black?" said his secretary. "A Mr. Tyrone is here to see you."

"Send him in, please," said Black, smoothing the scorn from his expression. He was wearing a look of polite deference when the door opened and Matthew Tyrone walked into the office.

They shook hands. Tyrone's grip was unreasonably firm, as though he was trying to remind Black of their relative positions of power. His bearing had all the spit and polish of an ex-marine, which Tyrone was. Only the thickening waist betrayed the fact that Tyrone's marine days had been left far behind.

"How was the flight from Washington?" inquired Black as they sat down.

"Terrible service. I tell you, commercial flights aren't what they used to be. To think the average American pays good money for the privilege."

"I imagine it can't compare with Air Force One."

Tyrone smiled. "Let's get down to business. Tell me where things stand with this little crisis of yours."

Black noted Tyrone's use of the word *yours. So now it's my problem,* he thought. Naturally. That's what they meant by deniability: When things go wrong, the other guy gets the blame. If any of this leaked out, Black's head would be the one to fall. But then, that's why this contract was so lucrative—because he—meaning Viratek—was willing to take that risk.

"We've recovered the documents," said Black. "And the film canisters. The negatives are being developed now."

"And your two employees?"

Black cleared his throat. "There's no need to take this any further."

"They're a risk to national security."

"You can't just kill them off!"

"Can't we?" Tyrone's eyes were a cold, gun-metal gray. An appropriate color for someone who called himself "the Cowboy." You didn't argue with anyone who had eyes like that. Not if you had an instinct for self-preservation.

Black dipped his head deferentially. "I'm not accustomed to this sort of...business. And I don't like dealing with your man Savitch."

"Mr. Savitch has performed well for us before."

"He killed one of my senior scientists!"

"I assume it was necessary."

Black looked down unhappily at his desk. Just the thought of that monster Savitch made him shudder.

"Why, exactly, did Martinique go bad?"

Because he had a conscience, thought Black. He looked at Tyrone. "There was no way to predict it. He'd worked in commercial R and D for ten years. He'd never presented a security problem before. We only found out last week that he'd taken classified documents. And then Victor Holland got involved...."

"How much does Holland know?"

"Holland wasn't involved with the project. But he's clever. If he looked over those papers, he might have pieced it together."

Now Tyrone was agitated, his fingers drumming the desktop. "Tell me about Holland. What do you know about him?"

"I've gone over his personnel file. He's forty-one years old, born and raised in San Diego. Entered the seminary but dropped out after a year. Went on to Stanford, then MIT. Doctorate in biochemistry. He was with Viratek for four years. One of our most promising researchers."

"What about his personal life?"

"His wife died three years ago of leukemia. Keeps pretty much to himself these days. Quiet kind of guy, likes classical jazz. Plays the saxophone in some amateur group."

Tyrone laughed. "Your typical nerd scientist." It was just the sort of moronic comment an ex-marine like Tyrone would make. It was an insult that grated on Black. Years ago, before he created Viratek Industries, Black too had been a research biochemist.

"He should be a simple matter to dispose of," said Tyrone. "Inexperienced. And probably scared." He reached for his briefcase. "Mr. Savitch is an expert on these matters. I suggest you let him take care of the problem."

"Of course." In truth, Black didn't think he had any choice. Nicholas Savitch was like some evil, frightening force that, once unleashed, could not be controlled.

The intercom buzzed. "Mr. Gregorian's here from the photo lab," said the secretary.

"Send him in." Black glanced at Tyrone. "The film's been developed. Let's see just what Martinique managed to photograph."

Gregorian walked in carrying a bulky envelope. "Here are those contact prints you requested," he said, handing the bundle across the desk to Black. Then he cupped his hand over his mouth, muffling a sound suspiciously like laughter.

"Yes, Mr. Gregorian?" inquired Black.

"Nothing, sir."

Tyrone cut in, "Well, let's see them!"

Black removed the five contact sheets and lay them out on the desk for everyone to see. The men stared.

For a long time, no one spoke. Then Tyrone said, "Is this some sort of joke?"

Gregorian burst out laughing.

Black said, "What the hell is this?"

"Those are the negatives you gave me, sir," Gregorian insisted. "I processed them myself."

"These are the photos you got back from Victor Holland?" Tyrone's voice started soft and rose slowly to a roar. "Five rolls of *naked women?*"

"There's been a mistake," said Black. "It's the wrong film—"

Gregorian laughed harder.

"Shut up!" yelled Black. He looked at Tyrone. "I don't know how this happened."

"Then the roll we want is still out there?"

Black nodded wearily.

Tyrone reached for the phone. "We need to clean things up. Fast."

"Who are you calling?" asked Black.

"The man who can do the job," said Tyrone as he punched in the numbers. "Savitch."

In his motel room on Lombard Street, Victor paced the avocado-green carpet, wracking his brain for a plan. Any plan. His well-organized scientist's mind had already distilled the situation into the elements of a research project. Identify the problem: someone is out to kill me. State your hypothesis: Jerry Martinique uncovered something dangerous and he was killed for it. Now they think I have the information—and the evidence. Which I don't. Goal: Stay alive. Method: *Any damn way I can!*

For the last two days, his only strategy had consisted of holing up in various cheap motel rooms and pacing the carpets. He couldn't hide out forever. If the feds were involved, and he had reason to believe they were, they'd soon have his credit card charges traced, would know exactly where to find him.

I need a plan of attack.

Going to the FBI was definitely out. Sam Polowski was the agent Victor had contacted, the one who'd arranged to meet him in Garberville. No one else should have known about that meeting. Sam Polowski had never shown up.

But someone else had. Victor's aching shoulder was a constant reminder of that near-disastrous rendezvous.

I could go to the newspapers. But how would he convince some skeptical reporter? Who would believe his stories of a project so dangerous it could kill millions? They would think his tale was some fabrication of a paranoid mind.

And I am not paranoid.

He paced over to the TV and switched it on to the five o'clock news. A perfectly coiffed anchorwoman smiled from the screen as she read a piece of fluff about the last day of school, happy children, Christmas vacation. Then her expression sobered. Transition. Victor found himself staring at the TV as the next story came on.

"And in Garberville, California, there have been no new leads in the murder investigation of a woman found slain Wednesday morning. A houseguest found Sarah Boylan, 39, lying in the driveway, dead of stab wounds to the neck. The victim was five months pregnant. Police say they are puzzled by the lack of motive in this terrible tragedy, and at the present time there are no suspects. Moving on to national news..."

No, no, no! Victor thought. She wasn't pregnant. Her name wasn't Sarah. It's a mistake....

Or was it?

My name is Catherine, she had told him.

Catherine Weaver. Yes, he was sure of the name. He'd remember it till the day he died.

He sat on the bed, the facts spinning around in his brain. Sarah. Cathy. A murder in Garberville.

When at last he rose to his feet, it was with a swelling sense of urgency, even panic. He grabbed the hotel room phone book and flipped to the *W*s. He understood now. The killer had made a mistake. If Cathy Weaver was still alive, she might have that roll of film—or know where to find it. Victor had to reach her.

Before someone else did.

Nothing could have prepared Cathy for the indescribable sense of gloom she felt upon returning to her flat in San Francisco. She had thought she'd cried out all her tears that night in the Garberville motel, the night after Sarah's death. But here she was, still bursting into tears, then sinking into deep, dark meditations. The drive to the city had been temporarily numbing. But as soon as she'd climbed the steps to her door and confronted the deathly silence of her second-story flat, she felt overwhelmed once again by grief.

And bewilderment. Of all the people in the world to die, why Sarah?

She made a feeble attempt at unpacking. Then, forcing herself to stay busy, she surveyed the refrigerator and saw that her shelves were practically empty. It was all the excuse she needed to flee her apartment. She pulled a sweater over her jeans and, with a sense of escape, walked the four blocks to the neighborhood grocery store. She bought only the essentials, bread and eggs and fruit. Enough to tide her over for a few days, until she was back on her feet and could think clearly about any sort of menu.

Carrying a sack of groceries in each arm, she walked through the gathering darkness back to her apartment building. The night was chilly, and she regretted not wearing a coat. Through an open window, a woman called, "Time for dinner!" and two children playing kickball in the street turned and scampered for home.

By the time Cathy reached her building, she was shivering and her arms were aching from the weight of the groceries. She trudged up the steps and, balancing one sack on her hip, managed to pull out her keys and unlock the security door. Just as she swung through, she heard footsteps, then glimpsed a blur of movement rushing toward her from the side. She was swept through the doorway, into the building. A grocery bag tumbled from her arms, spilling apples across the floor. She stumbled forward, catching herself on the wood banister. The door slammed shut behind her.

She spun around, ready to fight off her attacker.

It was Victor Holland.

"You!" she whispered in amazement.

He didn't seem so sure of *her* identity. He was frantically searching her face, as though trying to confirm he had the right woman. "Cathy Weaver?"

"What do you think you're—"

"Where's your apartment?" he cut in.

"What?"

"We can't stand around out here."

"It's—it's upstairs—"

"Let's go." He reached for her arm but she pulled away.

"My groceries," she said, glancing down at the scattered apples.

He quickly scooped up the fruit, tossed it in one of the bags, and nudged her toward the stairs. "We don't have a lot of time."

Cathy allowed herself to be herded up the stairs and halfway down the hall before she stopped dead in her tracks. "Wait a minute. You tell me what this is all about, Mr. Holland, and you tell me right now or I don't move another step!"

"Give me your keys."

"You can't just—"

"Give me your keys!"

She stared at him, shocked by the command. Suddenly she realized that what she saw in his eyes was panic. They were the eyes of a hunted man.

Automatically she handed him her keys.

"Wait here," he said. "Let me check the apartment first."

She watched in bewilderment as he unlocked her door and cautiously eased his way inside. For a few moments she heard nothing. She pictured him moving through the flat, tried to estimate how many seconds each room would require for inspection. It was a small flat, so why was he taking so long?

Slowly she moved toward the doorway. Just as she reached it, his head popped out. She let out a little squeak of surprise. He barely caught the bag of groceries as it slipped from her grasp.

"It's okay," he said. "Come on inside."

The instant she stepped over the threshold, he had the door locked and bolted behind her. Then he quickly circled the living room, closing the drapes, locking windows.

"Are you going to tell me what's going on?" she asked, following him around the room.

"We're in trouble."

"You mean *you're* in trouble."

"No. I mean *we*. Both of us." He turned to her, his gaze clear and steady. "Do you have the film?"

"What are you talking about?" she asked, utterly confused by the sudden shift of conversation.

"A roll of film. Thirty-five millimeter. In a black plastic container. Do you have it?"

She didn't answer. But an image from that last night with Sarah had already taken shape in her mind: a roll of film on the kitchen counter. Film she'd thought belonged to her friend Hickey. Film she'd slipped into her bathrobe pocket and later into her purse. But she wasn't about to reveal any of this, not until she found out why he wanted it. The gaze she returned to him was purposefully blank and unrevealing.

Frustrated, he forced himself to take a deep breath, and started over. "That night you found me—on the highway— I had it in my pocket. It wasn't with me when I woke up in the hospital. I might have dropped it in your car."

"Why do you want this roll of film?"

"I need it. As evidence—"

"For what?"

"It would take too long to explain."

She shrugged. "I've got nothing better to do at the moment—"

"Damn it!" He stalked over to her. Taking her by the shoulders, he forced her to look at him. "Don't you understand? That's why your friend was killed! The night they broke into your car, they were looking for that film!"

She stared at him, a look of sudden comprehension and horror. "Sarah..."

"Was in the wrong place at the wrong time. The killer must have thought she was *you*."

Cathy felt trapped by his unrelenting gaze. And by the inescapable threat of his revelation. Her knees wobbled, gave way. She sank into the nearest chair and sat there in numb silence.

"You have to get out of here," he said. "Before they find you. Before they figure out you're the Cathy Weaver they're looking for."

She didn't move. She couldn't move.

"Come on, Cathy. There isn't much time!"

"What was on that roll of film?" she asked softly.

"I told you. Evidence. Against a company called Viratek."

She frowned. "Isn't—isn't that the company you work for?"

"Used to work for."

"What did they do?"

"They're involved in some sort of illegal research project. I can't tell you the particulars."

"Why not?"

"Because I don't know them. I'm not the one who gathered the evidence. A colleague—a friend—passed it to me, just before he was killed."

"What do you mean by killed?"

"The police called it an accident. I think otherwise."

"You're saying he was murdered over a research project?" She shook her head. "Must have been dangerous stuff he was working on."

"I know this much. It involves biological weapons. Which makes the research illegal. And incredibly dangerous."

"Weapons? For what government?"

"Ours."

"I don't understand. If this is a federal project, that makes it all legal, right?"

"Not by a long shot. People in high places have been known to break the rules."

"How high are we talking about?"

"I don't know. I can't be sure of anyone. Not the police, not the Justice Department. Not the FBI."

Her eyes narrowed. The words she was hearing sounded like paranoid ravings. But the voice—and the eyes—were perfectly sane. They were sea-green, those eyes. They held an honesty, a steadiness that should have been all the assurance she needed.

It wasn't. Not by a long shot.

Quietly she said, "So you're telling me the FBI is after you. Is that correct?"

Sudden anger flared in his eyes, then just as quickly, it was gone. Groaning, he sank onto the couch and ran his hands through his hair. "I don't blame you for thinking I'm nuts. Sometimes I wonder if I'm all there. I thought if I could trust anyone, it'd be you...."

"Why me?"

He looked at her. "Because you're the one who saved my life. You're the one they'll try to kill next."

She froze. No, no, this was insane. Now he was pulling her into his delusion, making her believe in his nightmare world of murder and conspiracy. She wouldn't let him! She stood up and started to walk away, but his voice made her stop again.

"Cathy, think about it. Why was your friend Sarah killed? Because they thought she was *you*. By now they've figured out they killed the wrong woman. They'll have to come back and do the job right. Just in case you know something. In case you have evidence—"

"This is crazy!" she cried, clapping her hands over her ears. "No one's going to—"

"They already have!" He whipped out a scrap of newspaper from his shirt pocket. "On my way over here, I happened to pass a newsstand. This was on the front page." He handed her the piece of paper.

She stared in bewilderment at the photograph of a middle-aged woman, a total stranger. "San Francisco woman shot to death on front doorstep," read the accompanying headline.

"This has nothing to do with me," she said.

"Look at her name."

Cathy's gaze slid to the third paragraph, which identified the victim.

Her name was Catherine Weaver.

The scrap of newsprint slipped from her grasp and fluttered to the floor.

"There are three Catherine Weavers in the San Francisco phone book," he said. "That one was shot to death at nine o'clock this morning. I don't know what's happened to the second. She might already be dead. Which makes you next on the list. They've had enough time to locate you."

"I've been out of town—I only got back an hour ago—"

"Which explains why you're still alive. Maybe they came here earlier. Maybe they decided to check out the other two women first."

She shot to her feet, suddenly frantic with the need to flee. "I have to pack my things—"

"No. Let's just get the hell out of here."

Yes, do what he says! an inner voice screamed at her.

She nodded. Turning, she headed blindly for the door. Halfway there, she halted. "My purse—"

"Where is it?"

She headed back, past a curtained window. "I think I left it by the—"

Her next words were cut off by an explosion of shattering glass. Only the closed curtains kept the shards from piercing her flesh. Pure reflex sent Cathy diving to the floor just as the second gun blast went off. An instant later she found Victor Holland sprawled on top of her, covering her body with his as the third bullet slammed into the far wall, splintering wood and plaster.

The curtains shuddered, then hung still.

For a few seconds Cathy was paralyzed by terror, by the weight of Victor's body on hers. Then panic took hold. She squirmed free, intent on fleeing the apartment.

"Stay down!" Victor snapped.

"They're trying to kill us!"

"Don't make it easy for them!" He dragged her back to the floor. "We're getting out. But not through the front door."

"How—"

"Where's your fire escape?"

"My bedroom window."

"Does it go to the roof?"

"I'm not sure—I think so—"

"Then let's move it."

On hands and knees they crawled down the hall, into Cathy's unlit bedroom. Beneath the window they paused, listening. Outside, in the darkness, there was no sound. Then, from downstairs in the lobby, came the tinkle of breaking glass.

"He's already in the building!" hissed Victor. He yanked open the window. "Out, out!"

Cathy didn't need to be prodded. Hands shaking, she scrambled out and lowered herself onto the fire escape. Victor was right behind her.

"Up," he whispered. "To the roof."

And then what? she wondered, climbing the ladder to the third floor, past Mrs. Chang's flat. Mrs. Chang was out of town this week, visiting her son in New Jersey. The apartment was dark, the windows locked tight. No way in there.

"Keep going," said Victor, nudging her forward.

Only a few more rungs to go.

At last, she pulled herself up and over the edge and onto the asphalt roof. A second later, Victor dropped down beside her. Potted plants shuddered in the darkness. It was Mrs. Chang's rooftop garden, a fragrant mélange of Chinese herbs and vegetables.

Together, Victor and Cathy weaved their way through the plants and crossed to the opposite edge of the roof, where the next building abutted theirs.

"All the way?" said Cathy.

"All the way."

They hopped onto the adjoining roof and ran across to the other side, where three feet of emptiness separated them from the next building. She didn't pause to think of the perils of that leap, she simply flung herself across the gap and kept running, aware that every step took her farther and farther from danger.

On the roof of the fourth building, Cathy finally halted and stared over the edge at the street below. End of the line. It suddenly occurred to her that it was a very long drop to the ground below. The fire escape looked as sturdy as a Tinkertoy.

She swallowed. "This probably isn't a good time to tell you this, but—"

"Tell me what?"

"I'm afraid of heights."

He clambered over the edge. "Then don't look down."

Right, she thought, slithering onto the fire escape. *Don't look down.* Her palms were so slick with sweat she could barely grip the rungs. Suddenly seized by an attack of vertigo, she froze there, clinging desperately to that flimsy steel skeleton.

"Don't stop now!" Victor whispered up to her. "Just keep moving!"

Still she didn't move. She pressed her face against the rung, so hard she felt the rough edge bite into her flesh.

"You're okay, Cathy!" he said. "Come on."

The pain became all-encompassing, blocking out the dizziness, even the fear. When she opened her eyes again, the world had steadied. On rubbery legs, she descended the ladder, pausing on the third floor landing to wipe her sweaty palms on her jeans. She continued downward, to the second-floor landing. It was still a good fifteen-foot drop to the ground. She unlatched the extension ladder and started to slide it down, but it let out such a screech that Victor immediately stopped her.

"Too noisy. We have to jump!"

"But—"

To her astonishment, he scrambled over the railing and dropped to the ground. "Come on!" he hissed from below. "It's not that far. I'll catch you."

Murmuring a prayer, she lowered herself over the side and let go.

To her surprise he did catch her—but held on only for a second. The bullet wound had left his injured shoulder too weak to hold on. They both tumbled to the ground. She landed smack on top of him, her legs astride his hips, their faces inches apart. They stared at each other, so stunned they could scarcely breathe.

Upstairs, a window slid open and someone yelled, "Hey, you bums! If you don't clear out this instant, I'm calling the cops!"

Instantly Cathy rolled off Victor, only to stagger into a trash can. The lid fell off and slammed like a cymbal against the sidewalk.

"That's it for rest stops," Victor grunted and scrambled to his feet. *"Move it."*

They took off at a wild dash down the street, turned up an alley, and kept running. It was a good five blocks before they finally stopped to catch their breath. They glanced back.

The street was deserted.

They were safe!

Nicholas Savitch stood beside the neatly made bed and surveyed the room. It was every inch a woman's room, from the closet hung with a half-dozen simple but elegant dresses, to the sweetly scented powders and lotions lined up on the vanity table. It took only a single circuit around the room to tell him about the woman whose bedroom this was. She was slim, a size seven dress, size six-and-a-half shoe. The hairs on the brush were brown and shoulder-length. She owned only a few pieces of jewelry, and she favored natural scents, rosewater and lavender. Her favorite color was green.

Back in the living room, he continued to gather information. The woman subscribed to the Hollywood trade journals. Her taste in music, like her taste in books, was eclectic. He noticed a scrap of newspaper lying on the floor. He picked it up and glanced at the article. Now this was interesting. The death of Catherine Weaver I had not gone unnoticed by Catherine Weaver III.

He pocketed the article. Then he saw the purse, lying on the floor near the shattered window.

Bingo.

He emptied the contents on the coffee table. Out tumbled a wallet, checkbook, pens, loose change, and…an address book. He opened it to the *B*s. There he found the name he was looking for: Sarah Boylan.

He now knew this was the Catherine Weaver he'd been seeking. What a shame he'd wasted his time hunting down the other two.

He flipped through the address book and spotted a half dozen or so San Francisco listings. The woman may have been clever enough to slip away from him this time. But staying out of sight was a more difficult matter. And this little book, with its names of friends and relatives and colleagues, could lead him straight to her.

Somewhere in the distance, a police siren was wailing.

It was time to leave.

Savitch took the address book and the woman's wallet and headed out the door. Outside, his breath misted in the cold air as he walked at a leisurely pace down the street.

He could afford to take his time.

But for Catherine Weaver and Victor Holland, time was running out.

4

There was no time to rest. They jogged for the next six blocks, miles and miles, it seemed to Cathy. Victor moved tirelessly, leading her down side streets, avoiding busy intersections. She let him do the thinking and navigating. Her terror slowly gave way to numbness and a disorienting sense of unreality. The city itself seemed little more than a dreamscape, asphalt and streetlights and endless twists and turns of concrete. The only reality was the man striding close beside her, his gaze alert, his movements swift and sure. She knew he too must be afraid, but she couldn't see his fear.

He took her hand; the warmth of that grasp, the strength of those fingers, seemed to flow into her cold, exhausted limbs.

She quickened her pace. "I think there's a police substation down that street," she said. "If we go a block or two further—"

"We're not going to the police."

"What?" She stopped dead, staring at him.

"Not yet. Not until I've had a chance to think this through."

"Victor," she said slowly. "Someone is trying to kill us. Trying to kill *me*. What do you mean, you need time to *think this through?*"

"Look, we can't stand around talking about it. We have to get off the streets." He grabbed her hand again. "Come on."

"Where?"

"I have a room. It's only a few blocks away."

She let him drag her only a few yards before she mustered the will to pull free. "Wait a minute. Just *wait.*"

He turned, his face a mask of frustration, and confronted her. "Wait for what? For that maniac to catch up? For the bullets to start flying again?"

"For an explanation!"

"I'll explain it all. When we're safe."

She backed away. "Why are you afraid of the police?"

"I can't be sure of them."

"Do you have a reason to be afraid? What have you done?"

With two steps he closed the gap between them and grabbed her hard by the shoulders. "I just pulled you out of a death trap, remember? The bullets were going through your window, not mine!"

"Maybe they were aimed at you!"

"Okay!" He let her go, let her back away from him. "You want to try it on your own? Do it. Maybe the police'll be a help. Maybe not. But I can't risk it. Not until I know all the players behind this."

"You—you're letting me go?"

"You were never my prisoner."

"No." She took a breath—it misted in the cold air. She glanced down the street, toward the police substation. "It's...the reasonable thing to do," she muttered, almost to reassure herself. "That's what they're there for."

"Right."

She frowned, anticipating what lay ahead. "They'll ask a lot of questions."

"What are you going to tell them?"

She looked at him, her gaze unflinchingly meeting his. "The truth."

"Which'll be at best, incomplete. And at worst, unbelievable."

"I have broken glass all over my apartment to prove it."

"A drive-by shooting. Purely random."

"It's their job to protect me."

"What if they don't think you need protection?"

"I'll tell them about you! About Sarah."

"They may or may not take you seriously."

"They have to take me seriously! Someone's trying to kill me!" Her voice, shrill with desperation, seemed to echo endlessly through the maze of streets.

Quietly he said, "I know."

She glanced back toward the substation. "I'm going."

He said nothing.

"Where will you be?" she asked.

"On my own. For now."

She took two steps away, then stopped. "Victor?"

"I'm still here."

"You did save my life. Thank you."

He didn't respond. She heard his footsteps slowly walk away. She stood there thinking, wondering if she was doing the right thing. Of course she was. A man afraid of the police—with a story as paranoid as his was—had to be dangerous.

But he saved my life.

And once, on a rainy night in Garberville, she had saved his.

She replayed all the events of the last week. Sarah's murder, never explained. The other Catherine Weaver, shot to death on her front doorstep. The film canister that Sarah had retrieved from the car, the one Cathy had slipped into her bathrobe pocket...

Victor's footsteps had faded.

In that instant she realized she'd lost the only man who could help her find the answers to all those questions, the one man who'd stood by her in her darkest moment of terror. The one man she knew, by some strange intuition, she could trust. Facing that deserted street, she felt abandoned and utterly friendless. In sudden panic, she whirled around and called out: "Victor!"

At the far end of the block, a silhouette stopped and turned. He seemed an island of refuge in that crazy, dangerous world. She started toward him, her legs moving her faster and faster, until she was running, yearning for the safety of his arms, the arms of a man she scarcely knew. Yet it didn't feel like a stranger's arms gathering her to his chest, welcoming her into his protective embrace. She felt the pounding of his heart, the grip of his fingers against her back, and something told her that this was a man she could depend upon, a man who wouldn't fold when she needed him most.

"I'm right here," he murmured. "Right here." He stroked through her windblown hair, his fingers burying deep in the tangled strands. She felt the heat of his breath against her face, felt her own quick and shuddering response. And then, all at once, his mouth hungrily sought hers and he was kissing her. She responded with a kiss just as desperate, just as needy. Stranger though he was, he had been there for her and he was still here, his arms sheltering her from the terrors of the night.

She burrowed her face against his chest, longing to press ever deeper, ever closer. "I don't know what to do! I'm so afraid, Victor, and I don't know what to do...."

"We'll work this out together. Okay?" He cupped her face in his hands and tilted it up to his. "You and I, we'll beat this thing."

She nodded. Searching his eyes, connecting with that rock-solid gaze, she found all the assurance she needed.

A wind gusted down the street. She shivered in its wake. "What do we do first?" she whispered.

"First," he said, pulling off his windbreaker and draping it over her shoulders, "We get you warmed up. And inside." He took her hand. "Come on. A hot bath, a good supper, and you'll be operating on all cylinders again."

It was another five blocks to the Kon-Tiki Motel. Though not exactly a five-star establishment, the Kon-Tiki was comfortingly drab and anonymous, one of a dozen on motel row. They climbed the steps to Room 214, overlooking the half-empty parking lot. He unlocked the door and motioned her inside.

The rush of warmth against her cheeks was delicious. She stood in the center of that utterly charmless space and marveled at how good it felt to be safely surrounded by four walls. The furnishings were spare: a double bed, a dresser, two nightstands with lamps, and a single chair. On the wall was a framed print of some nameless South Pacific island. The only luggage she saw was a cheap nylon bag on the floor. The bedcovers were rumpled, recently napped in, the pillows punched up against the headboard.

"Not much," he said. "But it's warm. And it's paid for." He turned on the TV. "We'd better keep an eye on the news. Maybe they'll have something on the Weaver woman."

The Weaver woman, she thought. *It could have been me.* She was shivering again, but now it wasn't from the cold. Settling onto the bed she stared numbly at the TV, not really seeing what was on the screen. She was more aware of *him.* He was circling the room, checking the windows, fiddling with the lock on the door. He moved quietly, efficiently, his silence a testimony to the dangers of their situation. Most men she knew began to babble nonsense when they were scared; Victor Holland simply turned quiet. His mere presence was overwhelming. He seemed to fill the room.

He moved to her side. She flinched as he took her hands

and gently inspected them, palm side up. Looking down, she saw the bloodied scratches, the flakes of rust from the fire escape embedded in her skin.

"I guess I'm a mess," she murmured.

He smiled and stroked her face. "You could use some washing up. Go ahead. I'll get us something to eat."

She retreated into the bathroom. Through the door she could hear the drone of the TV, the sound of Victor's voice ordering a pizza over the phone. She ran hot water over her cold, numb hands. In the mirror over the sink she caught an unflattering glimpse of herself, her hair a tangled mess, her chin smudged with dirt. She washed her face, rubbing new life, new circulation into those frigid cheeks. Glancing down, she noticed Victor's razor on the counter. The sight of that blade cast her situation into a new focus—a frightening one. She picked up the razor, thinking how lethal that blade looked, how vulnerable she would be tonight. Victor was a large man, at least six foot two, with powerful arms. She was scarcely five foot five, a comparative weakling. There was only one bed in the next room. She had come here voluntarily. What would he assume about her? That she was a willing victim? She thought of all the ways a man could hurt her, kill her. It wouldn't take a razor to finish the job. Victor could use his bare hands. *What am I doing here?* she wondered. *Spending the night with a man I scarcely know?*

This was not the time to have doubts. She'd made the decision. She had to go by her instincts, and her instincts told her Victor Holland would never hurt her.

Deliberately she set down the razor. She would have to trust him. She was afraid not to.

In the other room, a door slammed shut. Had he left?

Opening the door a crack, she peered out. The TV was still on. There was no sign of Victor. Slowly she emerged, to find she was alone. She began to circle the room, searching for clues, anything that would tell her more about the man. The bureau drawers were empty, and so was the closet. Obviously he had not moved into this room for a long stay. He'd planned only one night, maybe two. She went to the nylon bag and glanced inside. She saw a clean pair of socks, an unopened package of underwear, and a day-old edition of the *San Francisco Chronicle*. All it told her was that the man kept himself informed and he traveled light.

Like a man on the run.

She dug deeper and came up with a receipt from an automatic teller machine. Yesterday he'd tried to withdraw cash. The machine had printed out the message: *Transaction cannot be completed. Please contact your bank.* Why had it refused him the cash? she wondered. Was he overdrawn? Had the machine been out of order?

The sound of a key grating in the lock caught her by surprise. She glanced up as the door swung open.

The look he gave her made her cheeks flush with guilt. Slowly she rose to her feet, unable to answer that look of accusation in his eyes.

The door swung shut behind him.

"I suppose it's a reasonable thing for you to do," he said. "Search my things."

"I'm sorry. I was just..." She swallowed. "I had to know more about you."

"And what terrible things have you dug up?"

"Nothing!"

"No deep dark secrets? Don't be afraid. Tell me, Cathy."

"Only...only that you had trouble getting cash out of your account."

He nodded. "A frustrating state of affairs. Since by my estimate I have a balance of six thousand dollars. And now

I can't seem to touch it." He sat down in the chair, his gaze still on her face. "What else did you learn?"

"You—you read the newspaper."

"So do a lot of people. What else?"

She shrugged. "You wear boxer shorts."

Amusement flickered in his eyes. "Now we're getting personal."

"You…" She took a deep breath. "You're on the run."

He looked at her a long time without saying a word.

"That's why you won't go to the police," she said. "Isn't it?"

He turned away, gazing not at her but at the far wall. "There are reasons."

"Give me one, Victor. One good reason is all I need and then I'll shut up."

He sighed. "I doubt it."

"Try me. I have every reason to believe you."

"You have every reason to think I'm paranoid." Leaning forward, he ran his hands over his face. "Lord, sometimes *I* think I must be."

Quietly she went to him and knelt down beside his chair. "Victor, these people who are trying to kill me—who are they?"

"I don't know."

"You said it might involve people in high places."

"It's just a guess. It's a case of federal money going to illegal research. Deadly research."

"And federal money has to be doled out by someone in authority."

He nodded. "This is someone who's bent the rules. Someone who could be hurt by a political scandal. He just might try to protect himself by manipulating the Bureau. Or even your local police. That's why I won't go to them. That's why I left the room to make my call."

"When?"

"While you were in the bathroom. I went to a pay phone and called the police. I didn't want it traced."

"You just said you don't want them involved."

"This call I had to make. There's a third Catherine Weaver in that phone book. Remember?"

A third victim on the list. Suddenly weak, she sat down on the bed. "What did you say?" she asked softly.

"That I had reason to think she might be in danger. That she wasn't answering her phone."

"You tried it?"

"Twice."

"Did they listen to you?"

"Not only did they listen, they demanded to know my name. That's when I picked up the cue that something must already have happened to her. At that point I hung up and hightailed it out of the booth. A call can be traced in seconds. They could've had me surrounded."

"That makes three," she whispered. "Those two other women. And me."

"They have no way of finding you. Not as long as you stay away from your apartment. Stay out of—"

They both froze in panic.

Someone was knocking on the door.

They stared at each other, fear mirrored in their eyes. Then, after a moment's hesitation, Victor said: "Who is it?"

"Domino's," called a thin voice.

Cautiously, Victor eased open the door. A teenage boy stood outside, wielding a bag and a flat cardboard box.

"Hi!" chirped the boy. "A large combo with the works, two Cokes and extra napkins. Right?"

"Right." Victor handed the boy a few bills. "Keep the change," he said and closed the door. Turning, he gave Cathy a sheepish look. "Well," he admitted. "Just goes to show you. Sometimes a knock at the door really is just the pizza man.''

They both laughed, a sound not of humor but of frayed nerves. The release of tension seemed to transform his face, melted his wariness to warmth. Erase those haggard lines, she thought, and he could almost be called a handsome man.

"I tell you what," he said. "Let's not think about this mess right now. Why don't we just get right down to the really important issue of the day. Food."

Nodding, she reached out for the box. "Better hand it over. Before I eat the damn bedspread."

While the ten o'clock news droned from the television set, they tore into the pizza like two ravenous animals. It was a greasy and utterly satisfying banquet on a motel bed. They scarcely bothered with conversation—their mouths were too busy devouring cheese and pepperoni. On the TV, a dapper anchorman announced a shakeup in the mayor's office, the resignation of the city manager, news that, given their current situation, seemed ridiculously trivial. Scarcely thirty seconds were devoted to that morning's killing of Catherine Weaver I; as yet, no suspects were in custody. No mention was made of any second victim by the same name.

Victor frowned. "Looks like the other woman didn't make it to the news."

"Or nothing's happened to her." She glanced at him questioningly. "What if the second Cathy Weaver is all right? When you called the police, they might've been asking you routine questions. When you're on edge, it's easy to—"

"Imagine things?" The look he gave her almost made her bite her tongue.

"No," she said quietly. "Misinterpret. The police can't

respond to every anonymous call. It's natural they'd ask for your name.''

"It was more than a request, Cathy. They were champing at the bit to interrogate me.''

"I'm not doubting your word. I'm just playing devil's advocate. Trying to keep things level and sane in a crazy situation.''

He looked at her long and hard. At last he nodded. "The voice of a rational woman,'' he sighed. "Exactly what I need right now. To keep me from jumping at my own shadow.''

"And remind you to eat.'' She held out another slice of pizza. "You ordered this giant thing. You'd better help me finish it.''

The tension between them instantly evaporated. He settled onto the bed and accepted the proffered slice. "That maternal look becomes you,'' he noted wryly. "So does the pizza sauce.''

"What?'' She swiped at her chin.

"You look like a two-year-old who's decided to finger-paint her face.''

"Good grief, can you hand me the napkins?''

"Let me do it.'' Leaning forward, he gently dabbed away the sauce. As he did, she studied his face, saw the laugh lines creasing the corners of his eyes, the strands of silver intertwined with the brown hair. She remembered the photo of that very face, pasted on a Viratek badge. How somber he'd looked, the unsmiling portrait of a scientist. Now he appeared young and alive and almost happy.

Suddenly aware that she was watching him, he looked up and met her gaze. Slowly his smile faded. They both went very still, as though seeing, in each other's eyes, something they had not noticed before. The voices on the television seemed to fade into a far-off dimension. She felt his fingers trace lightly down her cheek. It was only a touch, but it left her shivering.

She asked, softly, "What happens now, Victor? Where do we go from here?"

"We have several choices."

"Such as?"

"I have friends in Palo Alto. We could turn to them."

"Or?"

"Or we could stay right where we are. For a while."

Right where we are. In this room, on this bed. She wouldn't mind that. Not at all.

She felt herself leaning toward him, drawn by a force against which she could offer no resistance. Both his hands came up to cradle her face, such large hands, but so infinitely gentle. She closed her eyes, knowing that this kiss, too, would be a gentle one.

And it was. This wasn't a kiss driven by fear or desperation. This was a quiet melting together of warmth, of souls. She swayed against him, felt his arms circle behind her to pull her inescapably close. It was a dangerous moment. She could feel herself tottering on the edge of total surrender to this man she scarcely knew. Already, her arms had found their way around his neck and her hands were roaming through the silver-streaked thickness of his hair.

His kisses dropped to her neck, exploring all the tender rises and hollows of her throat. All the needs that had lain dormant these past few years, all the hungers and desires, seemed to stir inside her, awakening at his touch.

And then, in an instant, the magic slipped away. At first she didn't understand why he suddenly pulled back. He sat bolt upright. The expression on his face was one of frozen astonishment. Bewildered, she followed his gaze and saw that he was focused on the television set behind her. She turned to see what had captured his attention.

A disturbingly familiar face stared back from the screen.

She recognized the Viratek logo at the top, the straight-ahead gaze of the man in the photo. Why on earth would they be broadcasting Victor Holland's ID badge?

"...Sought on charges of industrial espionage. Evidence now links Dr. Holland to the death of a fellow Viratek researcher, Dr. Gerald Martinique. Investigators fear the suspect has already sold extensive research data to a European competitor...."

Neither one of them seemed able to move from the bed. They could only stare in disbelief at the newscaster with the Ken doll haircut. The station switched to a commercial break, raisins dancing crazily on a field, proclaiming the wonders of California sunshine. The lilting music was unbearable.

Victor rose to his feet and flicked off the television.

Slowly he turned to look at her. The silence between them grew agonizing.

"It's not true," he said quietly. "None of it."

She tried to read those unfathomable green eyes, wanting desperately to believe him. The taste of his kisses were still warm on her lips. The kisses of a con artist? *Is this just another lie? Has everything you've told me been nothing but lies? Who and what are you, Victor Holland?*

She glanced sideways, at the telephone on the bedside stand. It was so close. One call to the police, that's all it would take to end this nightmare.

"It's a frame-up," he said. "Viratek's releasing false information."

"Why?"

"To corner me. What easier way to find me than to have the police help them?"

She edged toward the phone.

"Don't, Cathy."

She froze, startled by the threat in his voice.

He saw the instant fear in her eyes. Gently he said,

"Please. Don't call. I won't hurt you. I promise you can walk right out that door if you want. But first listen to me. Let me tell you what happened. Give me a chance."

His gaze was steady and absolutely believable. And he was right beside her, ready to stop her from making a move. Or to break her arm, if need be. She had no other choice. Nodding, she settled back down on the bed.

He began to pace, his feet tracing a path in the dull green carpet.

"It's all some—some incredible lie," he said. "It's crazy to think I'd kill him. Jerry Martinique and I were the best of friends. We both worked at Viratek. I was in vaccine development, he was a microbiologist. His specialty was viral studies. Genome research."

"You mean—like chromosomes?"

"The viral equivalent. Anyway, Jerry and I, we helped each other through some bad times. He'd gone through a painful divorce and I..." He paused, his voice dropping. "I lost my wife three years ago. To leukemia."

So he'd been married. Somehow it surprised her. He seemed like the sort of man who was far too independent to have ever said, "I do."

"About two months ago," he continued, "Jerry was transferred to a new research department. Viratek had been awarded a grant for some defense project. It was top security—Jerry couldn't talk about it. But I could see he was bothered by something that was going on in that lab. All he'd say to me was, 'They don't understand the danger. They don't know what they're getting into.' Jerry's field was the alteration of viral genes. So I assume the project had something to do with viruses as weapons. Jerry was fully aware that those weapons are outlawed by international agreement."

"If he knew it was illegal, why did he take part in it?"

"Maybe he didn't realize at first what the project was

aiming for. Maybe they sold it to him as purely defensive research. In any event, he got upset enough to resign from the project. He went right to the top—the founder of Viratek. Walked into Archibald Black's office and threatened to go public if the project wasn't terminated. Four days later he had an accident." Anger flashed in Victor's eyes. It wasn't directed at her, but the fury in that gaze was frightening all the same.

"What happened to him?" she asked.

"His wrecked car was found at the side of the road. Jerry was still inside. Dead, of course." Suddenly, the anger was gone, replaced by overwhelming weariness. He sank onto the bed. "I thought the accident investigation would blow everything into the open. It was a farce. The local cops did their best, but then some federal transportation "expert" showed up on the scene and took over. He said Jerry must've fallen asleep at the wheel. Case closed. That's when I realized just how deep this went. I didn't know who to go to, so I called the FBI in San Francisco. Told them I had evidence."

"You mean the film?" asked Cathy.

Victor nodded. "Just before he was killed, Jerry told me about some duplicate papers he'd stashed away in his garden shed. After the...accident, I went over to his house. Found the place ransacked. But they never bothered to search the shed. That's how I got hold of the evidence, a single file and a roll of film. I arranged a meeting with one of the San Francisco agents, a guy named Sam Polowski. I'd already talked to him a few times on the phone. He offered to meet me in Garberville. We wanted to keep it private, so we agreed to a spot just outside of town. I drove down, fully expecting him to show. Well, someone showed up, all right. Someone who ran me off the road." He paused and looked straight at her. "That's the night you found me."

The night my whole life changed, she thought.

"You have to believe me," he said.

She studied him, her instincts battling against logic. The story was just barely plausible, halfway between truth and fantasy. But the man looked solid as stone.

Wearily she nodded. "I do believe you, Victor. Maybe I'm crazy. Or just gullible. But I do."

The bed shifted as he sat down beside her. They didn't touch, yet she could almost feel the warmth radiating between them.

"That's all that matters to me right now," he said. "That you know, in your heart, I'm telling the truth."

"In my heart?" She shook her head and laughed. "My heart's always been a lousy judge of character. No, I'm guessing. I'm going by the fact you kept me alive. By the fact there's another Cathy Weaver who's now dead..."

Remembering the face of that other woman, the face in the newspaper, she suddenly began to shake. It all added up to the terrible truth. The gun blasts into her apartment, the other dead Cathy. And Sarah, poor Sarah.

She was gulping in shaky breaths, hovering on the verge of tears.

She let him take her in his arms, let him pull her down on the bed beside him. He murmured into her hair, gentle words of comfort and reassurance. He turned off the lamp. In darkness they held each other, two frightened souls joined against a terrifying world. She felt safe there, tucked away against his chest. This was a place where no one could hurt her. It was a stranger's arms, but from the smell of his shirt to the beat of his heart, it all seemed somehow familiar. She never wanted to leave that spot, ever.

She trembled as his lips brushed her forehead. He was stroking her face now, her neck, warming her with his touch. When his hand slipped beneath her blouse, she didn't protest. Somehow it seemed so natural, that that hand would come to lie at her breast. It wasn't the touch of a marauder, it was simply a gentle reminder that she was in safekeeping.

And yet, she found herself responding....

Her nipple tingled and grew taut beneath his cupping hand. The tingling spread, a warmth that crept to her face and flushed her cheeks. She reached for his shirt and began to unbutton it. In the darkness she was slow and clumsy. By the time she finally slid her hand under the fabric, they were both breathing hard and fast with anticipation.

She brushed through the coarse mat of hair, stroking her way across that broad chest. He took in a sharp breath as her fingers skimmed a delicate circle around his nipple.

If playing with fire had been her intention, then she had just struck the match.

His mouth was suddenly on hers, seeking, devouring. The force of his kiss pressed her onto her back, trapping her head against the pillows. For a dizzy eternity she was swimming in sensations, the scent of male heat, the unyielding grip of his hands imprisoning her face. Only when he at last drew away did they both come up for air.

He stared down at her, as though hovering on the edge of temptation.

"This is crazy," he whispered.

"Yes. Yes, it is—"

"I never meant to do this—"

"Neither did I."

"It's just that you're scared. We're both scared. And we don't know what the hell we're doing."

"No." She closed her eyes, felt the unexpected bite of tears. "We don't. But I *am* scared. And I just want to be held. Please, Victor. Hold me, that's all. Just hold me."

He pulled her close, murmuring her name. This time the embrace was gentle, without the fever of desire. His shirt was still unbuttoned, his chest bared. And that's where she lay her head, against that curling nest of hair. Yes, he was right, so wise. They were crazy to be making love when they both knew it was fear, nothing else, that had driven their desire. And now the fever had broken.

A sense of peace fell over her. She curled up against him. Exhaustion robbed them both of speech. Her muscles gradually fell limp as sleep tugged her into its shadow. Even if she tried to, she could not move her arms or legs. Instead she was drifting free, like a wraith in the darkness, floating somewhere in a warm and inky sea.

Vaguely she was aware of light sliding past her eyelids. The warmth encircling her body seemed to melt away. No, she wanted it back, wanted *him* back! An instant later she felt him shaking her.

"Cathy. Come on, wake up!"

Through drowsy eyes she peered at him. "Victor?"

"Something's going on outside."

She tumbled out of bed and followed him to the window. Through a slit in the curtains she spotted what had alarmed him: a patrol car, its radio crackling faintly, parked by the motel registration door. At once she snapped wide awake, her mind going over the exits from their room. There was only one.

"Out, now!" he ordered. "Before we're trapped."

He eased open the door. They scrambled out onto the walkway. The frigid night air was like a slap in the face. She was already shivering, more from fear than from the cold. Running at a crouch, they moved along the walkway, away from the stairs, and ducked past the ice machine.

Below, they heard the lobby door open and the voice of the motel manager: "Yeah, that'll be right upstairs. Gee, he sure seemed like a nice-enough guy...."

Tires screeched as another patrol car pulled up, lights flashing.

Victor gave her a push. *"Go!"*

They slipped into a breezeway and scurried through, to the other side of the building. No stairways there! They climbed over the walkway railing and dropped into the parking lot.

Faintly they heard a banging, then the command: "Open up! This is the police."

At once they were sprinting instinctively for the shadows. No one spotted them, no one gave chase. Still they kept running, until they'd left the Kon-Tiki Motel blocks and blocks behind them, until they were so tired they were stumbling.

At last Cathy slowed to a halt and leaned back against a doorway, her breath coming out in clouds of cold mist. "How did they find you?" she said between gasps.

"It couldn't have been the call...." Suddenly he groaned. "My credit card! I had to use it to pay the bill."

"Where now? Should we try another motel?"

He shook his head. "I'm down to my last forty bucks. I can't risk a credit card again."

"And I left my purse at the apartment. I—I'm not sure I want to—"

"We're not going back for it. They'll be watching the place."

They. Meaning the killers.

"So we're broke," she said weakly.

He didn't answer. He stood with his hands in his pockets, his whole body a study in frustration. "You have friends you can go to?"

"I think so. Uh, no. She's out of town till Friday. And what would I tell her? How would I explain you?"

"You can't. And we can't handle any questions right now."

That leaves out most of my friends, she thought. Nowhere to go, no one to turn to. Unless...

No, she'd promised herself never to sink that low, never to beg for *that* particular source of help.

Victor glanced up the street. "There's a bus stop over there." He reached in his pocket and took out a handful of money. "Here," he said. "Take it and get out of the city. Go visit some friends on your own."

"What about you?"

"I'll be okay."

"Broke? With everyone after you?" She shook her head. "I'll only make things more dangerous for you." He pressed the money into her hand.

She stared down at the wad of bills, thinking: *This is all he has. And he's giving it to me.* "I can't," she said.

"You have to."

"But—"

"Don't argue with me." The look in his eyes left no alternative.

Reluctantly she closed her fingers around the money.

"I'll wait till you get on the bus. It should take you right past the station."

"Victor?"

He silenced her with a single look. Placing both hands on her shoulders, he stood her before him. "You'll be fine," he said. Then he pressed a kiss to her forehead. For a moment his lips lingered, and the warmth of his breath in her hair left her trembling. "I wouldn't leave you if I thought otherwise."

The roar of a bus down the block made them both turn.

"There's your limousine," he whispered. "Go." He gave her a nudge. "Take care of yourself, Cathy."

She started toward the bus stop. Three steps, four. She slowed and came to a halt. Turning, she saw that he had already edged away into the shadows.

"Get on it!" he called.

She looked at the bus. *I won't do it,* she thought.

Tess Gerritsen

She turned back to Victor. "I know a place! A place we can both stay!"

"What?"

"I didn't want to use it but—"

Her words were drowned out as the bus wheezed to the stop, then roared away.

"It's a bit of a walk," she said. "But we'd have beds and a meal. And I can guarantee no one would call the police."

He came out of the shadows. "Why didn't you think of this earlier?"

"I did think of it. But up till now, things weren't, well…desperate enough."

"Not desperate enough," he repeated slowly. He moved toward her, his face taut with incredulity. "Not *desperate* enough? Hell, lady. I'd like to know exactly what kind of crisis would qualify!"

"You have to understand, this is a last resort. It's not an easy place for me to turn to."

His eyes narrowed in suspicion. "This place is beginning to sound worse and worse. What are we talking about? A flophouse?"

"No, it's in Pacific Heights. You could even call the place a mansion."

"Who lives there? A friend?"

"Quite the opposite."

His eyebrow shot up. "An enemy?"

"Close." She let out a sigh of resignation. "My ex-husband."

5

"Jack, open up! Jack!" Cathy banged again and again on the door of the formidable Pacific Heights home. There was no answer. Through the windows they saw only darkness.

"Damn you, Jack!" She gave the door a slap of frustration. "Why aren't you *ever* home when I need you?"

Victor glanced around at the neighborhood of elegant homes and neatly trimmed shrubbery. "We can't stand around out here all night."

"We're not going to," she muttered. Crouching on her knees, she began to dig around in a red-brick planter.

"What are you doing?"

"Something I swore I'd never do." Her fingers raked the loamy soil, searching for the key Jack kept buried under the geraniums. Sure enough, there it was, right where it had always been. She rose to her feet, clapping the dirt off her hands. "But there are limits to my pride. Threat of death being one of them." She inserted the key and felt a momentary dart of panic when it didn't turn. But with a little jiggling, the lock at last gave way. The door swung open to the faint gleam of a polished wood floor, a massive bannister.

She motioned Victor inside. The solid thunk of the door closing behind them seemed to shut out all the dangers of the night. Cloaked in the darkness, they both let out a sigh of relief.

"Just what kind of terms are you on with your ex-husband?'' Victor asked, following her blindly through the unlit foyer.

"Speaking. Barely.''

"He doesn't mind you wandering around his house?''

"Why not?'' She snorted. "Jack lets half the human race wander through his bedroom. The only prerequisite being XX chromosomes.''

She felt her way into the pitch-dark living room and flipped on the light switch. There she froze in astonishment and stared at the two naked bodies intertwined on the polar bear rug.

"*Jack!*'' she blurted out.

The larger of the two bodies extricated himself and sat up. "Hello, Cathy!'' He raked his hand through his dark hair and grinned. "Seems like old times.''

The woman lying next to him spat out a shocking obscenity, scrambled to her feet, and stormed off in a blur of wild red hair and bare bottom toward the bedroom.

"That's Lulu,'' yawned Jack, by way of introduction.

Cathy sighed. "I see your taste in women hasn't improved.''

"No, sweetheart, my taste in women hit a high point when I married you.'' Unmindful of his state of nudity, Jack rose to his feet and regarded Victor. The contrast between the two men was instantly apparent. Though both were tall and lean, it was Jack who possessed the striking good looks, and he knew it. He'd always known it. Vanity wasn't a label one could ever pin on Victor Holland.

"I see you brought a fourth,'' said Jack, giving Victor the once-over. "So, what'll it be, folks? Bridge or poker?''

"Neither,'' said Cathy.

"That opens up all *sorts* of possibilities.''

"Jack, I need your help.''

He turned and looked at her with mock incredulity. "*No!*''

"You know damn well I wouldn't be here if I could avoid it!"

He winked at Victor. "Don't believe her. She's still madly in love with me."

"Can we get serious?"

"Darling, you never did have a sense of humor."

"*Damn you,* Jack!" Everyone had a breaking point and Cathy had reached hers. She couldn't help it; without warning she burst into tears. "For once in your life will you *listen* to me?"

That's when Victor's patience finally snapped. He didn't need a degree in psychology to know this Jack character was a first-class jerk. Couldn't he see that Cathy was exhausted and terrified? Up till this moment, Victor had admired her for her strength. Now he ached at the sight of her vulnerability.

It was only natural to pull her into his arms, to ease her tear-streaked face against his chest. Over her shoulder, he growled out an oath that impugned not only Jack's name but that of Jack's mother as well.

The other man didn't seem to take offense, probably because he'd been called far worse names, and on a regular basis. He simply crossed his arms and regarded Victor with a raised eyebrow. "Being protective, are we?"

"She needs protection."

"From what, pray tell?"

"Maybe you haven't heard. Three days ago, someone murdered her friend Sarah."

"Sarah...Boylan?"

Victor nodded. "Tonight, someone tried to kill Cathy."

Jack stared at him. He looked at his ex-wife. "Is this true? What he's saying?"

Cathy, wiping away tears, nodded.

"Why didn't you tell me this to begin with?"

"Because you were acting like an ass to begin with!" she shot back.

Down the hall came the *click-click* of high-heeled shoes. "She's absolutely right!" yelled a female voice from the foyer. "You *are* an ass, Jack Zuckerman!" The front door opened and slammed shut again. The thud seemed to echo endlessly through the mansion.

There was a long silence.

Suddenly, through her tears, Cathy laughed. "You know what, Jack? I *like* that woman."

Jack crossed his arms and gave his ex-wife the critical once-over. "Either I'm going senile or you forgot to tell me something. Why haven't you gone to the police? Why bother old Jack about this?"

Cathy and Victor glanced at each other.

"We can't go to the police," Cathy said.

"I assume this has to do with *him?*" He cocked a thumb at Victor.

Cathy let out a breath. "It's a complicated story...."

"It must be. If you're afraid to go to the police."

"I can explain it," said Victor.

"Mm-hm. Well." Jack reached for the bathrobe lying in a heap by the polar bear rug. "Well," he said again, calmly tying the sash. "I've always enjoyed watching creativity at work. So let's have it." He sat down on the leather couch and smiled at Victor. "I'm waiting. It's showtime."

Special Agent Sam Polowski lay shivering in his bed, watching the eleven o'clock news. Every muscle in his body ached, his head pounded, and the thermometer at his bedside read an irrefutable 101 degrees. So much for changing flat tires in the pouring rain. He wished he could get his hands on the joker who'd punched that nail in his tire while he was grabbing a quick bite at that roadside cafe. Not only had the culprit managed to keep Sam from his appointment in Garberville, thereby shredding the Viratek case into confetti, Sam had also lost track of his only contact in the affair: Victor Holland. And now, the flu.

Sam reached over for the bottle of aspirin. To hell with the ulcer. His head hurt. And when it came to headaches, there was nothing like Mom's time-tested remedy.

He was in the midst of gulping down three tablets when the news about Victor Holland flashed on the screen.

"...New evidence links the suspect to the murder of fellow Viratek researcher, Dr. Gerald Martinique...."

Sam sat up straight in bed. "What the hell?" he growled at the TV.

Then he grabbed the telephone.

It took six rings for his supervisor to answer. "Dafoe?" Sam said. "This is Polowski."

"Do you know what time it is?"

"Have you seen the late-night news?"

"I happen to be in bed."

"There's a story on Viratek."

A pause. "Yeah, I know. I cleared it."

"What's with this crap about industrial espionage? They're making Holland out to be a—"

"Polowski, drop it."

"Since when did he become a murder suspect?"

"Look, just consider it a cover story. I want him brought in. For his own good."

"So you sic him with a bunch of trigger-happy cops?"

"I said drop it."

"But—"

"You're off the case." Dafoe hung up.

Sam stared in disbelief at the receiver, then at the television, then back at the receiver.

Pull me off the case? He slammed the receiver down so hard the bottle of aspirin tumbled off the nightstand.

That's what you think.

* * *

"I think I've heard about enough," said Jack, rising to his feet. "I want this man out of my house. And I want him out now."

"Jack, please!" said Cathy. "Give him a chance—"

"You're buying this ridiculous tale?"

"I believe him."

"Why?"

She looked at Victor and saw the clear fire of honesty burning in his eyes. "Because he saved my life."

"You're a fool, babycakes." Jack reached for the phone. "You yourself saw the TV. He's wanted for murder. If you don't call the police, I will."

But as Jack picked up the receiver, Victor grabbed his arm. "No," he said. Though his voice was quiet, it held the unmistakable note of authority.

The two men stared at each other, neither willing to back down.

"This is more than just a case of murder," said Victor. "This is deadly research. The manufacture of illegal weapons. This could reach all the way to Washington."

"Who in Washington?"

"Someone in control. Someone with the federal funds to authorize that research."

"I see. Some lofty public servant is out knocking off scientists. With the help of the FBI."

"Jerry wasn't just any scientist. He had a conscience. He was a whistleblower who would've taken this to the press to stop that research. The political fallout would've been disastrous, for the whole administration."

"Wait. Are we talking Pennsylvania Avenue?"

"Maybe."

Jack snorted. "Holland, I *make* Grade B horror films. I don't live them."

"This isn't a film. This is real. Real bullets, real bodies."

"Then that's all the more reason I want nothing to do

with it." Jack turned to Cathy. "Sorry, sweetcakes. It's nothing personal, but I detest the company you keep."

"Jack," she said. "You have to help us!"

"You, I'll help. Him—no way. I draw the line at lunatics and felons."

"You heard what he said! It's a frame-up!"

"You are so gullible."

"Only about you."

"Cathy, it's all right," said Victor. He was standing very still, very calm. "I'll leave."

"No, you won't." Cathy shot to her feet and stalked over to her ex-husband. She stared him straight in the eye, a gaze so direct, so accusing, he seemed to wilt right down into a chair. "You owe it to me, Jack. You owe me for all the years we were married. All the years I put into *your* career, *your* company, *your* idiotic flicks. I haven't asked for anything. You have the house. The Jaguar. The bank account. I never asked because I didn't want to take a damn thing from this marriage except my own soul. But now I'm asking. This man saved my life tonight. If you ever cared about me, if you ever loved me, even a little, then you'll do me this favor."

"Harbor a criminal?"

"Only until we figure out what to do next."

"And how long might that take? Weeks? Months?"

"I don't know."

"Just the kind of definite answer I like."

Victor said, "I need time to find out what Jerry was trying to prove. What it is Viratek's working on—"

"You had one of his files," said Jack. "Why didn't you read the blasted thing?"

"I'm not a virologist. I couldn't interpret the data. It was some sort of RNA sequence, probably a viral genome. A lot of the data was coded. All I can be sure of is the name: Project Cerberus."

"Where is all this vital evidence now?"

"I lost the file. It was in my car the night I was shot. I'm sure they have it back."

"And the film?"

Victor sank into a chair, his face suddenly lined by weariness. "I don't have it. I was hoping that Cathy..." Sighing, he ran his hands through his hair. "I've lost that, too."

"Well," said Jack. "Give or take a few miracles, I'd say this puts your chances at just about zero. And I'm known as an optimist."

"I know where the film is," said Cathy.

There was a long silence. Victor raised his head and stared at her. "What?"

"I wasn't sure about you—not at first. I didn't want to tell you until I could be certain—"

Victor shot to his feet. *"Where is it?"*

She flinched at the sharpness of his voice. He must have noticed how startled she was—his next words were quiet but urgent. "I need that film, Cathy. Before they find it. Where is it?"

"Sarah found it in my car. I didn't know it was yours! I thought it was Hickey's."

"Who's Hickey?"

"A photographer—a friend of mine—"

Jack snorted. "Hickey. Now *there's* a ladies' man."

"He was in a rush to get to the airport," she continued. "At the last minute he left me with some rolls of film. Asked me to take care of them till he got back from Nairobi. But all his film was stolen from my car."

"And my roll?" asked Victor.

"It was in my bathrobe pocket the night Sarah—the night she—" She paused, swallowing at the mention of her friend. "When I got back here, to the city, I mailed it to Hickey's studio."

"Where's the studio?"

"Over on Union Street. I mailed it this afternoon—"

"So it should be there sometime tomorrow." He began to pace the room. "All we have to do is wait for the mail to arrive."

"I don't have a key."

"We'll find a way in."

"Terrific," sighed Jack. "Now he's turning my ex-wife into a burglar."

"We're only after the film!" said Cathy.

"It's still breaking and entering, sweetie."

"You don't have to get involved."

"But you're asking me to harbor the breakers and enterers."

"Just one night, Jack. That's all I'm asking."

"That sounds like one of *my* lines."

"And your lines always work, don't they?"

"Not this time."

"Then here's another line to chew on: 1988. Your federal tax return. Or lack of one."

Jack froze. He glowered at Victor, then at Cathy. "That's below the belt."

"Your most vulnerable spot."

"I'll get around to filing—"

"More words to chew on. Audit. IRS. Jail."

"Okay, okay!" Jack threw his arms up in surrender. "God, I *hate* that word."

"What, *jail?*"

"Don't laugh, babycakes. The word could soon apply to all of us." He turned and headed for the stairs.

"Where are you going?" Cathy demanded.

"To make up the spare beds. Seems I have houseguests for the night...."

"Can we trust him?" Victor asked after Jack had vanished upstairs.

Cathy sank back on the couch, all the energy suddenly

drained from her body, and closed her eyes. "We have to. I can't think of anywhere else to go...."

She was suddenly aware of his approach, and then he was sitting beside her, so close she could feel the overwhelming strength of his presence. He didn't say a word, yet she knew he was watching her.

She opened her eyes and met his gaze. So steady, so intense, it seemed to infuse her with new strength.

"I know it wasn't easy for you," he said. "Asking Jack for favors."

She smiled. "I've always wanted to talk tough with Jack." Ruefully she added, "Until tonight, I've never quite been able to pull it off."

"My guess is, talking tough isn't in your repertoire."

"No, it isn't. When it comes to confrontation, I'm a gutless wonder."

"For a gutless wonder, you did pretty well. In fact, you were magnificent."

"That's because I wasn't fighting for me. I was fighting for you."

"You don't consider yourself worth fighting for?"

She shrugged. "It's the way I was raised. I was always told that sticking up for yourself was unladylike. Whereas sticking up for other people was okay."

He nodded gravely. "Self-sacrifice. A fine feminine tradition."

That made her laugh. "Spoken like a man who knows women well."

"Only two women. My mother and my wife."

At the mention of his dead wife, she fell silent. She wondered what the woman's name was, what she'd looked like, how much he'd loved her. He must have loved her a great deal—she'd heard the pain in his voice earlier that evening when he'd mentioned her death. She felt an unexpected stab of envy that this unnamed wife had been so loved. What

Cathy would give to be as dearly loved by a man! Just as quickly she suppressed the thought, appalled that she could be jealous of a dead woman.

She turned away, her face tinged with guilt. "I think Jack will go along," she said. "Tonight, at least."

"That was blackmail, wasn't it? That stuff about the tax return?"

"He's a careless man. I just reminded him of his oversight."

Victor shook his head. "You are amazing. Jumping along rooftops one minute, blackmailing ex-husbands the next."

"You're so right," said Jack, who'd reappeared at the bottom of the stairs. "She is an amazing woman. I can't wait to see what she'll do next."

Cathy rose wearily to her feet. "At this point I'll do anything." She slipped past Jack and headed up the stairs. "Anything I have to to stay alive."

The two men listened to her footsteps recede along the hall. Then they regarded each other in silence.

"Well," said Jack with forced cheerfulness. "What's next on the agenda? Scrabble?"

"Try solitaire," said Victor, hauling himself off the couch. He was in no mood to share pleasantries with Jack Zuckerman. The man was slick and self-centered and he obviously went through women the way most men went through socks. Victor had a hard time imagining what Cathy had ever seen in the man. That is, aside from Jack's good looks and obvious wealth. There was no denying the fact he was a classic hunk, with the added attraction of money thrown in. Maybe it was that combination that had dazzled her.

A combination I'll certainly never possess, he thought.

He crossed the room, then stopped and turned. "Zuckerman?" he asked. "Do you still love your wife?"

Jack looked faintly startled by the question. "Do I still love her? Well, let me see. No, not exactly. But I suppose I have a sentimental attachment, based on ten years of marriage. And I respect her."

"Respect her? You?"

"Yes. Her talents. Her technical skill. After all, she's my number-one makeup artist."

That's what she meant to him. An asset he could use. *Thinking of himself, the jerk.* If there was anyone else Victor could turn to, he would. But the one man he would've trusted—Jerry—was dead. His other friends might already be under observation. Plus, they weren't in the sort of tax brackets that allowed private little hideaways in the woods. Jack, on the other hand, had the resources to spirit Cathy away to a safe place. Victor could only hope the man's sentimental attachment was strong enough to make him watch out for her.

"I have a proposition," said Victor.

Jack instantly looked suspicious. "What might that be?"

"I'm the one they're really after. Not Cathy. I don't want to make things any more dangerous for her than I already have."

"Big of you."

"It's better if I go off on my own. If I leave her with you, will you keep her safe?"

Jack shifted, looked down at his feet. "Well, sure. I guess so."

"Don't guess. Can you?"

"Look, we start shooting a film in Mexico next month. Jungle scenes, black lagoons, that sort of stuff. Should be a safe-enough place."

"That's next month. What about now?"

"I'll think of something. But first you get yourself out of the picture. Since you're the reason she's in danger in the first place."

Victor couldn't disagree with that last point. *Since the night I met her I've caused her nothing but trouble.*

He nodded. "I'm out of here tomorrow."

"Good."

"Take care of Cathy. Get her out of the city. Out of the country. Don't wait."

"Yeah. Sure."

Something about the way Jack said it, his hasty, whatever-you-say tone, made Victor wonder if the man gave a damn about anyone but himself. But at this point Victor had no choice. He had to trust Jack Zuckerman.

As he climbed the stairs to the guest rooms, it occurred to him that, come morning, it would be goodbye. A quiet little bond had formed between them. He owed his life to her and she to him. That was the sort of link one could never break.

Even if we never see each other again.

In the upstairs hall, he paused outside her closed door. He could hear her moving around the room, opening and closing drawers, squeaking bedsprings.

He knocked on the door. "Cathy?"

There was a pause. Then, "Come in."

One dim lamp lit the room. She was sitting on the bed, dressed in a ridiculously huge man's shirt. Her hair hung in damp waves to her shoulders. The scent of soap and shampoo permeated the shadows. It reminded him of his wife, of the shower smells and feminine sweetness. He stood there, pierced by a sense of longing he hadn't felt in over a year, longing for the warmth, the love, of a woman. Not just any woman. He wasn't like Jack, to whom a soft body with the right equipment would be sufficient. What Victor wanted was the heart and soul; the package they came wrapped in was only of minor importance.

His own wife Lily hadn't been beautiful; neither had she been unattractive. Even at the end, when the ravages of illness had left her shrunken and bruised, there had been a light in her eyes, a gentle spirit's glow.

The same glow he'd seen in Catherine Weaver's eyes the night she'd saved his life. The same glow he saw now.

She sat with her back propped up on pillows. Her gaze was silently expectant, maybe a little fearful. She was clutching a handful of tissues. *Why were you crying?* he wondered.

He didn't approach; he stood just inside the doorway. Their gazes locked together in the gloom. "I've just talked with Jack," he said.

She nodded but said nothing.

"We both agree. It's better that I leave as soon as possible. So I'll be taking off in the morning."

"What about the film?"

"I'll get it. All I need is Hickey's address."

"Yes. Of course." She looked down at the tissues in her fist.

He could tell she wanted to say something. He went to the bed and sat down. Those sweet woman smells grew intoxicating. The neckline of her oversized shirt sagged low enough to reveal a tempting glimpse of shadow. He forced himself to focus on her face.

"Cathy, you'll be fine. Jack said he'd watch out for you. Get you out of the city."

"Jack?" What sounded like a laugh escaped her throat.

"You'll be safer with him. I don't even know where I'll be going. I don't want to drag you into this—"

"But you already have. You've dragged me in over my head, Victor. What am I supposed to do now? I can't just— just sit around and wait for you to fix things. I owe it to Sarah—"

"And I owe it to you not to let you get hurt."

"You think you can hand me over to Jack and make everything be fine again? Well, it won't be fine. Sarah's dead. Her baby's dead. And somehow it's not just your fault. It's mine as well."

"No, it's not. Cathy—"

"It is my fault! Did you know she was lying there in the driveway all night? In the rain. In the cold. There she was, dying, and I slept through the whole damn thing...." She dropped her face in her hands. The guilt that had been tormenting her since Sarah's death at last burst through. She began to cry, silently, ashamedly, unable to hold back the tears any longer.

Victor's response was automatic and instinctively male. He pulled her against him and gave her a warm, safe place to cry. As soon as he felt her settle into his arms, he knew it was a mistake. It was too perfect a fit. She felt as if she belonged there, against his heart, felt that if she ever pulled away there would be left a hole so gaping it could never be filled. He pressed his lips to her damp hair and inhaled her heady scent of soap and warm skin. That gentle fragrance was enough to drown a man with need. So was the softness of her face, the silken luster of that shoulder peeking out from beneath the shirt. And all the time he was stroking her hair, murmuring inane words of comfort, he was thinking: *I have to leave her. For her sake I have to abandon this woman. Or I'll get us both killed.*

"Cathy," he said. It took all the willpower he could muster to pull away. He placed his hands on her shoulders, made her look at him. Her gaze was confused and brimming with tears. "We have to talk about tomorrow."

She nodded and swiped at the tears on her cheeks.

"I want you out of the city, first thing in the morning. Go to Mexico with Jack. Anywhere. Just keep out of sight."

"What will you do?"

"I'm going to take a look at that roll of film, see what kind of evidence it has."

"And then?"

"I don't know yet. Maybe I'll take it to the newspapers. The FBI is definitely out."

"How will I know you're all right? How do I reach you?"

He thought hard, fighting the distraction of her scent, her hair. He found himself stroking the bare skin of her shoulder, marveling at how smooth it felt beneath his fingers.

He focused on her face, on the look of worry in her eyes. "Every other Sunday I'll put an ad in the Personals. *Los Angeles Times*. It'll be addressed to, let's say, Cora. Anything I need to tell you will be there."

"Cora." She nodded. "I'll remember."

They looked at each other, a silent acknowledgment that this parting had to be. He cupped her face and pressed a kiss to her mouth. She barely responded; already, it seemed, she had said her goodbyes.

He rose from the bed and started for the door. There he couldn't resist asking, one more time: "You'll be all right?"

She nodded, but it was too automatic. The sort of nod one gave to dismiss an unimportant question. "I'll be fine. After all, I'll have Jack to watch over me."

He didn't miss the faint note of irony in her reply. Jack, it seemed, didn't inspire confidence in either of them. *What's my alternative? Drag her along with me as a moving target?*

He gripped the doorknob. No, it was better this way. He'd already ripped her life apart; he wasn't going to scatter the pieces as well.

As he was leaving, he took one last backward glance. She was still huddled on the bed, her knees drawn up to her chest. The oversized shirt had slid off one bare shoulder. For a moment he thought she was crying. Then she raised her head and met his gaze. What he saw in her eyes wasn't tears. It was something far more moving, something pure and bright and beautiful.

Courage.

In the pale light of dawn, Savitch stood outside Jack Zuckerman's house. Through the fingers of morning mist, Savitch studied the curtained windows, trying to picture the inhabitants within. He wondered who they were, in which room they slept, and whether Catherine Weaver was among them.

He'd find out soon.

He pocketed the black address book he'd taken from the woman's apartment. The name C. Zuckerman and this Pacific Heights address had been written on the inside front cover. Then the Zuckerman had been crossed out and replaced with Weaver. She was a divorcée, he concluded. Under Z, he'd found a prominent listing for a man named Jack, with various phone numbers and addresses, both foreign and domestic. Her ex-husband, he'd confirmed, after a brief chat with another name listed in the book. Pumping strangers for information was a simple matter. All it took was an air of authority and a cop's ID. The same ID he was planning to use now.

He gave the house one final perusal, taking in the manicured lawns and shrubbery, the trellis with its vines of winter-dormant wisteria. A successful man, this Jack Zuckerman. Savitch had always admired men of wealth. He gave his jacket a final tug to assure himself that the shoulder holster was concealed. Then he crossed the street to the front porch and rang the doorbell.

6

At first light, Cathy awakened. It wasn't a gentle return but a startling jerk back to consciousness. She was instantly aware that she was not in her own bed and that something was terribly wrong. It took her a few seconds to remember exactly what it was. And when she did remember, the sense of urgency was so compelling she rose at once from bed and began to dress in the semidarkness. *Have to be ready to run...*

The creak of floorboards in the next room told her that Victor was awake as well, probably planning his moves for the day. She rummaged through the closet, searching for things he might need in his flight. All she came up with was a zippered nylon bag and a raincoat. She searched the dresser next and found a few men's socks. She also found a collection of women's underwear. *Damn Jack and all his women,* she thought with sudden irritation and slammed the drawer shut. The thud was still resonating in the room when another sound echoed through the house.

The doorbell was ringing.

It was only seven o'clock, too early for visitors or deliverymen. Suddenly her door swung open. She turned to see Victor, his face etched with tension.

"What should we do?" she asked.

"Get ready to leave. Fast."

"There's a back door—"

"Let's go."

They hurried along the hall and had almost reached the

top of the stairs when they heard Jack's sleepy voice below, grumbling: "I'm coming, dammit! Stop that racket, I'm coming!"

The doorbell rang again.

"Don't answer it!" hissed Cathy. "Not yet—"

Jack had already opened the door. Instantly Victor snatched Cathy back up the hall, out of sight. They froze with their backs against the wall, listening to the voices below.

"Yeah," they heard Jack say. "I'm Jack Zuckerman. And who are you?"

The visitor's voice was soft. They could tell only that it was a man.

"Is that so?" said Jack, his voice suddenly edged with panic. "You're with the *FBI*, you say? And what on earth would the *FBI* want with my *ex-wife?*"

Cathy's gaze flew to Victor. She read the frantic message in his eyes: *Which way out?*

She pointed toward the bedroom at the end of the hall. He nodded. Together they tiptoed along the carpet, all the time aware that one misstep, one loud creak, might be enough to alert the agent downstairs.

"Where's your warrant?" they heard Jack demand of the visitor. "Hey, wait a minute! You can't just barge in here without a court order or something!"

No time left! thought Cathy in panic as she slipped into the last room. They closed the door behind them.

"The window!" she whispered.

"You mean jump?"

"No." She hurried across the room and gingerly eased the window open. "There's a trellis!"

He glanced down dubiously at the tangled vines of wisteria. "Are you sure it'll hold us?"

"I know it will," she said, swinging her leg over the sill. "I caught one of Jack's blondes hanging off it one night. And believe me, she was a *big* girl." She glanced down at the ground far below and felt a sudden wave of nausea as the old fear of heights washed through her. "God," she muttered. "Why do we always seem to be hanging out of windows?"

From somewhere in the house came Jack's outraged shout: "You can't go up there! You haven't shown me your warrant!"

"Move!" snapped Victor.

Cathy lowered herself onto the trellis. Branches clawed her face as she scrambled down the vine. An instant after she landed on the dew-soaked grass, Victor dropped beside her.

At once they were on their feet and sprinting for the cover of shrubbery. Just as they rolled behind the azalea bushes, they heard a second-floor window slide open, and then Jack's voice complaining loudly: "I know my rights! This is an illegal search! I'm going to call my lawyer!"

Don't let him see us! prayed Cathy, burrowing frantically into the bush. She felt Victor's body curl around her back, his arms pulling her tightly to him, his breath hot and ragged against her neck. For an eternity they lay shivering in the grass as mist swirled around them.

"You see?" they heard Jack say. "There's no one here but me. Or would you like to check the garage?"

The window slid shut.

Victor gave Cathy a little push. "Go," he whispered. "The end of the hedge. We'll run from there."

On hands and knees she crawled along the row of azalea bushes. Her soaked jeans were icy and her palms scratched and bleeding, but she was too numbed by terror to feel any pain. All her attention was focused on moving forward. Victor was crawling close behind her. When she felt him bump up against her hip, it occurred to her what a ridiculous view he had, her rump swaying practically under his nose.

She reached the last bush and stopped to shove a handful of tangled hair off her face. "That house next?" she asked.

"Go for it!"

They both took off like scared rabbits, dashing across the twenty yards of lawn between houses. Once they reached the cover of the next house, they didn't stop. They kept running, past parked cars and early-morning pedestrians. Five blocks later, they ducked into a coffee shop. Through the front window, they glanced out at the street, watching for signs of pursuit. All they saw was the typical Monday morning bustle: the stop-and-go traffic, the passersby bundled up in scarves and overcoats.

From the grill behind them came the hiss and sizzle of bacon. The smell of freshly brewed coffee wafted from the counter burner. The aromas were almost painful; they reminded Cathy that she and Victor probably had a total of forty dollars between them. Damn it, why hadn't she begged, borrowed or stolen some cash from Jack?

"What now?" she asked, half hoping he'd suggest blowing the rest of their cash on breakfast.

He scanned the street. "Let's go on."

"Where?"

"Hickey's studio."

"Oh." She sighed. Another long walk, and all on an empty stomach.

Outside, a car passed by bearing the bumper sticker: Today is the First Day of the Rest of Your Life.

Lord, I hope it gets better than this, she thought. Then she followed Victor out the door and into the morning chill.

Field Supervisor Larry Dafoe was sitting at his desk, pumping away at his executive power chair. Upper body strength, he always said, was the key to success as a man.

Bulk out those muscles *pull!*, fill out that size forty-four jacket *pull!*, and what you got was a pair of shoulders that'd impress any woman, intimidate any rival. And with this snazzy 700-buck model, you didn't even have to get out of your chair.

Sam Polowski watched his superior strain at the system of wires and pulleys and thought the device looked more like an exotic instrument of torture.

"What you gotta understand," gasped Dafoe, "is that there are other *pull!* issues at work here. Things you know nothing about."

"Like what?" asked Polowski.

Dafoe released the handles and looked up, his face sheened with a healthy sweat. "If I was at liberty to tell you, don't you think I already would've?"

Polowski looked at the gleaming black exercise handles, wondering whether he'd benefit from an executive power chair. Maybe a souped-up set of biceps was what he needed to get a little respect around this office.

"I still don't see what the point is," he said. "Putting Victor Holland in the hot seat."

"The point," said Dafoe, "is that you don't call the shots."

"I gave Holland my word he'd be left out of this mess."

"He's *part* of the mess! First he claims he has evidence, then he pulls a vanishing act."

"That's partly my fault. I never made it to the rendezvous."

"Why hasn't he tried to contact you?"

"I don't know." Polowski sighed and shook his head. "Maybe he's dead."

"Maybe we just need to find him." Dafoe reached for the exercise handles. "Maybe you need to get to work on the Lanzano file. Or maybe you should just go home. You look terrible."

"Yeah. Sure." Polowski turned. As he left the office, he could hear Dafoe once again huffing and puffing. He went to his desk, sat down and contemplated his collection of cold capsules, aspirin and cough syrup. He took a double dose of each. Then he reached in his briefcase and pulled out the Viratek file.

It was his own private collection of scrambled notes and phone numbers and news clippings. He sifted through them, stopping to ponder once again the link between Holland and the woman Catherine Weaver. He'd first seen her name on the hospital admission sheet, and had later been startled to hear of her connection to the murdered Garberville woman. Too many coincidences, too many twists and turns. Was there something obvious here he was missing? Might the woman have an answer or two?

He reached for the telephone and dialed the Garberville police department. They would know how to reach their witness. And maybe she would know how to find Victor Holland. It was a long shot but Sam Polowski was an inveterate horseplayer. He had a penchant for long shots.

The man ringing his doorbell looked like a tree stump dressed in a brown polyester suit. Jack opened the door and said, "Sorry, I'm not buying today."

"I'm not selling anything, Mr. Zuckerman," said the man. "I'm with the FBI."

Jack sighed. "Not again."

"I'm Special Agent Sam Polowski. I'm trying to locate a woman named Catherine Weaver, formerly Zuckerman. I believe she —"

"Don't you guys ever know when to quit?"

"Quit what?"

"One of your agents was here this morning. Talk to him!"

The man frowned. "One of *our* agents?"

"Yeah. And I just might register a complaint against him. Barged right in here without a warrant and started tramping all over my house."

"What did he look like?"

"Oh, I don't know! Dark hair, terrific build. But he could've used a course in charm school."

"Was he about my height?"

"Taller. Skinnier. Lots more hair."

"Did he give you his name? It wasn't Mac Braden, was it?"

"Naw, he didn't give me any name."

Polowski pulled out his badge. Jack squinted at the words: Federal Bureau of Investigation. "Did he show you one of these?" asked Polowski.

"No. He just asked about Cathy and some guy named Victor Holland. Whether I knew how to find them."

"Did you tell him?"

"That jerk?" Jack laughed. "I wouldn't bother to give him the time of day. I sure as hell wasn't going to tell him about—" Jack paused and cleared his throat. "I wasn't going to tell him anything. Even if I knew. Which I don't."

Polowski slipped his badge into his pocket, all the time gazing steadily at Jack. "I think we should talk, Mr. Zuckerman."

"What about?"

"About your ex-wife. About the fact she's in big trouble."

"That," sighed Jack, "I already know."

"She's going to get hurt. I can't fill you in on all the details because I'm still in the dark myself. But I do know one woman's already been hit. Your wife—"

"My ex-wife."

"Your ex-wife could be next."

Jack, unconvinced, merely looked at him.

"It's your duty as a citizen to tell me what you know," Polowski reminded him.

"My duty. Right."

"Look, cooperate, and you and me, we'll get along just fine. Give me grief, and I'll give *you* grief." Polowski smiled. Jack didn't. "Now, Mr. Zuckerman. Hey, can I call you Jack? Jack, why don't you tell me where she is? Before it's too late. For both of you."

Jack scowled at him. He drummed his fingers against the door frame. He debated. At last he stepped aside. "As a law-abiding citizen, I suppose it is my duty." Grudgingly, he waved the man in. "Oh, just come in, Polowski. I'll tell you what I know."

The window shattered, raining slivers into the gloomy space beyond.

Cathy winced at the sound. "Sorry, Hickey," she said under her breath.

"We'll make it up to him," said Victor, knocking off the remaining shards. "We'll send him a nice fat check. You see anyone?"

She glanced up and down the alley. Except for a crumpled newspaper tumbling past the trash cans, nothing moved. A few blocks away, car horns blared, the sounds of another Union Street traffic jam.

"All clear," she whispered.

"Okay." Victor draped his windbreaker over the sill. "Up you go."

He gave her a lift to the window. She clambered through and landed among the glass shards. Seconds later, Victor dropped down beside her.

They were standing in the studio dressing room. Against one wall hung a rack of women's lingerie; against the other were makeup tables and a long mirror.

Victor frowned at a cloud of peach silk flung over one

of the chairs. "What kind of photos does your friend take, anyway?"

"Hickey specializes in what's politely known as 'boudoir portraits.'"

Victor's startled gaze turned to a black lace negligee hanging from a wall hook. "Does that mean what I think it means?"

"What do you think it means?"

"You know."

She headed into the next room. "Hickey insists it's not pornography. It's tasteful erotic art...." She stopped in her tracks as she came face-to-face with a photo blowup on the wall. Naked limbs—eight, maybe more—were entwined in a sort of human octopus. Nothing was left to the imagination. Nothing at all.

"Tasteful," Victor said dryly.

"That must be one of his, uh, commercial assignments."

"I wonder what product they were selling."

She turned and found herself staring at another photograph. This time it was two women, drop-dead gorgeous and wearing not a stitch.

"Another commercial assignment?" Victor inquired politely over her shoulder.

She shook her head. "Don't ask."

In the front room they found a week's worth of mail piled up beneath the door slot, darkroom catalogues and advertising flyers. The roll of film Cathy had mailed the day before was not yet in the mound.

"I guess we just sit around and wait for the postman," she said.

He nodded. "Seems like a safe-enough place. Any chance your friend keeps food around?"

"I seem to remember a refrigerator in the other room."

She led Victor into what Hickey had dubbed his "shooting gallery." Cathy flipped the wall switch and the vast room was instantly illuminated by a dazzling array of spot-lights.

"So this is where he does it," said Victor, blinking in the sudden glare. He stepped over a jumble of electrical cords and slowly circled the room, regarding with humorous disbelief the various props. It was a strange collection of objects: a genuine English phone booth, a street bench, an exercise bicycle. In a place of honor sat a four-poster bed. The ruffled coverlet was Victorian; the handcuffs dangling from the bedposts were not.

Victor picked up one of the cuffs and let it fall again. "Just how good a friend *is* this Hickey guy, anyway?"

"None of this stuff was here when he shot me a month ago."

"He photographed *you?*" Victor turned and stared at her.

She flushed, imagining the images that must be flashing through his mind. She could feel his gaze undressing her, posing her in a sprawl across that ridiculous four-poster bed. With the handcuffs, no less.

"It wasn't like—like these other photos," she protested. "I mean, I just did it as a favor...."

"A favor?"

"It was a purely *commercial* shot!"

"Oh."

"I was fully dressed. In overalls, as a matter of fact. I was supposed to be a plumber."

"A lady plumber?"

"I was an emergency stand-in. One of his models didn't show up that day, and he needed someone with an ordinary face. I guess that's me. Ordinary. And it really was just my face."

"And your overalls."

"Right."

They looked at each other and burst out laughing.

"I can guess what you were thinking," she said.

"I don't even want to *tell* you what I was thinking." He turned and glanced around the room. "Didn't you say there was some food around here?"

She crossed the room to the refrigerator. Inside she found a shelf of film plus a jar of sweet pickles, some rubbery carrots and half a salami. In the freezer they discovered real treasures: ground Sumatran coffee and a loaf of sourdough bread.

Grinning, she turned to him. "A feast!"

They sat together on the four-poster bed and gnawed on salami and half-frozen sourdough, all washed down with cups of coffee. It was a bizarre little picnic, paper plates with pickles and carrots resting in their laps, the spotlights glaring down like a dozen hot suns from the ceiling.

"Why did you say that about yourself?" he asked, watching her munch a carrot.

"Say what?"

"That you're ordinary. So ordinary that you get cast as the lady plumber?"

"Because I am ordinary."

"I don't think so. And I happen to be a pretty good judge of character."

She looked up at a wall poster featuring one of Hickey's super models. The woman stared back with a look of glossy confidence. "Well, I certainly don't measure up to *that*."

"*That*," he said, "is pure fantasy. *That* isn't a real woman, but an amalgam of makeup, hairspray and fake eyelashes."

"Oh, I know that. That's my job, turning actors into some moviegoer's fantasy. Or nightmare, as the case may be." She reached into the jar and fished out the last pickle. "No, I really meant *underneath* it all. Deep inside, I *feel* ordinary."

"I think you're quite extraordinary. And after last night, I should know."

She gazed down, at the limp carrot stretched out like a little corpse across the paper plate. "There was a time—I suppose there's always that time, for everyone, when we're still young, when we feel special. When we feel the world's meant just for us. The last time I felt that way was when I married Jack." She sighed. "It didn't last long."

"Why did you marry him?"

"I don't know. Dazzle? I was only twenty-three, a mere apprentice on the set. He was the director." She paused. "He was *God.*"

"He impressed you, did he?"

"Jack can be very impressive. He can turn on the power, the charisma, and just overwhelm a gal. Then there was the champagne, the suppers, the flowers. I think what attracted him to me was that I didn't immediately fall for him. That I wasn't swooning at his every look. He thought of me as a challenge, the one he finally conquered." She gave him a rueful look. "That accomplished, he moved onto bigger and better things. That's when I realized that I wasn't particularly special. That I'm really just a perfectly ordinary woman. It's not a bad feeling. It's not as if I go through life longing to be someone different, someone special."

"Then who do you consider special?"

"Well, my grandmother. But she's dead."

"Venerable grandmothers always make the list."

"Okay, then. Mother Teresa."

"She's on everyone's list."

"Kate Hepburn. Gloria Steinem. My friend Sarah..." Her voice faded. Looking down, she added softly: "But she's dead, too."

Gently he took her hand. With a strange sense of wonder she watched his long fingers close over hers and thought about how the strength she felt in that grasp reflected the strength of the man himself. Jack, for all his dazzle and polish, had never inspired a fraction of the confidence she now felt in Victor. No man ever had.

He was watching her with quiet sympathy. "Tell me about Sarah," he said.

Cathy swallowed, trying to stem the tears. "She was absolutely lovely. I don't mean in *that* way." She nodded at the photo of Hickey's picture-perfect model. "I mean, in an inner sort of way. It was this look in her eyes. A perfect calmness. As though she'd found exactly what she wanted while all the rest of us were still grubbing around for lost treasure. I don't think she was born like that. She came to it, all by herself. In college, we were both pretty unsure of ourselves. Marriage certainly didn't help either of us. My divorce—it was nothing short of devastating. But Sarah's divorce only seemed to make her stronger. Better able to take care of herself. When she finally got pregnant, it was exactly as she planned it. There wasn't a father, you see, just a test tube. An anonymous donor. Sarah used to say that the primeval family unit wasn't man, woman and child. It was just woman and child. I thought she was brave, to take that step. She was a lot braver than I could ever be...." She cleared her throat. "Anyway, Sarah *was* special. Some people simply are."

"Yes," he said. "Some people are."

She looked up at him. He was staring off at the far wall, his gaze infinitely sad. What had etched those lines of pain in his face? She wondered if lines so deep could ever be erased. There were some losses one never got over, never accepted.

Softly she asked, "What was your wife like?"

He didn't answer at first. She thought: *Why did I ask that? Why did I have to bring up such terrible memories?*

He said, "She was a kind woman. That's what I'll always remember about her. Her kindness." He looked at

Cathy and she sensed it wasn't sadness she saw in those eyes, but acceptance.

"What was her name?"

"Lily. Lillian Dorinda Cassidy. A mouthful for such a tiny woman." He smiled. "She was about five foot one, maybe ninety pounds sopping wet. It used to scare me, how small she always seemed. Almost breakable. Especially toward the end, when she'd lost all that weight. It seemed as if she'd shrunk down to nothing but a pair of big brown eyes."

"She must have been young when she died."

"Only thirty-eight. It seemed so unfair. All her life, she'd done everything right. Never smoked, hardly ever touched a glass of wine. She even refused to eat meat. After she was diagnosed, we kept trying to figure out how it could've happened. Then it occurred to us what might have caused it. She grew up in a small town in Massachusetts. Directly downwind from a nuclear power plant."

"You think that was it?"

"One can never be sure. But we asked around. And we learned that, just in her neighborhood, at least twenty families had someone with leukemia. It took four years and a class-action suit to force an investigation. What they found was a history of safety violations going back all the way to the plant's opening."

Cathy shook her head in disbelief. "And all those years they allowed it to operate?"

"No one knew about it. The violations were hushed up so well even the federal regulators were kept in the dark."

"They shut it down, didn't they?"

He nodded. "I can't say I got much satisfaction, seeing the plant finally close. By that time Lily was gone. And all the families, well, we were exhausted by the fight. Even though it sometimes felt as though we were banging our heads against a wall, we knew it was something we had to

do. *Somebody* had to do it, for all the Lilys of the world."
He looked up, at the spotlights shining above. "And here
I am again, still banging my head against walls. Only this
time, it feels like the Great Wall of China. And the lives
at stake are yours and mine."

Their gazes met. She sat absolutely still as he lightly
stroked down the curve of her cheek. She took his hand,
pressed it to her lips. His fingers closed over hers, refusing
to release her hand. Gently he tugged her close. Their lips
met, a tentative kiss that left her longing for more.

"I'm sorry you were pulled into this," he murmured.
"You and Sarah and those other Cathy Weavers. None of
you asked to be part of it. And somehow I've managed to
hurt you all."

"Not you, Victor. You're not the one to blame. It's this
windmill you're tilting at. This giant, dangerous windmill.
Anyone else would have dropped his lance and fled. You're
still going at it."

"I didn't have much of a choice."

"But you did. You could have walked away from your
friend's death. Turned a blind eye to whatever's going on
at Viratek. That's what Jack would have done."

"But I'm not Jack. There are things I can't walk away
from. I'd always be thinking of the Lilys. All the thousands
of people who might get hurt."

At the mention once again of his dead wife, Cathy felt
some unbreachable barrier form between them—the
shadow of Lily, the wife she'd never met. Cathy drew back,
at once aching from the loss of his touch.

"You think that many people could die?" she asked.

"Jerry must have thought so. There's no way to predict
the outcome. The world's never seen the effects of all-out
biological warfare. I like to think it's because we're too
smart to play with our own self-destruction. Then I think

of all the crazy things people have done over the years and it scares me...."

"Are viral weapons that dangerous?"

"If you alter a few genes, make it just a little more contagious, raise the kill ratio, you'd end up with a devastating strain. The research alone is hazardous. A single slip-up in lab security and you could have millions of people accidentally infected. And no means of treatment. It's the kind of worldwide disaster a scientist doesn't want to think about."

"Armageddon."

He nodded, his gaze frighteningly sane. "If you believe in such a thing. That's exactly what it'd be."

She shook her head. "I don't understand why these things are allowed."

"They aren't. By international agreement, they're outlawed. But there's always some madman lurking in the shadows who wants that extra bit of leverage, that weapon no one else has."

A madman. That's what one would have to be, to even think of unleashing such a weapon on the world. She thought of a novel she'd read, about just such a plague, how the cities had lain dead and decaying, how the very air had turned poisonous. But those were only the nightmares of science fiction. This was real.

From somewhere in the building came the sound of whistling.

Cathy and Victor both sat up straight. The melody traveled along the hall, closer and closer, until it stopped right outside Hickey's door. They heard a rustling, then the slap of magazines hitting the floor.

"It's here!" said Cathy, leaping to her feet.

Victor was right behind her as she hurried into the front room. She spotted it immediately, sitting atop the pile: a padded envelope, addressed in her handwriting. She scooped it up and ripped the envelope open. Out slid the roll of film. The note she'd scribbled to Hickey fluttered to the floor. Grinning in triumph, she held up the canister. "Here's your evidence!"

"We hope. Let's see what we've got on the roll. Where's the darkroom?"

"Next to the dressing room." She handed him the film. "Do you know how to process it?"

"I've done some amateur photography. As long as I've got the chemicals I can—" He stopped and glanced over at the desk.

The phone was ringing.

Victor shook his head. "Ignore it," he said and turned for the darkroom.

As they left the reception room, they heard the answering machine click on. Hickey's voice, smooth as silk, spoke on the recording. "This is the studio of Hickman Von Trapp, specializing in tasteful and artistic images of the female form...."

Victor laughed. "Tasteful?"

"It depends on your taste," said Cathy as she followed him up the hall.

They had just reached the darkroom when the recording ended and was followed by the message beep. An agitated voice rattled from the speaker. "Hello? Hello, Cathy? If you're there, answer me, will you? There's an FBI agent looking for you—some guy named Polowski—"

Cathy stopped dead. "It's Jack!" she said, turning to retrace her steps toward the front room.

The voice on the speaker had taken on a note of panic. "I couldn't help it—he made me tell him about Hickey. Get out of there now!"

The message clicked off just as Cathy grabbed the receiver. "Hello? *Jack?*"

She heard only the dial tone. He'd already hung up.

Hands shaking, she began to punch in Jack's phone number.

"There's no time!" said Victor.

"I have to talk to him—"

He grabbed the receiver and slammed it down. "Later! We have to get out of here!"

She nodded numbly and started for the door. There she halted. "Wait. We need money!" She turned back to the reception desk and searched the drawers until she found the petty cash box. Twenty-two dollars was all it contained. "Always keep just enough for decent coffee beans," Hickey used to say. She pocketed the money. Then she reached up and yanked one of Hickey's old raincoats from the door hook. He wouldn't miss it. And she might need it for concealment. "Okay," she said, slipping on the coat. "Let's go."

They paused only a second to check the corridor. From another suite came the faint echo of laughter. Somewhere above, high heels clicked across a wooden floor. With Victor in the lead, they darted down the hall and out the front door.

The midday sun seemed to glare down on them like an accusing eye. Quickly they fell into step with the rest of the lunch crowd, the businessmen and artists, the Union Street chic. No one glanced their way. But even with people all around her, Cathy felt conspicuous. As though, in this bright cityscape of crowds and concrete, she was the focus of the painter's eye.

She huddled deeper into the raincoat, wishing it were a mantle of invisibility. Victor had quickened his pace, and she had to run to keep up.

"Where do we go now?" she whispered.

"We've got the film. Now I say we head for the bus station."

"And then?"

"Anywhere." He kept his gaze straight ahead. "As long as it's out of this city."

7

That pesky FBI agent was ringing his doorbell again.

Sighing, Jack opened the front door. "Back already?"

"Damn right I'm back." Polowski stamped in and shoved the door closed behind him. "I want to know where to find 'em next."

"I told you, Mr. Polowski. Over on Union Street there's a studio owned by Mr. Hickman—"

"I've been to Von Whats-his-name's studio."

Jack swallowed. "You didn't find them?"

"You knew I wouldn't. You warned 'em, didn't you?"

"Really, I don't know why you're harrassing me. I've tried to be—"

"They left in a hurry. The door was wide open. Food was still lying around. They left the empty cash box just sitting on the desk."

Jack drew himself up in outrage. "Are you calling my ex-wife a petty thief?"

"I'm calling her a desperate woman. And I'm calling you an imbecile for screwing things up. Now where is she?"

"I don't know."

"Who would she turn to?"

"No one I know."

"Think harder."

Jack stared down at Polowski's turgid face and marveled that any human being could be so unattractive. Surely the process of natural selection would have dictated against such unacceptable genes?

Jack shook his head. "I honestly don't know."

It was the truth, and Polowski must have sensed it. After a moment of silent confrontation, he backed off. "Then maybe you can tell me this. Why did you warn them?"

"It—it was—" Jack shrugged helplessly. "Oh, I don't know! After you left, I wasn't sure I'd done the right thing. I wasn't sure whether to trust you. *He* doesn't trust you."

"Who?"

"Victor Holland. He thinks you're in on some conspiracy. Frankly, the man struck me as just the slightest bit paranoid."

"He has a right to be. Considering what's happened to him so far." Polowski turned for the door.

"Now what happens?"

"I keep looking for them."

"Where?"

"You think I'd tell *you?*" He stalked out. "Don't leave town, Zuckerman," he snapped over his shoulder. "I'll be back to see you later."

"I don't think so," Jack muttered softly as he watched the other man lumber back to his car. He looked up and saw there wasn't a cloud in the sky. Smiling to himself, he shut the door.

It would be sunny in Mexico, as well.

Someone had left in a hurry.

Savitch strolled through the rooms of the photo studio, which had been left unlocked. He noted the scraps of a meal on the four-poster bed: crumbs of sourdough bread, part of a salami, an empty pickle jar. He also took note of the coffee cups: there were two of them. Interesting, since Savitch had spotted only one person leaving the studio, a squat little man in a polyester suit. The man hadn't been there long. Savitch had observed him climb into a dark green Ford parked at a fifteen-minute meter. The meter still had three minutes remaining.

Savitch continued his tour of the studio, eyeing the tawdry photos, wondering if this wasn't another waste of his time. After all, every other address he'd pulled from the woman's black book had turned up no sign of her. Why should Hickman Von Trapp's address be any different?

Still, he couldn't shake the instinct that he was getting close. Clues were everywhere. He read them, put them together. Today, this studio had been visited by two hungry people. They'd entered through a broken window in the dressing room. They'd eaten scraps taken from the refrigerator. They (or the man in the polyester suit) had emptied the petty cash box.

Savitch completed his tour and returned to the front room. That's when he noticed the telephone message machine blinking on and off.

He pressed the play button. The string of messages seemed endless. The calls were for someone named Hickey—no doubt the Hickman Von Trapp of the address book. Savitch lazily circled the room, half listening to the succession of voices. Business calls for the most part, inquiring about appointments, asking when proofs would be ready and would he like to do the shoot for *Snoop* magazine? Near the door, Savitch halted and stooped down to sift through the pile of mail. It was boring stuff, all addressed to Von Trapp. Then he noticed, off to the side, a loose slip of paper. It was a note, addressed to Hickey.

"Feel awful about this, but someone stole all those rolls of film from my car. This was the only one left. Thought I'd get it to you before it's lost, as well. Hope it's enough to save your shoot from being a complete waste—"

It was signed "Cathy."

He stood up straight. Catherine Weaver? It had to be! The roll of film—where the hell was the roll of film?

He rifled through the mail, searching, searching. He turned up only a torn envelope with Cathy Weaver's return address. The film was gone. In frustration, he began to fling magazines across the room. Then, in mid-toss, he froze.

A new message was playing on the recorder.

"Hello? Hello, Cathy? If you're there, answer me, will you? There's an FBI agent looking for you—some guy named Polowski. I couldn't help it—he made me tell him about Hickey. Get out of there now!"

Savitch stalked over to the answering machine and stared down as the mechanism automatically whirred back to the beginning. He replayed it.

Get out of there now!

There was now no doubt. Catherine Weaver had been here, and Victor Holland was with her. But who was this agent Polowski and why was he searching for Holland? Savitch had been assured that the Bureau was off the case. He would have to check into the matter.

He crossed over to the window and stared out at the bright sunshine, the crowded sidewalks. So many faces, so many strangers. Where, in this city, would two terrified fugitives hide? Finding them would be difficult, but not impossible.

He left the suite and went outside to a pay phone. There he dialed a Washington, D.C., number. He wasn't fond of asking the Cowboy for help, but now he had no choice. Victor Holland had his hands on the evidence, and the stakes had shot sky-high.

It was time to step up the pursuit.

The clerk yelled, "Next window, please!" and closed the grate.

"Wait!" cried Cathy, tapping at the pane. "My bus is leaving right now!"

"Which one?"

"Number 23 to Palo Alto—"

"There's another at seven o'clock."

"But—"

"I'm on my dinner break."

Cathy stared helplessly as the clerk walked away. Over the PA system came the last call for the Palo Alto express. Cathy glanced around just in time to see the Number 23 roar away from the curb.

"Service just ain't what it used to be," an old man muttered behind her. "Get there faster usin' yer damn thumb."

Sighing, Cathy shifted to the next line, which was eight-deep and slow as molasses. The woman at the front was trying to convince the clerk that her social security card was an acceptable ID for a check.

Okay, Cathy thought. *So we leave at seven o'clock. That puts us in Palo Alto at eight. Then what? Camp in a park? Beg a few scraps from a restaurant? What does Victor have in mind…?*

She glanced around and spotted his broad back hunched inside one of the phone booths. Whom could he possibly be calling? She saw him hang up and run his hand wearily through his hair. Then he picked up the receiver and dialed another number.

"Next!" Someone tapped Cathy on the shoulder. "Go ahead, Miss."

Cathy turned and saw that the ticket clerk was waiting. She stepped to the window.

"Where to?" asked the clerk.

"I need two tickets to…" Cathy's voice suddenly faded. "Where?"

Cathy didn't speak. Her gaze had frozen on a poster tacked right beside the ticket window. The words Have You seen This Man? appeared above an unsmiling photo of Victor Holland. And at the bottom were listed the charges: Industrial espionage and murder. If you have any information about this man, please contact your local police or the FBI.

"Lady, you wanna go somewhere or not?"

"What?" Cathy's gaze jerked back to the clerk, who was watching her with obvious annoyance. "Oh. Yes, I'm—I'd like two tickets. To Palo Alto." Numbly she handed over a fistful of cash. "One way."

"Two to Palo Alto. That bus will depart at 7:00, Gate 11."

"Yes. Thank you..." Cathy took the tickets and turned to leave the line. That's when she spotted the two policemen, standing just inside the front entrance. They seemed to be scanning the terminal, searching—for what?

In a panic, her gaze shot to the phone booth. It was empty. She stared at it with a sense of abandonment. *You left me! You left me with two tickets to Palo Alto and five bucks in my pocket!*

Where are you, Victor?

She couldn't stand here like an idiot. She had to do something, had to move. She pulled the raincoat tightly around her shoulders and forced herself to stroll across the terminal. *Don't let them notice me,* she prayed. *Please. I'm nobody. Nothing.* She paused at a chair and picked up a discarded *San Francisco Chronicle.* Then, thumbing through the Want Ads, she sauntered right past the two policemen. They didn't even glance at her as she went out the front entrance.

Now what? she wondered, pausing amidst the confusion of a busy sidewalk. Automatically she started to walk and had taken only half a dozen steps down the street when she was wrenched sideways, into an alley.

She reeled back against the trash cans and almost sobbed with relief. "Victor!"

"Did they see you?"

"No. I mean, yes, but they didn't seem to care—"

"Are you sure?" She nodded. He turned and slapped the wall in frustration. "What the hell do we do now?"

"I have the tickets."

"We can't use them."

"How are we going to get out of town? Hitchhike? Victor, we're down to our last five dollars!"

"They'll be watching every bus that leaves. And they've got my face plastered all over the damn terminal!" He slumped back against the wall and groaned. "*Have you seen this man?* God, I looked like some two-bit gangster."

"It wasn't the most flattering photo."

He managed to laugh. "Have you *ever* seen a flattering wanted poster?"

She leaned back beside him, against the wall. "We've got to get out of this city, Victor."

"Amend that. *You've* got to get out."

"What's that supposed to mean?"

"The police aren't looking for you. So *you* take that bus to Palo Alto. I'll put you in touch with some old friends. They'll see you make it somewhere safe."

"No."

"Cathy, they've probably got my mug posted in every airport and car rental agency in town! We've spent almost all our money for those bus tickets. I say you use them!"

"I'm not leaving you."

"You don't have a choice."

"Yes I do. I choose to stick to you like glue. Because you're the only one I feel safe with. The only one I can count on!"

"I can move faster on my own. Without you slowing me

MIRA

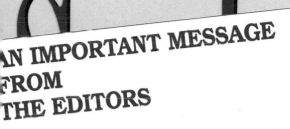

AN IMPORTANT MESSAGE
FROM
THE EDITORS

Dear Reader,

Because you've chosen to read one of our
fine novels, we'd like to say "thank you"!
And, as a **special** way to thank you, we've
selected <u>two more</u> of the books you love so
well, **and** a picture frame to send you
absolutely _FREE!_

Please enjoy them with our compliments...

Editor,
The Best of the Best

P.S. And because we value our
customers, we've attached something
extra inside ...

Peel off seal and
Place inside...

EDITOR'S
**FREE
GIFT
SEAL**
THANK YOU

HOW TO VALIDATE
YOUR
EDITOR'S FREE GIFT "THANK YOU"

1. Peel off gift seal from front cover. Place it in space provided at right. This automatically entitles you to receive two free books and a lovely picture frame decorated with celestial designs.

2. Send back this card and you'll get 2 "The Best of the Best™" novels. These books have a combined cover price of $11.00 or more, but they are yours to keep absolutely free.

3. There's no catch. You're under no obligation to buy anything. We charge nothing—ZERO—for your first shipment. And you don't have to make any minimum number of purchases—not even one!

4. We call this line "The Best of the Best" because each month you'll receive the best books by the world's hottest authors. These are authors whose names show up time and time again on all the major bestseller lists and whose books sell out as soon as they hit the stores. You'll love getting them conveniently delivered to your home...and you'll love our discount prices.

5. We hope that after receiving your free books you'll want to remain a subscriber. But the choice is yours—to continue or cancel, anytime at all! So why not take us up on our invitation, with no risk of any kind. You'll be glad you did!

6. Don't forget to detach your FREE BOOKMARK. And remember... just for validating your Editor's Free Gift Offer, we'll send you THREE MORE gifts, *ABSOLUTELY FREE!*

YOURS FREE!

This lovely picture frame is decorated with celestial designs—stars, moons and suns! It's perfect for displaying photographs of that "special someone" in your life and it's sure to please! And here's the best part: the frame is yours **absolutely free***, simply for accepting our no-risk offer!*

THE BEST OF THE BEST™: HERE'S HOW IT WORKS

Accepting free books places you under no obligation to buy anything. You may keep the books and gift and return the shipping statement marked "cancel". If you do not cancel, about a month later we will send you 3 additional novels, and bill you just $4.24 each plus 25¢ delivery per book and applicable sales tax, if any.* That's the complete price — and compared to cover prices of $5.50 each — quite a bargain! You may cancel at any time, but if you choose to continue, every month we'll send you 3 more books, which you may either purchase at the discount price…or return to us and cancel your subscription.

*Terms and prices subject to change without notice. Sales tax applicable in N.Y.

down." He looked off, toward the street. "Hell, I don't even *want* you around."

"I don't believe that."

"Why should I care what you believe?"

"Look at me! Look at me and say that!" She grabbed his arm, willing him to face her. "Say you don't want me around!"

He started to speak, to repeat the lie. She knew then that it *was* a lie; she could see it in his eyes. And she saw something else in that gaze, something that took her breath away.

He said, "I don't—I won't have you—"

She just stood there, looking up at him, waiting for the truth to come.

What she didn't expect was the kiss. She never remembered how it happened. She only knew that all at once his arms were around her and she was being swept up into some warm and safe and wonderful place. It started as an embrace more of desperation than passion, a coming together of two terrified people. But the instant their lips met, it became something much more. This went beyond fear, beyond need. This was a souls' joining, one that wouldn't be broken, even after this embrace was over, even if they never touched again.

When at last they drew apart and stared at each other, the taste of him was still fresh on her lips.

"You see?" she whispered. "I was right. You do want me around. You do."

He smiled and touched her cheek. "I'm not a very good liar."

"And I'm not leaving you. You need me. You can't show your face, but I can! I can buy bus tickets, run errands—"

"What I really need," he sighed, "is a new face." He glanced out at the street. "Since there's no plastic surgeon handy, I suggest we hoof it over to the BART station. It'll be crowded at this hour. We might make it to the East Bay—"

"God, I'm such an *idiot!*" she groaned. "A new face is exactly what you need!" She turned toward the street. "Come on. There isn't much time...."

"Cathy?" He followed her up the alley. They both paused, scanning the street for policemen. There were none in sight. "Where are we going?" he whispered.

"To find a phone booth."

"Oh. And who are we calling?"

She turned and the look she gave him was distinctly pained. "Someone we both know and love."

Jack was packing his suitcase when the phone rang. He considered not answering it, but something about the sound, an urgency that could only have been imagined, made him pick up the receiver. He was instantly sorry he had.

"Jack?"

He sighed. "Tell me I'm hearing things."

"Jack, I'm going to talk fast because your phone might be tapped—"

"You don't say."

"I need my kit. The whole shebang. And some cash. I swear I'll pay it all back. Get it for me right now. Then drop it off where we shot the last scene of *Cretinoid.* You know the spot."

"Cathy, you wait a minute! I'm in trouble enough as it is!"

"One hour. That's all I can wait."

"It's rush hour! I can't—"

"It's the last favor I'll ask of you." There was a pause. Then, softly, she added, "Please."

He let out a breath. "This is the absolute last time, right?"

"One hour, Jack. I'll be waiting."

Jack hung up and stared at his suitcase. It was only half packed, but it would have to do. He sure as hell wasn't coming back *here* tonight.

He closed the suitcase and carried it out to the Jaguar. As he drove away it suddenly occurred to him that he'd forgotten to cancel his date with Lulu tonight.

No time now, he thought. I've got more important things on my mind—like getting out of town.

Lulu would be mad as a hornet, but he'd make it up to her. Maybe a pair of diamond ear studs. Yeah, that would do the trick.

Good old Lulu, so easy to please. Now there was a woman he could understand.

The corner of Fifth and Mission was a hunker-down, chew-the-fat sort of gathering place for the street folk. At five forty-five it was even busier than usual. Rumor had it the soup kitchen down the block was fixing to serve beef Bourguignonne, which, as those who remembered better days and better meals could tell you, was made with red wine. No one passed up the chance for a taste of the grape, even if every drop of alcohol was simmered clean out of it. And so they stood around on the corner, talking of other meals they'd had, of the weather, of the long lines at the unemployment office.

No one noticed the two wretched souls huddled in the doorway of the pawnshop.

Lucky for us, thought Cathy, burying herself in the folds of the raincoat. The sad truth was, they were both beginning to fit right into this crowd. Just a moment earlier she'd caught sight of her own reflection in the pawnshop window and had almost failed to recognize the disheveled image staring back. *Has it been that long since I've combed my hair? That long since I've had a meal or a decent night's sleep?*

Victor looked no better. A torn shirt and two days' worth of stubble on his jaw only emphasized that unmistakable look of exhaustion. He could walk into that soup kitchen down the block and no one would look twice.

He's going to look a hell of a lot worse when I get through with him, she thought with a grim sense of humor.

If Jack ever showed up with the kit.

"It's 6:05," Victor muttered. "He's had an hour."

"Give him time."

"We're running out of time."

"We can still make the bus." She peered up the street, as though by force of will she could conjure up her ex-husband. But only a city bus barreled into view. *Come on, Jack, come on! Don't let me down this time....*

"Will ya lookit that!" came a low growl, followed by general murmurs of admiration from the crowd.

"Hey, pretty boy!" someone called as the group gathered on the corner to stare. "What'd you have to push to get yerself wheels like that?"

Through the gathering of men, Cathy spied the bright gleam of chrome and burgundy. "Get away from my car!" demanded a querulous voice. "I just had her waxed!"

"Looks like Pretty Boy got hisself lost. Turned down the wrong damn street, did ya?"

Cathy leaped to her feet. "He's here!"

She and Victor pushed through the crowd to find Jack standing guard over the Jaguar's gleaming finish.

"Don't—don't touch her!" he snapped as one man ran a grimy finger across the hood. "Why can't you people go find yourselves a job or something?"

"A job?" someone yelled. "What's that?"

"Jack!" called Cathy.

Jack let out a sigh of relief when he spotted her. "This is the last favor. The absolute *last* favor—"

"Where is it?" she asked.

Jack walked around to the trunk, where he slapped away another hand as it stroked the Jaguar's burgundy flank. "It's right here. The whole kit and kaboodle." He swung out the makeup case and handed it over. "Delivered as promised. Now I gotta run."

"Where are you going?" she called.

"I don't know." He climbed back into the car. "Somewhere. Anywhere!"

"Sounds like we're headed in the same direction."

"God, I hope not." He started the engine and revved it up a few times.

Someone yelled: "So long, Pretty Boy!"

Jack gazed out dryly at Cathy. "You know, you really should do something about the company you keep. Ciao, sweetcakes."

The Jaguar lurched away. With a screech of tires, it spun around the corner and vanished into traffic.

Cathy turned and saw that every eye was watching her. Automatically, Victor moved close beside her, one tired and hungry man facing a tired and hungry crowd.

Someone called out: "So who's the jerk in the Jag?"

"My ex-husband," said Cathy.

"Doin' a lot better than you are, honey."

"No kidding." She held up the makeup case and managed a careless laugh. "I ask the creep for my clothes, he throws me a change of underwear."

"Babe, now ain't that just the way it works?"

Already, the men were wandering away, regrouping in doorways, or over by the corner newsstands. The Jaguar was gone, and so was their interest.

Only one man stood before Cathy and Victor, and the look he gave them was distinctly sympathetic. "That's all he left you, huh? Him with that nice, fancy car?'' He turned to leave, then glanced back at them. ''Say, you two need a place to stay or somethin'? I got a lot of friends. And I hate to see a lady out in the cold.''

''Thanks for the offer,'' said Victor, taking Cathy's hand. ''But we've got a bus to catch.''

The man nodded and shuffled away, a kind but unfortunate soul whom the streets had not robbed of decency.

''We have a half hour to get on that bus,'' said Victor, hurrying Cathy along. ''Better get to work.''

They were headed up the street, toward the cover of an alley, when Cathy suddenly halted. ''Victor—''

''What's the matter?''

''Look.'' She pointed at the newsstand, her hand shaking.

Beneath the plastic cover was the afternoon edition of the *San Francisco Examiner.* The headline read: ''Two Victims, Same Name. Police Probe Coincidence.'' Beside it was a photo of a young blond woman. The caption was hidden by the fold, but Cathy didn't need to read it. She could already guess the woman's name.

''Two of them,'' she whispered. ''Victor, you were right....''

''All the more reason for us to get out of town.'' He pulled on her arm. ''Hurry.''

She let him lead her away. But even as they headed down the street, even as they left the newsstand behind them, she carried that image in her mind: the photograph of a blond woman, the second victim.

The second Catherine Weaver.

Patrolman O'Hanley was a helpful soul. Unlike too many of his colleagues, O'Hanley had joined the force out of a true desire to serve and protect. The ''Boy Scout'' was what the other men called him behind his back. The epithet both annoyed and pleased him. It told him he didn't fit in with the rough-and-tumble gang on the force. It also told him he was above it all, above the petty bribe-taking and backbiting and maneuverings for promotion. He wasn't out to glorify the badge on his chest. What he wanted was the chance to pat a kid on the head, rescue an old granny from a mugging.

That's why he found this particular assignment so frustrating. All this standing around in the bus depot, watching for a man some witness *might* have spotted a few hours ago. O'Hanley hadn't noticed any such character. He'd eye-balled every person who'd walked in the door. A sorry lot, most of them. Not surprising since, these days, anyone with the cash to spare took a plane. By the looks of these folks, none of 'em could spare much more than pennies. Take that pair over there, huddled together in the waiting area. A father and daughter, he figured, and both of 'em down on their luck. The daughter was bundled up in an old raincoat, the collar pulled up to reveal only a mop of wind-blown hair. The father was an even sorrier sight, gaunt-faced, white-whiskered, about as old as Methuselah. Still, there was a remnant of pride in the old codger—O'Hanley could see it in the way the man held himself, stiff and straight. Must've been an impressive fellow in his younger years since he was still well over six feet tall.

The public speaker announced final boarding for number fourteen to Palo Alto.

The old man and his daughter rose to their feet.

O'Hanley watched with concern as the pair shuffled across the terminal toward the departure gate. The woman was carrying only one small case, but it appeared to be a heavy one. And she already had her hands full, trying to guide the old man in the right direction. But they were making progress, and O'Hanley figured they'd make it to the bus okay.

That is, until the kid ran into them.

He was about six, the kind of kid no mother wants to admit she produced, the kind of kid who gives all six-year-olds a bad name. For the last half hour the boy had been tearing around the terminal, scattering ashtray sand, tipping over suitcases, banging locker doors. Now he was running. Only this kid was doing it *backward.*

O'Hanley saw it coming. The old man and his daughter were crossing slowly toward the departure gate. The kid was scuttling toward them. Intersecting paths, inevitable collision. The kid slammed into the woman's knees; the case flew out of her grasp. She stumbled against her companion. O'Hanley, paralyzed, expected the codger to keel over. To his surprise, the old man simply caught the woman in his arms and handily set her back on her feet.

By now O'Hanley was hurrying to their aid. He got to the woman just as she'd regained her footing. "You folks okay?" he asked.

The woman reacted as though he'd slapped her. She stared up at him with the eyes of a terrified animal. "What?" she said.

"Are you okay? Looked to me like he hit you pretty hard."

She nodded.

"How 'bout you, Gramps?"

The woman glanced at her companion. It seemed to O'Hanley that there was a lot being said in that glance, a lot he wasn't privy to.

"We're both fine," the woman said quickly. "Come on, Pop. We'll miss our bus."

"Can I give you a hand with him?"

"That's mighty kind of you, officer, but we'll do fine." The woman smiled at O'Hanley. Something about that smile wasn't right. As he watched the pair shuffle off toward bus number fourteen, O'Hanley kept trying to figure it out. Kept trying to put his finger on what was wrong with that pair of travelers.

He turned away and almost tripped over the fallen case. The woman had forgotten it. He snatched it up and started to run for the bus. Too late; the number fourteen to Palo Alto was already pulling away. O'Hanley stood helplessly on the curb, watching the taillights vanish around the corner.

Oh, well.

He turned in the makeup case at Lost and Found. Then he stationed himself once again at the entrance. Seven o'clock already and still no sighting of the suspect Victor Holland.

O'Hanley sighed. What a waste of a policeman's time.

Five minutes out of San Francisco, aboard the number fourteen bus, the old man turned to the woman in the raincoat and said, "This beard is killing me."

Laughing, Cathy reached up and gave the fake whiskers a tug. "It did the trick, didn't it?"

"No kidding. We practically got a police escort to the getaway bus." He scratched furiously at his chin. "Geez, how do those actors stand this stuff, anyway? The itch is driving me up a wall."

"Want me to take it off?"

"Better not. Not till we get to Palo Alto."

Another hour, she thought. She sat back and gazed out at the highway gliding past the bus window. "Then what?" she asked softly.

"I'll knock on a few doors. See if I can dig up an old friend or two. It's been a long time, but I think there are still a few in town."

"You used to live there?"

"Years ago. Back when I was in college."

"Oh." She sat up straight. "A *Stanford* man."

"Why do you make it sound just a tad disreputable?"

"I rooted for the Bears, myself."

"I'm consorting with the arch enemy?"

Giggling, she burrowed against his chest and inhaled the warm, familiar scent of his body. "It seems like another lifetime. Berkeley and blue jeans."

"Football. Wild parties."

"Wild parties?" she asked. "You?"

"Well, *rumors* of wild parties."

"Frisbee. Classes on the lawn…"

"Innocence," he said softly.

They both fell silent.

"Victor?" she asked. "What if your friends aren't there any longer? Or what if they won't take us in?"

"One step at a time. That's how we have to take it. Otherwise it'll all seem too overwhelming."

"It already does."

He squeezed her tightly against him. "Hey, we're doing okay. We made it out of the city. In fact, we waltzed out right under the nose of a cop. I'd call that pretty damn impressive."

Cathy couldn't help grinning at the memory of the earnest young Patrolman O'Hanley. "All policemen should be so helpful."

"Or blind," Victor snorted. "I can't believe he called me *Gramps*."

"When I set out to change a face, I do it right."

"Apparently."

She looped her arm through his and pressed a kiss to one scowling, bewhiskered cheek. "Can I tell you a secret?"

"What's that?"

"I'm crazy about older men."

The scowl melted away, slowly reformed into a dubious smile. "How much older are we talking about?"

She kissed him again, this time full on the lips. "Much older."

"Hm. Maybe these whiskers aren't so bad, after all." He took her face in his hands. This time he was the one kissing her, long and deeply, with no thought of where they were or where they were going. Cathy felt herself sliding back against the seat, into a space that was inescapable and infinitely safe.

Someone behind them hooted: "Way to go, Gramps!"

Reluctantly, they pulled apart. Through the flickering shadows of the bus, Cathy could see the twinkle in Victor's eyes, the gleam of a wry smile.

She smiled back and whispered, "Way to go, Gramps."

The posters with Victor Holland's face were plastered all over the bus station.

Polowski couldn't help a snort of irritation as he gazed at that unflattering visage of what he knew in his gut was an innocent man. A damn witchhunt, that's what this'd turned into. If Holland wasn't already scared enough, this public stalking would surely send him diving for cover, beyond the reach of those who could help him. Polowski only hoped it'd also be beyond the reach of those with less benign intentions.

With all these posters staring him in the face, Holland would've been a fool to stroll through this bus depot. Still, Polowski had an instinct about these things, a sense of how people behaved when they were desperate. If he were in Holland's shoes, a killer on his trail and a woman companion to worry about, he knew what *he'd* do —get the hell out of San Francisco. A plane was unlikely. According to Jack Zuckerman, Holland was operating on a thin wallet. A credit card would've been out of the question. That also knocked out a rental car. What was left? It was either hitch-hike or take the bus.

Polowski was betting on the bus.

His last piece of info supported that hunch. The tap on Zuckerman's phone had picked up a call from Cathy Weaver. She'd arranged some sort of drop-off at a site Polowski couldn't identify at first. He'd spent a frustrating hour asking around the office, trying to locate someone who'd not only seen Zuckerman's forgettable film, *Cretinoid,* but could also pinpoint where the last scene was filmed. The Mission District, some movie nut file clerk had finally told him. Yeah, she was sure of it. The monster came up through the manhole cover right at the corner of Fifth and Mission and slurped down a derelict or two just before the hero smashed him with a crated piano. Polowski hadn't stayed to hear the rest; he'd made a run for his car.

By that time, it was too late. Holland and the woman were gone, and Zuckerman had vanished. Polowski found himself cruising down Mission, his doors locked, his windows rolled up, wondering when the local police were going to clean up the damn streets.

That's when he remembered the bus depot was only a few blocks away.

Now, standing among the tired and slack-jawed travelers at the bus station, he was beginning to think he'd wasted his time. All those wanted posters staring him in the face. And there was a cop standing over by the coffee machine, taking furtive sips from a foam cup.

Polowski strolled over to the cop. "FBI," he said, flashing his badge.

The cop—he was scarcely more than a boy—instantly straightened. "Patrolman O'Hanley, sir."

"Seeing much action?"

"Uh—you mean today?"

"Yeah. Here."

"No, sir." O'Hanley sighed. "Pretty much a bust. I

mean, I could be out on patrol. Instead they got me hanging around here eyeballing faces."

"Surveillance?"

"Yes, sir." He nodded at the poster of Holland. "That guy. Everyone's hot to find him. They say he's a spy."

"Do they, now?" Polowski took a lazy glance around the room. "Seen anyone around here who looks like him?"

"Not a one. I been watching every minute."

Polowski didn't doubt it. O'Hanley was the kind of kid who, if you asked him to, would scrub the Captain's boots with a toothbrush. He'd do a good job of it, too.

Obviously Holland hadn't come through here. Polowski turned to leave. Then another thought came to mind, and he turned back to O'Hanley. "The suspect may be traveling with a woman," he said. He pulled out a photo of Cathy Weaver, one Jack Zuckerman had been persuaded to donate to the FBI. "Have you seen her come through here?"

O'Hanley frowned. "Gee. She sure does look like... Naw. That can't be her."

"Who?"

"Well, there was this woman in here 'bout an hour ago. Kind of a down and outer. Some little brat ran smack into her. I sort've brushed her off and sent her on her way. She looked a lot like this gal, only in a lot worse shape."

"Was she traveling alone?"

"She had an old guy with her. Her pop, I think."

Suddenly Polowski was all ears. That instinct again—it was telling him something. "What did this old man look like?"

"Real old. Maybe seventy. Had this bushy beard, lot of white hair."

"How tall?"

"Pretty tall. Over six feet..." O'Hanley's voice trailed off as his gaze focused on the wanted poster. Victor Holland was six foot three. O'Hanley's face went white. "Oh, God…"

"Was it him?"

"I—I can't be sure—"

"Come on, come on!"

"I just don't know… Wait. The woman, she dropped a makeup case! I turned it in at that window there—"

It took only a flash of an FBI badge for the clerk in Lost and Found to hand over the case. The instant Polowski opened the thing, he knew he'd hit pay dirt. It was filled with theatrical makeup supplies. Stenciled inside the lid was: Property of Jack Zuckerman Productions.

He slammed the lid shut. "Where did they go?" he snapped at O'Hanley.

"They—uh, they boarded a bus right over there. That gate. Around seven o'clock."

Polowski glanced up at the departure schedule. At seven o'clock, the number fourteen had departed for Palo Alto.

It took him ten minutes to get hold of the Palo Alto depot manager, another five minutes to convince the man this wasn't just another Prince-Albert-in-the-can phone call.

"The number fourteen from San Francisco?" came the answer. "Arrived twenty minutes ago."

"What about the passengers?" pressed Polowski. "You see any of 'em still around?"

The manager only laughed. "Hey, man. If you had a choice, would *you* hang around a stinking bus station?"

Muttering an oath, Polowski hung up.

"Sir?" It was O'Hanley. He looked sick. "I messed up, didn't I? I let him walk right past me. I can't believe—"

"Forget it."

"But—"

Polowski headed for the exit. "You're just a rookie," he called over his shoulder. "Chalk it up to experience."

"Should I call this in?"

"I'll take care of it. I'm headed there, anyway."

"Where?"

Polowski shoved open the station door. "Palo Alto."

8

The front door was answered by an elderly oriental woman whose command of English was limited.

"Mrs. Lum? Remember me? Victor Holland. I used to know your son."

"Yes, yes!"

"Is he here?"

"Yes." Her gaze shifted to Cathy now, as though the woman didn't want her second visitor to feel left out of the conversation.

"I need to see him," said Victor. "Is Milo here?"

"Milo?" At last here was a word she seemed to know. She turned and called out loudly in Chinese.

Somewhere a door squealed open and footsteps stamped up the stairs. A fortyish oriental man in blue jeans and chambray shirt came to the front door. He was a dumpling of a fellow, and he brought with him the vague odor of chemicals, something sharp and acidic. He was wiping his hands on a rag.

"What can I do for you?" he asked.

Victor grinned. "Milo Lum! Are you still skulking around in your mother's basement?"

"Excuse me?" Milo inquired politely. "Am I supposed to know you, sir?"

"Don't recognize an old horn player from the Out of Tuners?"

Milo stared in disbelief. "Gershwin? That can't be *you?*"

"Yeah, I know," Victor said with a laugh. "The years haven't been kind."

"I didn't want to say anything, but..."

"I won't take it personally. Since—" Victor peeled off his false beard "—the face isn't all mine."

Milo gazed down at the lump of fake whispers, hanging like a dead animal in Victor's grasp. Then he stared up at Victor's jaw, still blotchy with spirit gum. "This is some kind of joke on old Milo, right?" He stuck his head out the door, glancing past Victor at the sidewalk. "And the other guys are hiding out there somewhere, waiting to yell *surprise!* Aren't they? Some big practical joke."

"I wish it were a joke," said Victor.

Milo instantly caught the undertone of urgency in Victor's voice. He looked at Cathy, then back at Victor. Nodding, he stepped aside. "Come in, Gersh. Sounds like I have some catching up to do."

Over a late supper of duck noodle soup and jasmine tea, Milo heard the story. He said little; he seemed more intent on slurping down the last of his noodles. Only when the ever-smiling Mrs. Lum had bowed good-night and creaked off to bed did Milo offer his comment.

"When you get in trouble, man, you sure as hell do it right."

"Astute as always, Milo," sighed Victor.

"Too bad we can't say the same for the cops," Milo snorted. "If they'd just bothered to ask around, they would've learned you're harmless. Far as I know, you're guilty of only one serious crime."

Cathy looked up, startled. "What crime?"

"Assaulting the ears of victims unlucky enough to hear his saxophone."

"This from a piccolo player who practises with earplugs," observed Victor.

"That's to drown out extraneous noise."

"Yeah. Mainly your own."

Cathy grinned. "I'm beginning to understand why you called yourselves the Out of Tuners."

"Just some healthy self-deprecating humor," said Milo. "Something we needed after we failed to make the Stanford band." Milo rose, shoving away from the kitchen table. "Well, come on. Let's see what's on that mysterious roll of film."

He led them along the hall and down a rickety set of steps to the basement. The chemical tang of the air, the row of trays lined up on a stainless-steel countertop and the slow drip, drip of water from the faucet told Cathy she was standing in an enormous darkroom. Tacked on the walls was a jumble of photos. Faces, mostly, apparently snapped around the world. Here and there she spotted a newsworthy shot: soldiers storming an airport, protestors unfurling a banner.

"Is this your job, Milo?" she asked.

"I wish," said Milo, agitating the developing canister. "No, I just work in the ol' family business."

"Which is?"

"Shoes. Italian, Brazilian, leather, alligator, you name it, we import it." He cocked his head at the photos. "That's how I get my exotic faces. Shoe-buying trips. I'm an expert on the female arch."

"For that," said Victor, "he spent four years at Stanford."

"Why not? Good a place as any to study the fine feet of the fair sex." A timer rang. Milo poured out the developer, removed the roll of film, and hung it up to dry. "Actually," he said, squinting at the negatives, "it was my dad's dying request. He wanted a son with a Stanford degree. I wanted four years of nonstop partying. We both got our wishes." He paused and gazed off wistfully at his photos. "Too bad I can't say the same of the years since then."

"What do you mean?" asked Cathy.

"I mean the partying's long since over. Gotta earn those profits, keep up those sales. Never thought life'd come down to the bottom line. Whatever happened to all that rabble-rousing potential, hey, Gersh? We sort of lost it along the way. All of us, Bach and Ollie and Roger. The Out of Tuners finally stepped into line. Now we're all marching to the beat of the same boring drummer." He sighed and glanced at Victor. "You make out anything on those negatives?"

Victor shook his head. "We need prints."

Milo flipped off the lights, leaving only the red glow of the darkroom lamp. "Coming up."

As Milo laid out the photographic paper, Victor asked, "What happened to the other guys? They still around?"

Milo flipped the exposure switch. "Roger's VP at some multinational bank in Tokyo. Into silk suits and ties, the whole nine yards. Bach's got an electronics firm in San José."

"And Ollie?"

"What can I say about Ollie?" Milo slipped the first print into the bath. "He's still lurking around in that lab over at Stanford Med. I doubt he ever sees the light of day. I figure he's got some secret chamber in the basement where he keeps his assistant Igor chained to the wall."

"This guy I have to meet," said Cathy.

"Oh, he'd love you." Victor laughed and gave her arm a squeeze. "Seeing as he's probably forgotten what the female of the species looks like."

Milo slid the print into the next tray. "Yeah, Ollie's the one who never changed. Still the night owl. Still plays a mean clarinet." He glanced at Victor. "How's the sax, Gersh? You keeping it up?"

"Haven't played in months."

"Lucky neighbors."

"How did you ever get that name?" asked Cathy. "Gersh?"

"Because," said Milo, wielding tongs as he transferred another batch of prints between trays, "he's a firm believer in the power of George Gershwin to win a lady's heart. 'Someone to Watch Over Me,' wasn't that the tune that made Lily say…" Milo's voice suddenly faded. He looked at his friend with regret.

"You're right," said Victor quietly. "That was the tune. And Lily said yes."

Milo shook his head. "Sorry. Guess I still have a hard time remembering she's gone."

"Well, she is," said Victor, his voice matter-of-fact. Cathy knew there was pain buried in the undertones. But he hid it well. "And right now," Victor said, "we've got other things to think about."

"Yeah." Milo, chastened, turned his attention back to the prints he'd just developed. He fished them out and clipped the first few sheets on the line to dry. "Okay, Gersh. Tell us what's on this roll that's worth killing for."

Milo switched on the lights.

Victor stood in silence for a moment, frowning at the first five dripping prints. To Cathy, the data was meaningless, only a set of numbers and codes, recorded in an almost illegible hand.

"Well," grunted Milo. "That sure tells me a lot."

Victor's gaze shifted quickly from one page to the next. He paused at the fifth photo, where a column ran down the length of the page. It contained a series of twenty-seven entries, each one a date followed by the same three letters: EXP.

"Victor?" asked Cathy. "What does it mean?"

He turned to them. It was the look in his eyes that worried her. The stillness. Quietly he said, "We need to call Ollie."

"You mean tonight?" asked Milo. "Why?"

"This isn't just some experiment in test tubes and petri dishes. They've gone beyond that, to clinical trials." Victor pointed to the last page. "These are monkeys. Each one was infected with a new virus. A manmade virus. And in every case the results were the same."

"You mean this?" Milo pointed to the last column. "EXP?"

"It stands for expired," said Victor. "They all died."

Sam Polowski sat on a bench in the Palo Alto bus terminal and wondered: If I wanted to disappear, where would I go next? He watched a dozen or so passengers straggle off to board the 210 from San José, noting they were by and large the Birkenstock and backpack set. Probably Stanford students heading off for Christmas break. He wondered why it was that students who could afford such a pricey university couldn't seem to scrape up enough to buy a decent pair of jeans. Or even a decent haircut, for that matter.

At last Polowski rose and automatically dusted off his coat, a habit he'd picked up from his early years of hanging around the seamier side of town. Even if the grime wasn't actually visible, he'd always *felt* it was there, coating any surface he happened to brush against, ready to cling to him like wet paint.

He made one phone call—to Dafoe's answering machine, to tell him Victor Holland had moved on to Palo Alto. It was, after all, his responsibility to keep his supervisor informed. He was glad he only had to talk to a recording and not to the man himself.

He left the bus station and strolled down the street, heading Lord knew where, in search of a spark, a hunch. It was a nice-enough neighborhood, a nice-enough town. Palo Alto had its old professors' houses, its bookshops and coffee houses where university types, the ones with the beards and wire-rim glasses, liked to sit and argue the meaning of Proust and Brecht and Goethe. Polowski remembered his own university days, when, after being subjected to an hour of such crap from the students at the next table, he had finally stormed over to them and yelled, "Maybe Brecht meant it that way, maybe not. But can you guys answer this? *What the hell difference does it make?*"

This did not, needless to say, enhance his reputation as a serious scholar.

Now, as he paced along the street, no doubt in the footsteps of more serious philosophers, Polowski turned over in his head the question of Victor Holland. More specifically the question of where such a man, in his desperation, would hide. He stalked past the lit windows, the glow of TVs, the cars spilling from garages. Where in this warren of suburbia was the man hiding?

Holland was a scientist, a musician, a man of few but lasting friendships. He had a Ph.D. from MIT, a B.S. from Stanford. The university was right up the road. The man must know his way around here. Maybe he still had friends in the neighborhood, people who'd take him in, keep his secrets.

Polowski decided to take another look at Holland's file. Somewhere in the Viratek records, there had to be some employment reference, some recommendation from a Stanford contact. A friend Holland might turn to.

Sooner or later, he would have to turn to *someone*.

It was after midnight when Dafoe and his wife returned home. He was in an excellent mood, his head pleasantly abuzz with champagne, his ears still ringing with the heart-wrenching aria from *Samson and Delilah*. Opera was a passion for him, a brilliant staging of courage and conflict and *amore,* a vision of life so much grander than the petty little world in which he found himself. It launched him to a plane of such thrilling intensity that even his own wife took on exciting new aspects. He watched her peel off her coat and kick off her shoes. Forty pounds overweight, hair streaked with silver, yet she had her attractions. *It's been three weeks. Surely she'll let me tonight....*

But his wife ignored his amorous looks and wandered off to the kitchen. A moment later, the rumble of the automatic dishwasher announced another of her fits of house-cleaning.

In frustration, Dafoe turned and stabbed the blinking button on his answering machine. The message from Polowski completely destroyed any amorous intentions he had left.

"...Reason to believe Holland is in, or has just left, the Palo Alto area. Following leads. Will keep you informed...."

Polowski, you half-wit. Is following orders so damn difficult?

It was 3:00 a.m. Washington time. An ungodly hour, but he made the phone call.

The voice that answered was raspy with sleep. "Tyrone here."

"Cowboy, this is Dafoe. Sorry to wake you."

The voice became instantly alert, all sleep shaken from it. "What's up?"

"New lead on Holland. I don't know the particulars, but he's headed south, to Palo Alto. May still be there."

"The university?"

"It is the Stanford area."

"That may be a very big help."

"Anything for an old buddy. I'll keep you posted."

"One thing, Dafoe."

"Yeah?"

"I can't have any interference. Pull all your people out. We'll take it from here."

Dafoe paused. "I might...have a problem."

"A problem?" The voice, though quiet, took on a razor's edge.

"It's, uh, one of my men. Sort of a wild card. Sam Polowski. He's got this Holland case under his skin, wants to go after him."

"There's such a thing as a direct order."

"At the moment, Polowski's unreachable. He's in Palo Alto, digging around in God knows what."

"Loose cannons. I don't like them."

"I'll pull him back as soon as I can."

"Do that. And keep it quiet. It's a matter of utmost security."

After Dafoe hung up, his gaze shifted automatically to the photo on the mantelpiece. It was a '68 snapshot of him and the Cowboy: two young marines, both of them grinning, their rifles slung over their shoulders as they stood ankle-deep in a rice paddy. It was a crazy time, when one's very life depended on the loyalty of buddies. When Semper Fi applied not only to the corps in general but to each other in particular. Matt Tyrone was a hero then, and he was a hero now. Dafoe stared at that smiling face in the photo, disturbed by the threads of envy that had woven into his admiration for the man. Though Dafoe had much to be proud of—a solid eighteen years in the FBI, maybe even a shot at assistant director somewhere in his stars, he couldn't match the heady climb of Matt Tyrone in the NSA. Though Dafoe wasn't clear as to exactly what position the Cowboy held in the NSA, he had heard that Tyrone regularly attended cabinet meetings, that he held the trust of the president, that he dealt in secrets and shadows and security. He was the sort of man the country needed, a man for whom patriotism was more than mere flag-waving and rhetoric; it was a way of life. Matt Tyrone would do more than die for his country; he'd live for it.

Dafoe couldn't let such a man, such a friend, down.

He dialed Sam Polowski's home phone and left a message on the recorder.

This is a direct order. You are to withdraw from the Holland case immediately. Until further notice you are on suspension.

He was tempted to add, *by special request from my friends in Washington,* but thought better of it. No room for vanity here. The Cowboy had said national security was at stake.

Dafoe had no doubt it truly was. He'd gotten the word from Matt Tyrone. And Matt Tyrone's authority came direct from the President himself.

"This does not look good. This does not look good at all."

Ollie Wozniak squinted through his wire-rim glasses at the twenty-four photographs strewn across Milo's dining table. He held one up for a closer look. Through the bottle-glass lens, one pale blue eye stared out, enormous. One only saw Ollie's eyes; everything else, hollow cheeks, pencil lips and baby-fine hair, seemed to recede into the background pallor. He shook his head and picked up another photo.

"You're right, of course," he said. "Some of these I can't interpret. I'd like to study 'em later. But these here are definitely raw mortality data. Rhesus monkeys, I suspect." He paused and added quietly, "I hope."

"Surely they wouldn't use people for this sort of thing," said Cathy.

"Not officially." Ollie put down the photo and looked at her. "But it's been done."

"Maybe in Nazi Germany."

"Here, too," said Victor.

"What?" Cathy looked at him in disbelief.

"Army studies in germ warfare. They released colonies

of Serratia Marcescens over San Francisco and waited to see how far the organism spread. Infections popped up in a number of Bay Area hospitals. Some of the cases were fatal.''

"I can't believe it," murmured Cathy.

"The damage was unintentional, of course. But people died just the same.''

"Don't forget Tuskegee," said Ollie. "People died in those experiments, too. And then there was that case in New York. Mentally retarded kids in a state hospital who were deliberately exposed to hepatitis. No one died there, but the ethics were just as shaky. So it's been done. Sometimes in the name of humanity.''

"Sometimes not," said Victor.

Ollie nodded. "As in this particular case.''

"What exactly are we talking about here?" asked Cathy, nodding at the photos. "Is this medical research? Or weapons development?''

"Both." Ollie pointed to one of the photos on the table. "By all appearances, Viratek's engaged in biological weapons research. They've dubbed it Project Cerberus. From what I can tell, the organism they're working on is an RNA virus, extremely virulent, highly contagious, producing over eighty-percent mortality in its lab animal hosts. This photo here—'' he tapped one of the pages ''—shows the organism produces vesicular skin lesions on the infected subjects.''

"Vesicular?''

"Blisterlike. That could be one route of transmission, the fluid in those lesions." He sifted through the pile and pulled out another page. "This shows the time course of the illness. The viral counts, periods of infectiousness. In almost every case the course is the same. The subject's exposed here." He pointed to Day One on the time graph. "Minor signs of illness here at Day Seven. Full-blown pox on Day

Twelve. And here—'' he tapped the graph at Day Fourteen ''—the deaths begin. The time varies, but the result's the same. They all die.''

"You used the word *pox*,'' said Cathy.

Ollie turned to her, his eyes like blue glass. "Because that's what it is.''

"You mean like chickenpox?''

"I wish it was. Then it wouldn't be so deadly. Almost everyone gets exposed to chickenpox as a kid, so most of us are immune. But this one's a different story.''

"Is it a new virus?'' asked Milo.

"Yes and no.'' He reached for an electron micrograph. "When I saw this I thought there was something weirdly familiar about all this. The appearance of the organism, the skin lesions, the course of illness. The whole damn picture. It reminded me of something I haven't read about in decades. Something I never dreamed I'd see again.''

"You're saying it's an old virus?'' said Milo.

"Ancient. But they've made some modifications. Made it more infectious. And deadlier. Which turns this into a real humdinger of a weapon, considering the millions of folks it's already killed.''

"*Millions?*'' Cathy stared at him. "What are we talking about?''

"A killer we've known for centuries. Smallpox.''

"That's impossible!'' said Cathy. "From what I've read, we conquered smallpox. It's supposed to be extinct.''

"It was,'' said Victor. "For all practical purposes. Worldwide vaccination wiped it out. Smallpox hasn't been reported in decades. I'm not even sure they still make the vaccine. Ollie?''

"Not available. No need for it since the virus has vanished.''

"So where did *this* virus come from?'' asked Cathy.

Ollie shrugged. "Probably someone's closet.''

"Come on."

"I'm serious. After smallpox was eradicated, a few samples of virus were kept alive in government labs, just in case someone needed it for future research. It's the scientific skeleton in the closet, so to speak. I'd assume those labs are top security. Because if any of the virus got out, there could be a major epidemic." He looked at the stack of photos. "Looks like security's already been breached. Someone obviously got hold of the virus."

"Or had it handed to them," said Victor. "Courtesy of the U.S. government."

"I find that incredible, Gersh," said Ollie. "This is a powderkeg experiment you're talking about. No committee would approve this sort of project."

"Right. That's why I think this is a maverick operation. It's easy to come up with a scenario. Bunch of hardliners cooking this up over at NSA. Or joint chiefs of staff. Or even the Oval Office. Someone says: 'World politics have changed. We can't get away with nuking the enemy. We need a new weapons option, one that'll work well against a Third World army. Let's find one.' And some guy in that room, some red, white and blue robot, will take that as the go-ahead. International law be damned."

"And since it's unofficial," said Cathy, "it'd be completely deniable."

"Right. The administration could claim it knew nothing."

"Sounds like Iran-Contra all over again."

"With one big difference," said Ollie. "When Iran-Contra fell apart, all you had were a few ruined political careers. If Project Cerberus goes awry, what you'll have is a few million dead people."

"But Ollie," said Milo. "I got vaccinated for smallpox when I was a kid. Doesn't that mean I'm safe?"

"Probably. Assuming the virus hasn't been altered too

much. In fact, everyone over 35 is probably okay. But remember, there's a whole generation after us that never got
the vaccine. Young adults and kids. By the time you could
manufacture enough vaccine for them all, we'd have a rag-
ing epidemic.''

''I'm beginning to see the logic of this weapon,'' said
Victor. ''In any war, who makes up the bulk of combat
soldiers? Young adults.''

Ollie nodded. ''They'd be hit bad. As would the kids.''

''A whole generation,'' Cathy murmured. ''And only the
old would be spared.'' She glanced at Victor and saw, mirrored in his eyes, the horror she felt.

''They chose an appropriate name,'' said Milo.

Ollie frowned. ''What?''

''Cerberus. The three-headed dog of Hades.'' Milo
looked up, visibly shaken. ''Guardian of the dead.''

It wasn't until Cathy was fast asleep and Milo had retired
upstairs that Victor finally broached the subject to Ollie. It
had troubled him all evening, had shadowed his every moment since they'd arrived at Milo's house. He couldn't look
at Cathy, couldn't listen to the sound of her voice or inhale
the scent of her hair without thinking of the terrible possibilities. And in the deepest hours of night, when it seemed
all the world was asleep except for him and Ollie, he made
the decision.

''I need to ask you a favor,'' he said.

Ollie gazed at him across the dining table, steam wafting
up from his fourth cup of coffee. ''What sort of favor?''

''It has to do with Cathy.''

Ollie's gaze shifted to the woman lying asleep on the
living room floor. She looked very small, very defenseless,
curled up beneath the comforter. Ollie said, ''She's a nice
woman, Gersh.''

''I know.''

"There hasn't really been anyone since Lily. Has there?"

Victor shook his head. "I guess I haven't felt ready for it. There were always other things to think about...."

Ollie smiled. "There are always excuses. I should know. People keep telling me there's a glut of unattached female baby boomers. I haven't noticed."

"And I never bothered to notice." Victor looked at Cathy. "Until now."

"What're you gonna do with her, Gersh?"

"That's what I need you for. I'm not the safest guy to hang around with these days. A woman could get hurt."

Ollie laughed. "Hell, a *guy* could get hurt."

"I feel responsible for her. And if something happened to her, I'm not sure I could ever..." He let out a long sigh and rubbed his bloodshot eyes. "Anyway, I think it's best if she leaves."

"For where?"

"She has an ex-husband. He'll be working down in Mexico for a few months. I think she'd be pretty safe."

"You're sending her to her ex-husband?"

"I've met him. He's a jerk, but at least she won't be alone down there."

"Does Cathy agree to this?"

"I didn't ask her."

"Maybe you should."

"I'm not giving her a choice."

"What if she wants the choice?"

"I'm not in the mood to take any crap, Okay? I'm doing this for her own good."

Ollie took off his glasses and cleaned them on the table-cloth. "Excuse me for saying this, Gersh, but if it was me, I'd want her nearby, where I could sort of keep an eye on her."

"You mean where I can watch her get killed?" Victor

shook his head. "Lily was enough. I won't go through it with Cathy."

Ollie thought it over for a moment, then he nodded. "What do you want me to do?"

"Tomorrow I want you to take her to the airport. Buy her a ticket to Mexico. Let her use your name. Mrs. Wozniak. Make sure she gets safely off the ground. I'll pay you back when I can."

"What if she won't get on the plane? Do I just shove her aboard?"

"Do whatever it takes, Ollie. I'm counting on you."

Ollie sighed. "I guess I can do it. I'll call in sick tomorrow. That'll free up my day." He looked at Victor. "I just hope you know what you're doing."

So do I, thought Victor.

Ollie rose to his feet and tucked the envelope with the photos under his arm. "I'll get back to you in the morning. After I show these last two photos to Bach. Maybe he can identify what those grids are."

"If it's anything electronic, Bach'll figure it out."

Together they walked to the door. There they paused and regarded each other, two old friends who'd grown a little grayer and, Victor hoped, a little wiser.

"Somehow it'll all work out," said Ollie. "Remember. The system's there to be beaten."

"Sounds like the old Stanford radical again."

"It's been a long time." Grinning, Ollie gave Victor a clap on the back. "But we're still not too old to raise a little hell, hey, Gersh? See you in the morning."

Victor waved as Ollie walked away into the darkness. Then he closed the door and turned off all the lights.

In the living room he sat beside Cathy and watched her sleep. The glow of a streetlight spilled in through the window onto her tumbled hair. *Ordinary,* she had called herself. Perhaps, if she'd been a stranger he'd merely passed on the street, he might have thought so, too. A chance meeting on a rainy highway in Garberville had made it impossible for him to ever consider this woman ordinary. In her gentleness, her kindness, she was very much like Lily.

In other ways, she was very different.

Though he'd cared about his wife, though they'd never stopped being good friends, he'd found Lily strangely passionless, a pristine, spiritual being trapped by human flesh. Lily had never been comfortable with her own body. She'd undress in the dark, make love—the rare times they did—in the dark. And then, the illness had robbed her of what little desire she had left.

Gazing at Cathy, he couldn't help wondering what passions might lie harbored in her still form.

He cut short the speculation. What did it matter now? Tomorrow, he'd send her away. *Get rid of her,* he thought brutally. It was necessary. He couldn't think straight while she was around. He couldn't stay focused on the business at hand: exposing Viratek. Jerry Martinique had counted on him. Thousands of potential victims counted on him. He was a scientist, a man who prided himself on logic. His attraction to this particular woman was, in the grand scheme of things, clearly unimportant.

That was what the scientist in him said.

That problem finally settled, he decided to get some rest while he could. He kicked off his shoes and stretched out beside her to sleep. The comforter was large enough—they could share it. He climbed beneath it and lay for a moment, not touching her, almost afraid to share her warmth.

She whimpered in her sleep and turned toward him, her silky hair tumbling against his face.

This was more than he could resist. Sighing, he wrapped his arms around her and felt her curl up against his chest. It was their last night together. They might as well spend it keeping each other warm.

That was how he fell asleep, with Cathy in his arms.

Only once during the night did he awaken. He had been dreaming of Lily. They were walking together, in a garden of pure white flowers. She said absolutely nothing. She simply looked at him with profound sadness, as if to say, *Here I am, Victor. I've come back to you. Why doesn't that make you happy?* He couldn't answer her. So he simply took her in his arms and held her.

He'd awakened to find he was holding Cathy, instead.

Joy instantly flooded his heart, warmed the darkest corners of his soul. It took him by surprise, that burst of happiness; it also made him feel guilty. But there it was. And the joy was all too short-lived. He remembered that today she'd be going away.

Cathy, Cathy. What a complication you've become.

He turned on his side, away from her, mentally building a wall between them.

He concentrated on the dream, trying to remember what had happened. He and Lily had been walking. He tried to picture Lily's face, her brown eyes, her curly black hair. It was the face of the woman he'd been married to for ten years, a face he should know well.

But the only face he saw when he closed his eyes was that of Catherine Weaver.

It took Nicholas Savitch only two hours to pack his bags and drive down to Palo Alto. The word from Matt Tyrone was that Holland had slipped south to the Stanford area, perhaps to seek out old friends. Holland was, after all, a Stanford man. Maybe not the red-and-white rah-rah Cardinals type, but a Stanford man nonetheless. These old school ties could run deep. It was only a guess on Savitch's part; he'd never gone beyond high school. His education consisted of what a hungry and ambitious boy could pick up on Chicago's south side. Mainly a keen, almost uncanny knack for crawling into another man's head, for sensing what a particular man would think and do in a given situation. Call it advanced street psychology. Without spending a day in college, Savitch had earned his degree.

Now he was putting it to use.

The *finder,* they called him. He liked that name. He grinned as he drove, his leather-gloved hands expertly handling the wheel. Nicholas Savitch, diviner of human souls, the hunter who could ferret a man out of deepest hiding.

In most cases it was a simple matter of logic. Even while on the run, most people conformed to old patterns. It was the fear that did it. It made them seek out their old comforts, cling to their usual habits. In a strange town, the familiar was precious, even if it was only the sight of those ubiquitous golden arches.

Like every other fugitive, Victor Holland would seek the familiar.

Savitch turned his car onto Palm Drive and pulled up in front of the Stanford Arch. The campus was silent; it was 2:00 a.m. Savitch sat for a moment, regarding the silent buildings, Holland's alma mater. Here, in his former stomping grounds, Holland would turn to old friends, revisit old haunts. Savitch had already done his homework. He carried, in his briefcase, a list of names he'd culled from the man's file. In the morning he'd start in on those names, knock on neighbors' doors, flash his government ID, ask about new faces in the neighborhood.

The only possible complication was Sam Polowski. By last report, the FBI agent was also in town, also on Holland's trail. Polowski was a dogged operator. It'd be messy business, taking out a Bureau man. But then, Polowski was only a cog, the way the Weaver woman was only a cog, in a much bigger wheel.

Neither of them would be missed.

9

In the cold, clear hours before dawn, Cathy woke up shaking, still trapped in the threads of a nightmare. She had been walking in a world of concrete and shadow, where doorways gaped and silhouettes huddled on street corners. She drifted among them, one among the faceless, taking refuge in obscurity, instinctively avoiding the light. No one pursued her; no attacker lunged from the alleys. The real terror lay in the unending maze of concrete, the hard echoes of the streets, the frantic search for a safe place.

And the certainty that she would never find it.

For a moment she lay in the darkness, curled up beneath a down comforter on Milo's living room floor. She barely remembered having crawled under the covers; it must have been sometime after three when she'd fallen asleep. The last she remembered, Ollie and Victor were still huddled in the dining room, discussing the photographs. Now there was only silence. The dining room, like the rest of the house, lay in shadow.

She turned on her back, and her shoulder thumped against something warm and solid. Victor. He stirred, murmuring something she couldn't understand.

"Are you awake?" she whispered.

He turned toward her and in his drowsiness enfolded her in his arms. She knew it was only instinct that drew him to her, the yearning of one warm body for another. Or perhaps it was the memory of his wife sleeping beside him, in his mind always there, always waiting to be held. For the moment, she let him cling to the dream. *While he's still half asleep, let him believe I'm Lily,* she thought. *What harm can there be? He needs the memory. And I need the comfort.*

She burrowed into his arms, into the safe spot that once had belonged to another. She took it without regard for the consequences, willing to be swept up into the fantasy of being, for this moment, the one woman in the world he loved. How good it felt, how protected and cared for. From the soap-and-sweat smell of his chest to the coarse fabric of his shirt, it was sanctuary. He was breathing warmly into her hair now, whispering words she knew were for another, pressing kisses to the top of her head. Then he trapped her face in his hands and pressed his lips to hers in a kiss so undeniably needy it ignited within her a hunger of her own. Her response was instinctive and filled with all the yearning of a woman too long a stranger to love.

She met his kiss with one just as deep, just as needy.

At once she was lost, whirled away into some grand and glorious vortex. He stroked down her face, her neck. His hands moved to the buttons of her blouse. She arched against him, her breasts suddenly aching to be touched. It had been so long, so long.

She didn't know how the blouse fell open. She knew only that one moment his fingers were skimming the fabric, and the next moment, they were cupping her flesh. It was that unexpected contact of skin on forbidden skin, the magic torment of his fingers caressing her nipple, that made any last resistance fall away. How many chances were left to them? How many nights together? She longed for so many more, an eternity, but this might be all they had. She welcomed it, welcomed him, with all the passion of a woman granted one last taste of love.

With a knowing touch, she slid her hands down his shirt, undoing buttons, stroking her way through the dense hair of his chest, to the top of his trousers. There she paused, feeling his startled intake of breath, knowing that he too was past retreat.

Together they fumbled at buttons and zippers, both of them suddenly feverish to be free. It all fell away in a tumult of cotton and lace. And when the last scrap of clothing was shed, when nothing came between them but the velvet darkness, she reached up and pulled him to her, on her.

It was a joyful filling, as if, in that first deep thrust within her, he also reached some long-empty hollow in her soul.

"Please," she murmured, her voice breaking into a whimper.

He fell instantly still. "Cathy?" he asked, his hands anxiously cupping her face. "What—"

"Please. Don't stop...."

His soft laughter was all the reassurance she needed. "I have no intention of stopping," he whispered. "None whatsoever..."

And he didn't stop. Not until he had taken her with him all the way, higher and further than any man ever could, to a place beyond thought or reason. Only when release came, wave flooding upon wave, did she know how very high and far they had climbed.

A sweet exhaustion claimed them.

Outside, in the grayness of dawn, a bird sang. Inside, the silence was broken only by the sound of their breathing.

She sighed into the warmth of his shoulder. "Thank you."

He touched her face. "For what?"

"For making me feel...wanted again."

"Oh, Cathy."

"It's been such a long time. Jack and I, we—we stopped making love way before the divorce. It was me, actually. I couldn't bear having him..." She swallowed. "When you don't love someone anymore, when they don't love you, it's hard to let yourself be...touched.''

He brushed his fingers down her cheek. "Is it still hard? Being touched?''

"Not by you. Being touched by you is like...being touched the very first time.''

By the window's pale light she saw him smile. "I hope your very first time wasn't too awful.''

Now she smiled. "I don't remember it very well. It was such a frantic, ridiculous thing on the floor of a college dorm room.''

He reached out and patted the carpet. "I see you've come a long way.''

"Haven't I?" she laughed. "But floors can be terribly romantic places.''

"Goodness. A carpet connoisseur. How do dorm room and living room floors compare?''

"I couldn't tell you. It's been such a long time since I was eighteen.'' She paused, hovering on the edge of baring the truth. "In fact,'' she admitted, "it's been a long time since I've been with anyone.''

Softly he said, "It's been a long time for both of us.''

She let that revelation hang for a moment in the semi-darkness. "Not—not since Lily?" she finally asked.

"No.'' A single word, yet it revealed so much. The three years of loyalty to a dead woman. The grief, the loneliness. How she wanted to fill that womanless chasm for him! To be his savior, and he, hers. Could she make him forget? No, not forget; she couldn't expect him ever to forget Lily. But she wanted a space in his heart for herself, a very large space designed for a lifetime. A space to which no other woman, dead or alive, could ever lay claim.

"She must have been a very special woman," she said.

He ran a strand of her hair through his fingers. "She was

very wise, very aware. And she was kind. That's something I don't always find in a person.''

She's still part of you, isn't she? She's still the one you love.

''It's the same sort of kindness I find in you,'' he said.

His fingers had slid to her face and were now stroking her cheek. She closed her eyes, savoring his touch, his warmth. ''You hardly know me,'' she whispered.

''But I do. That night, after the accident, I survived purely on the sound of your voice. And the touch of your hand. I'd know them both, anywhere.''

She opened her eyes and gazed at him. ''Would you really?''

He pressed his lips to her forehead. ''Even in my sleep.''

''But I'm not Lily. I could never be Lily.''

''That's true. You can't be. No one can.''

''I can't replace what you lost.''

''What makes you think that's what I want? Some sort of replacement? She was my wife. And yes, I loved her.'' By the way he said it, his answer invited no exploration.

She didn't try.

From somewhere in the house came the jingle of a telephone. After two rings it stopped. Faintly they heard Milo's voice murmuring upstairs.

Cathy sat up and reached automatically for her clothes. She dressed in silence, her back turned to Victor. A new modesty had sprung up between them, the shyness of strangers.

''Cathy,'' he said. ''People do move on.''

''I know.''

''You've gotten over Jack.''

She laughed, a small, tired sound. ''No woman ever really gets over Jack Zuckerman. Yes, I'm over the worst of it. But every time a woman falls in love, really falls in love, it takes something out of her. Something that can never be put back.''

''It also gives her something.''

''That depends on who you fall in love with, doesn't it?''

Footsteps thumped down the stairs, creaked across the dining room. A wide-awake Milo stood in the doorway, his uncombed hair standing out like a brush. ''Hey, you two!'' he hissed. ''Get up! Hurry.''

Cathy rose to her feet in alarm. ''What is it?''

''That was Ollie on the phone. He called to say some guy's in the area, asking questions about you. He's already been down to Bach's neighborhood.''

''What?'' Now Victor was on his feet and hurriedly stuffing his legs into his trousers.

''Ollie figures the guy'll be knocking around here next. Guess they know who your friends are.''

''Who was asking the questions?''

''Claimed he was FBI.''

''Polowski,'' muttered Victor, pulling his shirt on. ''Has to be.''

''You know him?''

''The same guy who set me up. The guy who's been tailing us ever since.''

''How did he know we're here?'' said Cathy. ''No one could've followed us—''

''No one had to. They have my profile. They know I have friends here.'' Victor glanced at Milo. ''Sorry, buddy. Hope this doesn't get you into trouble.''

Milo's laugh was distinctly tense. ''Hey, I didn't do nothin' wrong. Just harbored a felon.'' The bravado suddenly melted away. He asked, ''Exactly what kind of trouble should I expect?''

''Questions,'' said Victor, quickly buttoning his shirt. ''Lots of 'em. Maybe they'll even take a look around. Just keep cool, tell 'em you haven't heard from me. Think you can do it?''

"Sure. But I don't know about Ma—"

"Your Ma's no problem. Just tell her to stick to Chinese." Victor grabbed the envelope of photos and glanced at Cathy. "Ready?"

"Let's get out of here. Please."

"Back door," Milo suggested.

They followed him through the kitchen. A glance told them the way was clear. As he opened the door, Milo added, "I almost forgot. Ollie wants to see you this afternoon. Something about those photos."

"Where?"

"The lake. Behind the boathouse. You know the place."

They stepped out into the chill dampness of morning. Fog-borne silence hung in the air. *Will we ever stop running?* thought Cathy. *Will we never stop listening for footsteps?*

Victor clapped his friend on the shoulder. "Thanks, Milo. I owe you a big one."

"And one of these days I plan to collect!" Milo hissed as they slipped away.

Victor held up his hand in farewell. "See you around."

"Yeah," Milo muttered into the mist. "Let's hope not in jail."

The Chinese man was lying. Though the man betrayed nothing in his voice, no hesitation, no guilty waver, still Savitch knew this Mr. Milo Lum was hiding something. His eyes betrayed him.

He was seated on the living room couch, across from Savitch. Off to the side sat Mrs. Lum in an easy chair, smiling uncomprehendingly. Savitch might be able to use the old biddy; for now, it was the son who held his interest.

"I can't see why you'd be after him," said Milo. "Victor's as clean as they come. At least, he was when I knew him. But that was a long time ago."

"How far back?" asked Savitch politely.

"Oh, years. Yeah. Haven't seen him since. No, sir."

Savitch raised an eyebrow. Milo shifted on the couch, shuffled his feet, glanced pointlessly around the room.

"You and your mother live here alone?" Savitch asked.

"Since my dad died."

"No tenants? No one else lives here?"

"No. Why?"

"There were reports of a man fitting Holland's description in the neighborhood."

"Believe me, if Victor was wanted by the police, he wouldn't hang around here. You think I'd let a murder suspect in the house? With just me and my old Ma?"

Savitch glanced at Mrs. Lum, who merely smiled. The old woman had sharp, all-seeing eyes. A survivor's eyes.

It was time for Savitch to confirm his hunch. "Excuse me," he said, rising to his feet. "I had a long drive from the city. May I use your restroom?"

"Uh, sure. Down that hall."

Savitch headed into the bathroom and closed the door. Within seconds he'd spotted the evidence he was looking for. It was lying on the tiled floor: a long strand of brown hair. Very silky, very fine.

Catherine Weaver's shade.

It was all the proof he needed to proceed. He reached under his jacket for the shoulder holster and pulled out the semiautomatic. Then he gave his crisp white shirt a regretful pat. Messy business, interrogation. He would have to watch the bloodstains.

He stepped out into the hall, casually holding his pistol at his side. He'd go for the old woman first. Hold the barrel to her head, threaten to pull the trigger. There was an uncommonly strong bond between this mother and son. They would protect each other at all costs.

Savitch was halfway down the hall when the doorbell rang. He halted. The front door was opened and a new voice said, "Mr. Milo Lum?"

"And who the hell are you?" came Milo's weary reply.

"The name's Sam Polowski. FBI."

Every muscle in Savitch's body snapped taut. No choice now; he had to take the man out.

He raised his pistol. Soundlessly, he made his way down the hall toward the living room.

"*Another* one?" came Milo's peevish voice. "Look, one of your guys is already here—"

"What?"

"Yeah, he's back in the—"

Savitch stepped out and was swinging his pistol toward the front doorway when Mrs. Lum shrieked.

Milo froze. Polowski didn't. He rolled sideways just as the bullet thudded into the door frame, splintering wood.

By the time Savitch got off a second shot, Polowski was crawling somewhere behind the couch and the bullet slammed uselessly into the stuffing. That was it for chances—Polowski was armed.

Savitch decided it was time to vanish.

He turned and darted back up the hall, into a far bedroom. It was the mother's room; it smelled of incense and old-lady perfume. The window slid open easily. Savitch kicked out the screen, scrambled over the sill and sank heel-deep into the muddy flower bed. Cursing, he slogged away, trailing clumps of mud across the lawn.

He heard, faintly, "Halt! FBI!" but continued running.

He nursed his rage all the way back to the car.

Milo stared in bewilderment at the trampled pansies. "What the hell was that all about?" he demanded. "Is this some sort of FBI practical joke?''

Sam Polowski didn't answer; he was too busy tracking the footprints across the grass. They led to the sidewalk, then faded into the road's pebbly asphalt.

"Hey!" yelled Milo. "What's going on?"

Polowski turned. "I didn't really see him. What did he look like?"

Milo shrugged. "I dunno. Efrem Zimbalist-type."

"Meaning?"

"Tall, clean-cut, great build. Typical FBI."

There was a silence as Milo regarded Polowski's sagging belly.

"Well," amended Milo, "maybe not *typical*..."

"What about his face?"

"Lemme think. Brown hair? Maybe brown eyes?"

"You're not sure."

"You know how it is. All you white guys look alike to me."

An eruption of rapid Chinese made them both turn. Mrs. Lum had followed them out onto the lawn and was jabbering and gesticulating.

"What's she saying?" asked Polowski.

"She says the man was about six foot one, had straight dark brown hair parted on the left, brown eyes, almost black, a high forehead, a narrow nose and thin lips, and a small tattoo on his inside left wrist."

"Uh—is that all?"

"The tattoo read PJX."

Polowski shook his head in amazement. "Is she always this observant?"

"She can't exactly converse in English. So she does a lot of watching."

"Obviously." Polowski took out a pen and began to jot the information in a notebook.

"So who was this guy?" prodded Milo.

"Not FBI."

"How do I know *you're* FBI."

"Do I look like it?"

"No."

"Only proves my point."

"What?"

"If I wanted to pretend I was an agent, wouldn't I at least try to *look* like one? Whereas, if I *am* one, I wouldn't bother to try and look like one."

"Oh."

"Now." Polowski slid the notebook in his pocket. "You're still going to insist you haven't seen, or heard from, Victor Holland?"

Milo straightened. "That's right."

"And you don't know how to get in touch with him?"

"I have no idea."

"That's too bad. Because I could be the one to save his life. I've already saved yours."

Milo said nothing.

"Just why the hell do you think that guy was here? To pay a social visit? No, he was after information." Polowski paused and added, ominously, "And believe me, he would've gotten it."

Milo shook his head. "I'm confused."

"So am I. That's why I need Holland. He has the answers. But I need him alive. That means I need to find him before the other guy does. Tell me where he is."

Polowski and Milo looked at each other long and hard.

"I don't know," said Milo. "I don't know what to do."

Mrs. Lum was chattering again. She pointed to Polowski and nodded.

"Now what's she saying?" asked Polowski.

"She says you have big ears."

"For that, I can look in the mirror."

"What she means is, the size of your ears indicates sagacity."

"Come again?"

"You're a smart dude. She thinks I should listen to you."

Polowski turned and grinned at Mrs. Lum. "Your mother is a great judge of character." He looked back at Milo. "I wouldn't want anything to happen to her. Or you. You both have to get out of town."

Milo nodded. "On that particular point, we both agree." He turned toward the house.

"What about Holland?" called Polowski. "Will you help me find him?"

Milo took his mother by the arm and guided her across the lawn. Without even a backward look he said, "I'm thinking about it."

"It was those two photos. I just couldn't figure them out," said Ollie.

They were standing on the boathouse pier, overlooking the bed of Lake Lagunita. The lake was dry now, as it was every winter, drained to a reedy marsh until spring. They were alone, the three of them, sharing the lake with only an occasional duck. In the spring, this would be an idyllic spot, the water lapping the banks, lovers drifting in rowboats, here and there a poet lolling under the trees. But today, under black clouds, with a cold mist rising from the reeds, it was a place of utter desolation.

"I knew they weren't biological data," said Ollie. "I kept thinking they looked like some sort of electrical grid. So this morning, right after I left Milo's, I took 'em over to Bach's, down in San José. Caught him at breakfast."

"Bach?" asked Cathy.

"Another member of the Out of Tuners. Great bassoon player. Started an electronics firm a few years back and now he's working with the big boys. Anyway, the first thing he says as I walk in the door is, 'Hey, did the FBI get to you yet?' And I said, 'What?' and he says, 'They just called. For some reason they're looking for Gershwin. They'll probably get around to you next.' And that's when I knew I had to get you two out of Milo's house, stat.''

"So what did he say about those photos?"

"Oh, yeah." Ollie reached into his briefcase and pulled out the photos. "Okay. This one here, it's a circuit diagram An electronic alarm system. Very sophisticated, very secure. Designed to be breached by use of a keypad code, punched in at this point here. Probably at an entryway. You seen anything like it at Viratek?"

Victor nodded. "Building C-2. Where Jerry worked. The keypad's in the hall, right by the Special Projects door."

"Ever been inside that door?"

"No. Only those with top clearance can get through. Like Jerry."

"Then we'll have to visualize what comes next. Going by the diagram, there's another security point here, probably another keypad. Right inside the first door, they've stationed a camera system."

"You mean like a bank camera?" asked Cathy.

"Similar. Only I'd guess this one's being monitored twenty-four hours a day."

"They went first class, didn't they?" said Victor. "Two secured doors, plus inspection by a guard. Not to mention the guard at the outside gate."

"Don't forget the laser lattice."

"What?"

"This inner room here." Ollie pointed to the diagram's core. "Laser beams, directed at various angles. They'll detect movement of just about anything bigger than a rat."

"How do the lasers get switched off?"

"Has to be done by the security guard. The controls are on his panel."

"You can tell all this from the diagram?" asked Cathy. "I'm impressed."

"No problem." Ollie grinned. "Bach's firm designs security systems."

Victor shook his head. "This looks impossible. We can't get through all that."

Cathy frowned at him. "Wait a minute. What are you talking about? You aren't considering going into that building, are you?"

"We discussed it last night," said Victor. "It may be the only way—"

"Are you crazy? Viratek's out to kill us and you want to break *in?*"

"It's the proof we need," said Ollie. "You try going to the newspapers or the Justice Department and they'll demand evidence. You can bet Viratek's going to deny everything. Even if someone does launch an investigation, all Viratek has to do is toss the virus and, *poof!* your evidence is gone. No one can prove a thing."

"You have photos—"

"Sure. A few pages of animal data. The virus is never identified. And all that evidence could've been fabricated by, say, some disgruntled ex-employee."

"So what *is* proof? What do you need, another dead body? Victor's, for instance?"

"What we need is the virus—a virus that's supposed to be extinct. Just a single vial and the case against them is nailed shut."

"Just a single vial. Right." Cathy shook her head. "I don't know what I'm worried about. No one can get through those doors. Not without the keypad codes."

"Ah, but those we have!" Ollie flipped to the second photo. "The mysterious numbers. See, they finally make sense. Two sets of seven digits. Not phone numbers at all! Jerry was pointing the way through Viratek's top security.''

''What about the lasers?'' she pointed out, her agitation growing. They couldn't be serious! Surely they could see the futility of this mission. She didn't care if her fear showed; she had to be their voice of reason. ''And then there's the guards,'' she said. ''Two of them. Do you have a way past them? Or did Jerry also leave you the formula for invisibility?''

Ollie glanced uneasily at Victor. ''Uh, maybe I should let you two discuss this first. Before we make any other plans.''

''I thought I was part of all this,'' said Cathy. ''Part of every decision. I guess I was wrong.''

Neither man said a thing. Their silence only fueled Cathy's anger. She thought: *So you left me out of this. You didn't respect my opinion enough to ask me what I think, what I want.*

Without a word she turned and walked away.

Moments later, Victor caught up with her. She was standing on the dirt path, hugging herself against the cold. She heard his approach, sensed his uncertainty, his struggle to find the right words. For a moment he simply stood beside her, not speaking.

''I think we should run,'' she said. She gazed over the dry lake bed and shivered. The wind that swept across the reeds was raw and biting; it sliced right through her sweater. ''I want to get away,'' she said. ''I want to go somewhere warm. Some place where the sun's shining, where I can lie on a beach and not worry about who's watching me from the bushes....'' Suddenly reminded of the terrible possibilities, she turned and glanced at the oaks hulking behind them. She saw only the fluttering of dead leaves.

''I agree with you,'' said Victor quietly.

"You do?" She turned to him, relieved. "Let's go, Victor! Let's leave now. Forget this crazy idea. We can catch the next bus south—"

"This very afternoon. You'll be on your way."

"*I* will?" She stared at him, at first not willing to accept what she'd heard. Then the meaning of his words sank in. "You're not coming."

Slowly he shook his head. "I can't."

"You mean you won't."

"Don't you see?" He took her by the shoulders, as though to shake some sense into her. "We're backed into a corner. Unless we do something—I do something—we'll always be running."

"Then let's *run!*" She reached for him, her fingers clutching at his windbreaker. She wanted to scream at him, to tear away his cool mask of reason and get to the raw emotions beneath. They had to be there, buried deep in that logical brain of his. "We could go to Mexico," she said. "I know a place on the coast—in Baja. A little hotel near the beach. We could stay there a few months, wait until things are safer—"

"It'll never be safer."

"Yes, it will! They'll forget about us—"

"You're not thinking straight."

"I am. I'm thinking I want to stay alive."

"And that's exactly why I have to do this." He took her face in his hands, trapping it so she could look nowhere but at him. No longer was he the lover, the friend—his voice now held the cold, steady note of authority and she hated the sound of it. "I'm trying to keep you alive," he said. "With a future ahead of you. And the only way I can do that is to blow this thing wide open so the world knows about it. I owe it to you. And I owe it to Jerry."

She wanted to argue with him, to plead with him to go with her, but she knew it was useless. What he said was true. Running would only be a temporary solution, one that would give them a few sweet months of safety, but a temporary one just the same.

"I'm sorry, Cathy," he said softly. "I can't think of any other way—"

"—But to get rid of me," she finished for him.

He released her. She stepped back, and the sudden gulf between them left her aching. She couldn't bear to look at him, knowing that the pain she felt wouldn't be reflected in his eyes. "So how does it work?" she said dully. "Do I leave tonight? Will it be plane, train or automobile?"

"Ollie will drive you to the airport. I've asked him to buy you the ticket under his name—Mrs. Wozniak. He'll have to be the one to see you off. We thought it'd be safer if I didn't come along to the airport."

"Of course."

"That'll get you to Mexico. Ollie'll give you enough cash to keep you going for a while. Enough to get you anywhere you want to go from there. Baja. Acapulco. Or just hang around with Jack if you think that's best."

"Jack." She turned away, unwilling to show her tears. "Right."

"Cathy." She felt his hand on her shoulder, as though he wanted to turn her toward him, to pull her back one last time into his arms. She refused to move.

Footsteps approached. They both glanced around to see Ollie, standing a few feet away. "Ready to go?" he asked.

There was a long silence. Then Victor nodded. "She's ready."

"Uh, look," Ollie mumbled, suddenly aware that he'd stepped in at a bad time. "My car's over by the boathouse. If you want, I can, uh, wait for you there...."

Cathy furiously dashed away her tears. "No," she said with sudden determination. "I'm coming."

Victor stood watching her, his gaze veiled by some cool, impenetrable mist.

"Goodbye, Victor," she said.

He didn't answer. He just kept looking at her through that terrible mist.

"If I—if I don't see you again..." She stopped, struggling to be just as brave, just as invulnerable. "Take care of yourself," she finished. Then she turned and followed Ollie down the path.

Through the car window, she glimpsed Victor, still standing on the lake path, his hands jammed in his pockets, his shoulders hunched against the wind. He didn't wave goodbye; he merely watched them drive away.

It was an image she'd carry with her forever, that last, fading view of the man she loved. The man who'd sent her away.

As Ollie turned the car onto the road, she sat stiff and silent, her fists balled in her lap, the pain in her throat so terrible she could scarcely breathe. Now he was behind them. She couldn't see him, but she knew he was still standing there, as unmoving as the oaks that surrounded him. *I love you,* she thought. *And I will never see you again.*

She turned to look out. He was a distant figure now, almost lost among the trees. In a gesture of farewell, she reached up and gently touched the window.

The glass was cold.

"I have to stop off at the lab," said Ollie, turning into the hospital parking lot. "I just remembered I left the checkbook in my desk. Can't get you a plane ticket without it."

Cathy nodded dully. She was still in a state of shock, still trying to accept the fact that she was now on her own. That Victor had sent her away.

Ollie pulled into a stall marked Reserved, Wozniak. "This'll only take a sec."

"Shall I come in with you?"

"You'd better wait in the car. I work with a very nosy bunch. They see me with a woman and they want to know everything. Not that there's ever anything to know." He climbed out and shut the door. "Be right back."

Cathy watched him stride away and vanish into a side entrance. She had to smile at the thought of Ollie Wozniak squiring around a woman—any woman. Unless it was someone with a Ph.D. who could sit through his scientific monologues.

A minute passed.

Outside, a bird screeched. Cathy glanced out at the trees lining the hospital driveway and spotted the jay, perched among the lower branches. Nothing else moved, not even the leaves.

She leaned back and closed her eyes.

Too little sleep, too much running, had taken its toll. Exhaustion settled over her, so profound she thought she would never again be able to move her limbs. *A beach,* she thought. *Warm sand. Waves washing at my feet...*

The jay's cry cut off in mid-screech. Only vaguely did Cathy register the sudden silence. Then, even through her half sleep, she sensed the shadowing of the window, like a cloud passing before the sun.

She opened her eyes. A face was staring at her through the glass.

Panic sent her lunging for the lock button. Before she could jam it down, the door was wrenched open. A badge was thrust up to her face.

"FBI!" the man barked. "Out of the car, please."

Slowly Cathy emerged, to stand weak-kneed against the door. *Ollie,* she thought, her gaze darting toward the hospital entrance. *Where are you?* If he appeared, she had to be ready to bolt, to flee across the parking lot and into the woods. She doubted the man with the badge would be able to keep up; his stubby legs and thick waist didn't go along with a star athlete.

But he must have a gun. If I bolt, would he shoot me in the back?

"Don't even think about it, Miss Weaver," the man said. He took her arm and gave her a nudge toward the hospital entrance. "Go on. Inside."

"But—"

"Dr. Wozniak's waiting for us in the lab."

Waiting didn't exactly describe Ollie's predicament. Bound and trussed would have been a better description. She found Ollie bent over double in his office, handcuffed to the foot of his desk, while three of his lab colleagues stood by gaping in amazement.

"Back to work, folks," said the agent as he herded the onlookers out of the office. "Just a routine matter." He shut the door and locked it. Then he turned to Cathy and Ollie. "I have to find Victor Holland," he said. "And I have to find him fast."

"Man," Ollie muttered into his chest. "This guy sounds like a broken record."

"Who are you?" demanded Cathy.

"The name's Sam Polowski. I work out of the San Francisco office." He pulled out his badge and slapped it on the desk. "Take a closer look if you want. It's official."

"Uh, excuse me?" called Ollie. "Could I maybe, possibly, get into a more comfortable position?"

Polowski ignored him. His attention was focused on Cathy. "I don't think I need to spell it out for you, Miss Weaver. Holland's in trouble."

"And you're one of his biggest problems," she retorted.

"That's where you're wrong." Polowski moved closer,

his gaze unflinching, his voice absolutely steady. "I'm one of his hopes. Maybe his only hope."

"You're trying to kill him."

"Not me. Someone else, someone who's going to succeed. Unless I can stop it."

She shook her head. "I'm not stupid! I know about you. What you've been trying to—"

"Not me. The other guy." He reached for the telephone on the desk. "Here," he said, holding the receiver out to her. "Call Milo Lum. Ask him what happened at his house this morning. Maybe he'll convince you I'm on your side."

Cathy stared at the man, wondering what sort of game he was playing. Wondering why she was falling for it. *Because I want so much to believe him.*

"He's alone out there," said Polowski. "One man trying to buck the U.S. government. He's new to the game. Sooner or later he's going to slip, do something stupid. And that'll be it." He dialed the phone for her and again held out the receiver. "Go on. Talk to Lum."

She heard the phone ring three times, followed by Milo's answer "Hello? Hello?"

Slowly she took the receiver. "Milo?"

"Is that you? Cathy? God, I was hoping you'd call—"

"Listen, Milo. I need to ask you something. It's about a man named Polowski."

"I've met him."

"You *have?*" She looked up and saw Polowski nodding.

"Lucky for me," said Milo. "The guy's got the charm of an old shoe but he saved my life. I don't know what Gersh was talking about. Is Gersh around? I have to—"

"Thanks, Milo," she murmured. "Thanks a lot." She hung up.

Polowski was still looking at her.

"Okay," she said. "I want your side of it. From the beginning."

"You gonna help me out?"

"I haven't decided." She crossed her arms. "Convince me."

Polowski nodded. "That's just what I plan to do."

10

For Victor it was a long and miserable afternoon. After leaving the lake, he wandered around the campus for a while, ending up at last in the main quad. There in the courtyard, standing among the buildings of sandstone and red tile, Victor struggled to keep his mind on the business at hand: exposing Viratek. But his thoughts kept shifting back to Cathy, to that look she'd given him, full of hurt abandonment.

As if I'd betrayed her.

If she could just see the good sense in his actions. He was a scientist, a man whose life and work was ruled by logic. Sending her away was the logical thing to do. The authorities were closing in, the noose was growing ever tighter. He could accept the danger to himself. After all, he'd chosen to take on Jerry's battle, to see this through to the end.

What he hadn't chosen was to put Cathy in danger. *Now she's out of the mess and on her way to a safe place. One less thing to worry about. Time to put her out of my mind.*

As if I could.

He stared up at one of the courtyard's Romanesque arches and reminded himself, once again, of the wisdom of his actions. Still, the uneasiness remained. Where was she? Was she safe? She'd been gone only an hour and he missed her already.

He gave a shrug, as though by that gesture, he could somehow cast off the fears. Still they remained, constant

and gnawing. He found a place under the eaves and huddled on the steps to wait for Ollie's return.

At dusk he was still waiting. By the last feeble light of
day, he paced the stone courtyard. He counted and re-
counted the number of hours it should've taken Ollie to
drive to San José Airport and return. He added in traffic
time, red lights, ticket-counter delays. Surely three hours
was enough. Cathy had to be on a plane by now, jetting
for warmer climes.

Where was Ollie?

At the sound of the first footstep, he spun around. For a
moment he couldn't believe what he was seeing, couldn't
understand how she could be standing there, silhouetted
beneath the sandstone archway. "Cathy?" he said in
amazement.

She stepped out, into the courtyard. "Victor," she said
softly. She started toward him, slowly at first, and then, in
a jubilant burst of flight, ran toward his waiting arms. He
swept her up, swung her around, kissed her hair, her face.
He didn't understand why she was here but he rejoiced that
she was.

"I don't know if I've done the right thing," she murmured. "I hope to God I have."

"Why did you come back?"

"I wasn't sure—I'm still not sure—"

"Cathy, what are you doing here?"

"You can't fight this alone! And he can help you—"

"Who can?"

From out of the twilight came another voice, gruff and
startling. "*I* can."

At once Victor stiffened. His gaze shifted back to the
arch behind Cathy. A man emerged and walked slowly toward him. Not a tall man, he had the sort of body that, in
a weight-loss ad, would've been labeled Before. He came

up to Victor and planted himself squarely on the courtyard stones.

"Hello, Holland," he said. "I'm glad we've finally met. The name is Sam Polowski."

Victor turned and looked in disbelief at Cathy. "Why?" he asked in quiet fury. "Just tell me that. *Why?*"

She reacted as though he'd delivered a physical blow. Tentatively she reached for his arm; he pulled away from her at once.

"He wants to help," she said, her voice wretched with pain. "*Listen* to him!"

"I'm not sure there's any point to listening. Not now." He felt his whole body go slack in defeat. He didn't understand it, would never understand it. It was over, the running, the scraping along on fear and hope. All because Cathy had betrayed him. He turned matter-of-factly to Polowski. "I take it I'm under arrest," he said.

"Hardly," said Polowski, nodding toward the archway. "Seeing as he's got my gun."

"What?"

"Hey, Gersh! Over here!" Ollie yelled. "See, I got him covered!"

Polowski winced. "Geez, do ya have to wave the damn thing?"

"Sorry," said Ollie.

"Now, does that convince you, Holland?" asked Polowski. "You think I'd hand my piece over to an idiot like him if I didn't want to talk to you?"

"He's telling the truth," insisted Cathy. "He gave the gun to Ollie. He was willing to take the risk, just to meet you face-to-face."

"Bad move, Polowski," said Victor bitterly. "I'm wanted for murder, remember? Industrial espionage? How do you know I won't just blow you away?"

"'Cause I know you're innocent."

"That makes a difference, does it?"

"It does to me."

"Why?"

"You're caught up in something big, Holland. Something that's going to eat you up alive. Something that's got my supervisor doing backflips to keep me off the case. I don't like being pulled off a case. It hurts my delicate ego."

The two men gazed at each other through the gathering darkness, each sizing up the other.

At last Victor nodded. He looked at Cathy, a quiet plea for forgiveness, for not believing in her. When at last she came into his arms, he felt the world had suddenly gone right again.

He heard a deliberate clearing of a throat. Turning, he saw Polowski hold out his hand. Victor took it in a handshake that could very well be his doom—or his salvation.

"You've led me on a long, hard chase," said Polowski. "I think it's time we worked together."

"Basically," said Ollie, "What we have here is just your simple, everyday mission impossible."

They were assembled in Polowski's hotel room, a five-member team that Milo had just dubbed the "Older, Crazier Out of Tuners," or Old COOTS for short. On the table in the center of the room lay potato chips, beer and the photos detailing Viratek's security system. There was also a map of the Viratek compound, forty acres of buildings and wooded grounds, all of it surrounded by an electrified fence. They had been studying the photos for an hour now, and the job that lay before them looked hopeless.

"No easy way in," said Ollie, shaking his head. "Even if those keypad codes are still valid, you're faced with the human element of recognition. Two guards, two positions. No way they're gonna let you pass."

"There has to be a way," said Polowski. "Come on,

Holland. You're the egghead. Use that creative brain of yours."

Cathy looked at Victor. While the others had tossed ideas back and forth, he had said very little. *And he's the one with the most at stake—his life,* she thought. It took incredible courage—or foolhardiness—even to consider such a desperate move. Yet here he was, calmly scanning the map as though he were planning nothing more dangerous than a Sunday drive.

He must have felt her gaze, for he slung his arm around her and tugged her close. Now that they were reunited, she savored every moment they shared, committed to memory every look, every caress. Soon he could be wrenched away from her. Even now he was making plans to enter what looked like a death trap.

He pressed a kiss to the top of her head. Then, reluctantly, he turned his attention back to the map.

"The electronics I'm not worried about," he said. "It's the human element. The guards."

Milo cocked his head toward Polowski. "I still say ol' J. Edgar here should get a warrant and raid the place."

"Right," snorted Polowski. "By the time that order gets through the judge and Dafoe and your Aunt Minnie's cousin, Viratek'll have that lab turned into a baby-milk factory. No, we need to get in on our own. Without anyone getting word of it." He looked at Ollie. "And you're sure this is the only evidence we'll need?"

Ollie nodded. "One vial should do it. Then we take it to a reputable lab, have them confirm it's smallpox, and your case is airtight."

"They'll have no way around it?"

"None. The virus is officially extinct. Any company caught playing with a live sample is, ipso facto, dead meat."

"I like that," said Polowski. "That ipso facto stuff. No fancy Viratek attorney can argue that one away."

"But first you gotta get hold of a vial," said Ollie. "And from where I'm standing, it looks impossible. Unless we're willing to try armed robbery."

For one frightening moment, Polowski actually seemed to give that thought serious consideration. "Naw," he conceded. "Wouldn't go over well in court."

"Besides which," said Ollie, "I refuse to shoot another human being. It's against my principles."

"Mine, too," said Milo.

"But theft," said Ollie, "that's acceptable."

Polowski looked at Victor. "A group with high moral standards."

Victor grinned. "Holdovers from the sixties."

"Sounds like we're back to the first option," said Cathy. "We have to steal the virus." She focused on the map of the compound, noting the electrified fence that circled the entire complex. The main road led straight to the front gate. Except for an unpaved fire road, labeled *not maintained,* no other approaches were apparent.

"All right," she said. "Assume you do get through the front gate. You still have to get past two locked doors, two separate guards and a laser grid. Come on."

"The doors are no problem," said Victor. "It's the two guards."

"Maybe a diversion?" suggested Milo. "How about we set a fire?"

"And bring in the town fire department?" said Victor. "Not a good idea. Besides, I've dealt with this night guard at the front gate. I know him. And he goes strictly by the book. Never leaves the booth. At the first hint of anything suspicious, he'll hit the alarm button."

"Maybe Milo could whip up a fake security pass," said

Ollie. "You know, the way he used to fix us up with those fake drivers' licenses."

"He falsified IDs?" said Polowski.

"Hey, I just changed the age to twenty-one!" protested Milo.

"Made great passports, too," said Ollie. "I had one from the kingdom of Booga Booga. It got me right past the customs official in Athens."

"Yeah?" Polowski looked impressed. "So what about it, Holland? Would it work?"

"Not a chance. The guard has a master list of top-security employees. If he doesn't know the face, he'll do a double check."

"But he does let some people through automatically?"

"Sure. The bigwigs. The ones he recognizes on—" Victor suddenly paused and turned to stare at Cathy "—on sight. Lord. It just might work."

Cathy took one look at his face and immediately read his mind. "No," she said. "It's not that easy! I need to see the subject! I need molds of his face. Detailed photos from every angle—"

"But you *could* do it. You do it all the time."

"On film it works! But this is face-to-face!"

"It's at night, through a car window. Or through a video camera. If you could just make me pass for one of the exec's—"

"What are you talking about?" demanded Polowski.

"Cathy's a makeup artist. You know, horror films, special effects."

"This is different!" Cathy said. The difference being it was Victor's life on the line. No, he couldn't ask her to do this. If anything went wrong, she would be responsible. Having his death on her conscience would be more than she could live with.

She shook her head, praying he'd read the deadly earnestness in her gaze. "There's too much at stake," she insisted. "It's not as simple as—as filming *Slimelords*!"

"You did *Slimelords*?" asked Milo. "Terrific flick!"

"Besides," said Cathy, "it's not that easy, copying a face. I have to cast a mold, to get the features just right. For that I need a model."

"You mean the real guy?" asked Polowski.

"Right. The real guy. And I hardly think you're going to get some Viratek executive to sit down and let me slap plaster all over his face."

There was a long silence.

"That does present a problem," said Milo.

"Not necessarily."

They all turned and looked at Ollie.

"What are you thinking?" asked Victor.

"About this guy who works with me once in a while. Down in the lab..." Ollie looked up, and the grin on his face was distinctly smug. "He's a veterinarian."

The events of the past few weeks had weighed heavily on Archibald Black, so heavily, in fact, that he found it difficult to carry on with those everyday tasks of life. Just driving to and from his office at Viratek was an ordeal. And then, to sit down at his desk and face his secretary and pretend that nothing, absolutely nothing, was wrong—that was almost more than he could manage. He was a scientist, not an actor.

Not a criminal.

But that's what they would call him, if the experiments in C wing ever came to light. His instinct was to shut the lab down, to destroy the contents of those incubators. But Matthew Tyrone insisted the work continue. They were so close to completion. After all, Defense had underwritten the project, and Defense expected a product. This matter of

Victor Holland was only a minor glitch, soon to be solved. The thing to do was carry on.

Easy for Tyrone to say, thought Black. *Tyrone had no conscience to bother him.*

These thoughts had plagued him all day. Now, as Black packed up his briefcase, he felt desperate to flee forever this teak-and-leather office, to take refuge in some safe and anonymous job. It was with a sigh of relief that he walked out the door.

It was dark when he pulled into his gravel driveway. The house, a saltbox of cedar and glass tucked among the trees, looked cold and empty and in need of a woman. Perhaps he should call his neighbor Muriel. She always seemed to appreciate an impromptu dinner together. Her snappy wit and green Jell-O salad almost made up for the fact she was 75. What a shame his generation didn't produce many Muriels.

He stepped out of his car and started up the path to the front door. Halfway there, he heard a soft *whht!* and almost simultaneously, a sharp pain stung his neck. Reflexively he slapped at it; something came away in his hands. In wonderment, he stared down at the dart, trying to understand where it had come from and how such a thing had managed to lodge in his neck. But he found he couldn't think straight. And then he found he was having trouble seeing, that the night had suddenly darkened to a dense blackness, that his legs were being sucked into some sort of quagmire. His briefcase slipped from his grasp and thudded to the ground.

I'm dying, he thought. And then, *Will anyone find me here?*

It was his last conscious thought before he collapsed onto the leaf-strewn path.

"Is he dead?"

Ollie bent forward and listened for Archibald Black's

breathing. "He's definitely alive. But out cold." He looked up at Polowski and Victor. "Okay, let's move it. He'll be out for only an hour or so."

Victor grabbed the legs, Ollie and Polowski, the arms. Together they carried the unconscious man a few dozen yards through the woods, toward the clearing where the van was parked.

"You—you sure we got an hour?" gasped Polowski.

"Plus or minus," said Ollie. "The tranquilizer's designed for large animals, so the dose was only an estimate. And this guy's heavier than I expected." Ollie was panting now. "Hey, Polowski, he's slipping. Pull your weight, will ya?"

"I am! I think his right arm's heavier than his left."

The van's side door was already open for them. They rolled Black inside and slid the door closed. A bright light suddenly glared, but the unconscious man didn't even twitch.

Cathy knelt down at his side and critically examined the man's face.

"Can you do it?" asked Victor.

"Oh, I can do it," she said. "The question is, will you pass for him?" She glanced up and down the man's length, then back at Victor. "Looks about your size and build. We'll have to darken your hair, give you a widow's peak. I think you'll pass." She turned and glanced at Milo, who was already poised with his camera. "Take your photos. A few shots from every angle. I need lots of hair detail."

As Milo's strobe flashed again and again, Cathy donned gloves and an apron. She pointed to a sheet. "Drape him for me," she directed. "Everything but his face. I don't want him to wake up with plaster all over his clothes."

"Assuming he wakes up at all," said Milo, frowning down at Black's inert form.

"Oh, he'll wake up," said Ollie. "Right where we found him. And if we do the job right, Mr. Archibald Black will never know what hit him."

It was the rain that awakened him. The cold droplets pelted his face and dribbled into his open mouth. Groaning, Black turned over and felt gravel bite into his shoulder. Even in his groggy state it occurred to him that this did not make sense. Slowly he took stock of all the things that were not as they should be: the rain falling from the ceiling, the gravel in his bed, the fact he was still wearing his shoes...

At last he managed to shake himself fully awake. He found to his puzzlement that he was sitting in his driveway, and that his briefcase was lying right beside him. By now the rain had swelled to a downpour—he had to get out of the storm. Half crawling, half walking, Black managed to make it up the porch steps and into the house.

An hour later, huddled in his kitchen, a cup of coffee in hand, he tried to piece together what had happened. He remembered parking his car. He'd taken out his briefcase and apparently had managed to make it halfway up the path. And then...what?

A vague ache worried its way into his awareness. He rubbed his neck. That's when he remembered something strange had happened, just before he blacked out. Something associated with that ache in his neck.

He went to a mirror and looked. There it was, a small puncture in the skin. An absurd thought popped into his head: *Vampires.* Right. *Damn it, Archibald. You are a scientist. Come up with a rational explanation.*

He went to the laundry hamper and fished out his damp shirt. To his alarm he spotted a droplet of blood on the lapel. Then he saw what had caused it: a common, everyday tailor's pin. It was still lodged in the collar, no doubt left there by the dry cleaners. There was his rational explanation. He'd been pricked by a collar pin and the pain had sent him into a faint.

In disgust, he threw the shirt down. First thing in the morning, he was going to complain to the Tidy Girl cleaners and demand they do his suit for free.

Vampires, indeed.

"Even with bad lighting, you'll be lucky if you pass," said Cathy.

She stood back and gave Victor a long, critical look. Slowly she walked around him, eyeing the newly darkened hair, the resculpted face, the new eye color. It was as close as she could make it, but it wasn't good enough. It would never be good enough, not when Victor's life was at stake.

"I think he's the spitting image," said Polowski. "What's the problem now?"

"The problem is, I suddenly realize it's a crazy idea. I say we call it off."

"You've been working on him all afternoon. You got it right down to the damn freckles on his nose. What else can you improve on?"

"I don't know. I just don't feel *good* about this!"

There was a silence as she confronted the four men.

Ollie shook his head. "Women's intuition. That's a dangerous thing to disregard."

"Well, here's *my* intuition," said Polowski. "I think it'll work. And I think it's our best option. Our chance to nail the case."

Cathy turned to Victor. "You're the one who'll get hurt. It's your decision." What she really wanted to say was, *Please. Don't do it. Stay with me. Stay alive and safe and mine.* But she knew, looking into his eyes, that he'd already made his decision, and no matter how much she might wish for it, he would never really be hers.

"Cathy," he said. "It'll work. You have to believe that."

"The only thing I believe," she said, "is that you're going to get killed. And I don't want to be around to watch it."

Without another word, she turned and walked out the door.

Outside, in the parking lot of the Rockabye Motel, she stood in the darkness and hugged herself. She heard the door shut, and then his footsteps moved toward her across the blacktop.

"You don't have to stay," he said. "There's still that beach in Mexico. You could fly there tonight, be out of this mess."

"Do you want me to go?"

A pause, then, "Yes."

She shrugged, a poor attempt at nonchalance. "All right. I suppose it all makes perfect sense. I've done my part."

"You saved my life. At the very least, I owe you a measure of safety."

She turned to him. "Is that what weighs most on your mind, Victor? The fact that you *owe* me?"

"What weighs most on my mind is that you might get caught in the crossfire. I'm prepared to walk through those doors at Viratek. I'm prepared to do a lot of stupid things. But I'm not prepared to watch you get hurt. Does that make any sense?" He pulled her against him, into a place that felt infinitely warm and safe. "Cathy, Cathy. I'm not crazy. I don't want to die. But I don't see any way around this...."

She pressed her face against his chest, felt his heartbeat, so steady, so regular. She was afraid to think of that heart not beating, of those arms no longer alive to hold her. He was brave enough to go through with this crazy scheme; couldn't she somehow dredge up the same courage? She thought, *I've come this far with you. How could I dream of walking away? Now that I know I love you?*

The motel door opened, and light arced across the parking lot. "Gersh?" said Ollie. "It's getting late. If we want to go ahead, we'll have to leave now."

Victor was still looking at her. "Well?" he said. "Do you want Ollie to take you to the airport?"

"No." She squared her shoulders. "I'm coming with you."

"Are you sure that's what you want to do?"

"I'm never sure of anything these days. But on this I've decided. I'll stick it out." She managed a smile. "Besides, you might need me on the set. In case your face falls off."

"I need you for a hell of a lot more than that."

"Gersh?"

Victor reached out for Cathy's hand. She let him take it. "We're coming," he said. "Both of us."

"I'm approaching the front gate. One guard in the booth. No one else around. Copy?"

"Loud and clear," said Polowski.

"Okay. Here I go. Wish me luck."

"We'll be tuned in. Break a leg." Polowski clicked off the microphone and glanced at the others. "Well, folks, he's on his way."

To what? Cathy wondered. She glanced around at the other faces. There were four of them huddled in the van. They'd parked a half mile from Viratek's front gate. Close enough to hear Victor's transmissions, but too far away to do him much good. With the microphone link, they could mark his progress.

They could also mark his death.

In silence, they waited for the first hurdle.

"Evening," said Victor, pulling up at the gate.

The guard peered out through the booth window. He was

in his twenties, cap on straight, collar button fastened. This was Pete Zahn, Mr. By-the-book Extraordinaire. If anyone was to cut the operation short, it would be this man. Victor made a brave attempt at a smile and prayed his mask wouldn't crack. It seemed an eternity, that exchange of looks. Then, to Victor's relief, the man smiled back.

"Working late, Dr. Black?"

"Forgot something at the lab."

"Must be important, huh? To make a special trip at midnight."

"These government contracts. Gotta be done on time."

"Yeah." The guard waved him through. "Have a nice night."

Heart pounding, Victor pulled through the gate. Only when he'd rounded the curve into the empty parking lot did he manage a sigh of relief. "First base," he said into the microphone. "Come on, guys. Talk to me."

"We're here," came the response. It was Polowski.

"I'm heading into the building—can't be sure the signal will get through those walls. So if you don't hear from me—"

"We'll be listening."

"I've got a message for Cathy. Put her on."

There was a pause, then he heard, "I'm here, Victor."

"I just wanted to tell you this. I'm coming back. I promise. Copy?"

He wasn't sure if it was just the signal's waiver, but he thought he heard the beginning of tears in her reply. "I copy."

"I'm going in now. Don't leave without me."

It took Pete Zahn only a minute to look up Archibald Black's license plate number. He kept a Rolodex in the booth, though he seldom referred to it as he had a good memory for numbers. He knew every executive's license by heart. It was his own little mind game, a test of his cleverness. And the plate on Dr. Black's car just didn't seem right.

He found the file card. The auto matched up okay: a gray 1991 Lincoln sedan. And he was fairly certain that *was* Dr. Black sitting in the driver's seat. But the license number was all wrong.

He sat back and thought about it for a while, trying to come up with all the possible explanations. That Black was simply driving a different auto. That Black was playing a joke on him, testing him.

That it hadn't been Archibald Black, at all.

Pete reached for the telephone. The way to find out was to call Black's home. It was after midnight, but it had to be done. If Black didn't answer the phone, then that must be him in the Lincoln. And if he *did* answer, then something was terribly wrong and Black would want to know about it.

Two rings. That's all it took before a groggy voice answered, "Hello?"

"This is Pete Zahn, night man at Viratek. Is this—is this Dr. Black?"

"Yes."

"Dr. *Archibald* Black?"

"Look, it's late! What is it?"

"I don't know how to tell you this, Dr. Black, but..." Pete cleared his throat. "Your double just drove through the gate...."

"I'm through the front door. Heading up the hall to the security wing. In case anyone's listening." Victor didn't expect a reply, and he heard none. The building was a concrete monstrosity, designed to last forever. He doubted a radio signal would make it through these walls. Though he'd been on his own from the moment he'd entered the front gate, at least he'd had the comfort of knowing his friends were listening in on the progress. Now he was truly alone.

He moved at a casual pace to the locked door marked Authorized Personnel Only. A camera hung from the ceiling, its lens pointed straight at him. He pointedly ignored it and turned his attention to the security keypad mounted on the wall. The numbers Jerry had given him had gotten him through the front door; would the second combination get him through this one? His hands were sweating as he punched in the seven digits. He felt a dart of panic as a beep sounded and a message flashed on the screen: *Incorrect security code. Access denied.*

He could feel the sweat building up beneath the mask. Were the numbers wrong? Had he simply transposed two digits? He knew someone was watching him through the camera, wondering why he was taking so long. He took a deep breath and tried again. This time, he entered the digits slowly, deliberately. He braced himself for the warning beep. To his relief, it didn't go off.

Instead, a new message appeared. *Security code accepted. Please enter.*

He stepped through, into the next room.

Third hurdle, he thought in relief as the door closed behind him. Now for the home run.

Another camera, mounted in a corner, was pointed at him. Acutely conscious of that lens, he made his way across the room to the inner lab door. He turned the knob and a warning bell sounded.

Now what? he thought. Only then did he notice the red light glowing over the door, and the warning *Laser grid activated.* He needed a key to shut it off. He saw no other way to deactivate it, no way to get past it, into the room beyond.

It was time for desperate measures, time for a little chutzpah. He patted his pockets, then turned and faced the camera. "Hello?" He waved.

A voice answered over an intercom. "Is there a problem, Dr. Black?"

"Yes. I can't seem to find my keys. I must have left them at home...."

"I can cut the lasers from here."

"Thanks. Gee, I don't know how this happened."

"No problem."

At once the red warning light shut off. Cautiously Victor tried the door; it swung open. He gave the camera a goodbye wave and entered the last room.

Inside, to his relief, there were no cameras anywhere—at least, none that he could spot. A bit of breathing space, he thought. He moved into the lab and took a quick survey of his surroundings. What he saw was a mind-numbing display of space-age equipment—not just the expected centrifuges and microscopes, but instruments he'd never seen before, all of them brand-new and gleaming. He headed through the decontamination chamber, past the laminar flow unit, and went straight to the incubators. He opened the door.

Glass vials tinkled in their compartments. He took one out. Pink fluid glistened within. The label read Lot #341. Active.

This must be it, he thought. This was what Ollie had told him to look for. Here was the stuff of nightmares, the grim reaper distilled to sub-microscopic elements.

He removed two vials, fitted them into a specially padded cigarette case, and slipped it into his pocket. *Mission accomplished,* he thought in triumph as he headed back through the lab. All that lay before him was a casual stroll back to his car. Then the champagne...

He was halfway across the room when the alarm bell went off.

He froze, the harsh ring echoing in his ears.

"Dr. Black?" said the guard's voice over some hidden intercom. "Please don't leave. Stay right where you are."

Victor spun around wildly, trying to locate the speaker. "What's going on?"

"I've just been asked to detain you. If you'll hold on, I'll find out what—"

Victor didn't wait to hear the reason—he bolted for the door. Even as he reached it, he heard the whine of the lasers powering on, felt something slash his arm. He shoved through the first door, dashed across the anteroom and out the security door, into the hallway.

Everywhere, alarms were going off. The whole damn building had turned into an echo chamber of ringing bells. His gaze shot right, to the front entrance. No, not that way—the guard was stationed there.

He sprinted left, toward what he hoped was a fire exit. Somewhere behind him a voice yelled, "Halt!" He ignored it and kept running. At the end of the hall he slammed against the opening bar and found himself in a stairwell. No exit, only steps leading up and down. He wasn't about to be trapped like a rat in the basement. He headed up the stairs.

One flight into his climb, he heard the stairwell door slam open on the first floor. Again a voice commanded, "Halt or I'll shoot!"

A bluff, he thought.

A pistol shot exploded, echoing up the concrete stairwell.

Not a bluff. With new desperation, he pushed through the landing door, into the second-floor hallway. A line of closed doors stretched before him. Which one, which one? There was no time to think. He ducked into the third room and softly shut the door behind him.

In the semidarkness, he spotted the gleam of stainless steel and glass beakers. Another lab. Only this one had a large window, now shimmering with moonlight, looming over the far countertop.

From down the hall came the slam of a door being kicked open and the guard's shouted command: "Freeze!"

He was down to one last escape route. Victor grabbed a chair, raised it over his head, and flung it at the window. The glass shattered, raining moonlight-silvered shards into the darkness below. He scarcely bothered to look before he leapt. Bracing himself for the impact, he jumped from the window and landed in a tangle of shrubbery.

"Halt!" came a shout from above.

That was enough to jar Victor back to his feet. He sprinted off across a lawn, into the cover of trees. Glancing back, he saw no pursuing shadow. The guard wasn't about to risk his neck leaping out any window.

Got to make it out the gate...

Victor circled around the building, burrowing his way through bushes and trees to a stand of oaks. From there he could view the front gate, way off in the distance. What he saw made his heart sink.

Floodlights illuminated the entrance, glaring down on the four security cars blocking the driveway. Now a panel truck pulled up. The driver went around to the back and opened the doors. At his command two German shepherds leaped out and danced around, barking at his feet.

Victor backed away, stumbling deeper into the grove of oaks. *No way out,* he thought, glancing behind him at the fence, topped with coils of barbed wire. Already, the dogs' barking was moving closer. *Unless I can sprout wings and fly, I'm a dead man....*

11

"Something's wrong!" Cathy cried as the first security car drove past.

Polowski touched her arm. "Easy. It could be just a routine patrol."

"No. Look!" Through the trees, they spotted three more cars, all roaring down the road at top speed toward Viratek.

Ollie muttered a surprisingly coarse oath and reached for the microphone.

"Wait!" Polowski grabbed his hand. "We can't risk a transmission. Let him contact us first."

"If he's in trouble—"

"Then he already knows it. Give him a chance to make it out on his own."

"What if he's trapped?" said Cathy. "Are we just going to sit here?"

"We don't have a choice. Not if they've blockaded the front gate—"

"We *do* have a choice!" said Cathy, scrambling forward into the driver's seat.

"What the hell are you doing?" demanded Polowski.

"Giving him a fighting chance. If we don't—"

They all fell instantly silent as a transmission suddenly hissed over the receiver. "Looks like I got myself in a bind, guys. Don't see a way out. You copy?"

Ollie snatched up the microphone. "Copy, Gersh. What's your situation?"

"Bad."

"Specify."

"Front gate's blocked and lit up like a football field. Big time alarms going off. They just brought in the dogs—"

"Can you get over the fence?"

"Negative. It's electrified. Low voltage, but more than ˙can handle. You guys better hit the road without me."

Polowski grabbed the microphone and barked, "Did you get the stuff?"

Cathy turned and snapped: "Forget that! Ask him where he is. *Ask him!*"

"Holland?" said Polowski. "Where are you?"

"At the northeast perimeter. Fence goes all the way around. Look, get moving. I'll manage—"

"Tell him to head for the east fence!" Cathy said. "Near the midpoint!"

"What?"

"Just tell him!"

"Go to the east fence," Polowski said into the microphone. "Midpoint."

"I copy."

Polowski looked up at Cathy in puzzlement. "What the hell are you thinking of?"

"This is a getaway car, right?" she muttered as she turned on the engine. "I say we put it to its intended use!" She threw the van into gear and spun it around, onto the road.

"Hey, you're going the wrong way!" yelled Milo.

"No, I'm not. There's a fire road, just off to the left somewhere. There it is." She made a sharp turn, onto what was little more than a dirt track. They bounced along, crashing through tree branches and shrubs, a ride so violently spine-shaking it was all they could do to hang on.

"How did you find this *wonderful* road?" Polowski managed to ask.

"It was on the map. I saw it when we were studying the plans for Viratek."

"Is this a scenic route? Or does it go somewhere?"

"The east fence. Used to be the construction entrance for the compound. I'm hoping it's still clear enough to get through...."

"And then what happens?"

Ollie sighed. "Don't ask."

Cathy steered around a bush that had sprung up in her path and ran head-on into a sapling. Her passengers tumbled to the floor. "Sorry," she muttered. Reversing gear, she spun them back on the road. "It should be just ahead...."

A barrier of chain link suddenly loomed before them. Instantly she cut the lights. Through the darkness, they could hear dogs barking, moving in. Where was he?

Then they saw him, flitting through the moonlight. He was running. Somewhere off to the side, a man shouted and gunfire spat the ground.

"Brace yourselves!" yelled Cathy. She snapped on her seatbelt and gripped the steering wheel. Then she stepped on the gas.

The van jerked forward like a bronco, barreled through the underbrush, and slammed into the fence. The chain link sagged; electrical sparks hissed in the night. Cathy threw the gears into reverse, backed up, and hit the gas again.

The fence toppled; barbed wire scraped across the windshield.

"We're through!" said Ollie. He yanked open the sliding door and yelled: "Come on, Gersh! Come on!"

The running figure zigzagged across the grass. All around him, gunfire exploded. He made a last flying leap across the coil of barbed wire and stumbled.

"Come on, Gersh!"

Gunfire spattered the van.

Victor struggled back to his feet. They heard the rip of clothing, then he was reaching up to them, being dragged inside, to safety.

The door slammed shut. Cathy backed up, wheeled the van around and slammed on the gas pedal.

They leaped forward, bouncing through the bushes and across ruts. Another round of bullets pinged the van. Cathy was oblivious to it. She focused only on getting them back to the main road. The sound of gunfire receded. At last the trees gave way to a familiar band of blacktop. She turned left and gunned the engine, anxious to put as many miles as possible between them and Viratek.

Off in the distance, a siren wailed.

"We got company!" said Polowski.

"Which way now?" Cathy cried. Viratek lay behind them; the sirens were approaching from ahead.

"I don't know! Just get the hell out of here!"

As yet her view of the police cars was blocked by trees, but she could hear the sirens moving rapidly closer. *Will they let us pass? Or will they pull us over?*

Almost too late she spotted a clearing, off to the side. On sudden impulse she veered off the pavement, and the van bounced onto a stubbly field.

"Don't tell me," groaned Polowski. "Another fire road?"

"Shut up!" she snapped and steered straight for a clump of bushes. With a quick turn of the wheel, she circled behind the shrubbery and cut her lights.

It was just in time. Seconds later, two patrol cars, lights flashing, sped right past the concealing bushes. She sat frozen, listening as the sirens faded in the distance. Then, in the darkness, she heard Milo say softly, "Her name is Bond. Jane Bond."

Half laughing, half crying, Cathy turned as Victor scrambled beside her, onto the front seat. At once she was in his arms, her tears wetting his shirt, her sobs muffled in the depths of his embrace. He kissed her damp cheeks, her mouth. The touch of his lips stilled her tremors.

From the back came the sound of a throat being cleared. "Uh, Gersh?" inquired Ollie politely. "Don't you think we ought to get moving?"

Victor's mouth was still pressed against Cathy's. Reluctantly he broke contact but his gaze never left her face. "Sure," he murmured, just before he pulled her back for another kiss. "But would somebody else mind driving...?"

"Here's where things get dangerous," said Polowski. He was at the wheel now, as they headed south toward San Francisco. Cathy and Victor sat in front with Polowski; in the back of the van, Milo and Ollie lay curled up asleep like two exhausted puppies. From the radio came the soft strains of a country western song. The dials glowed a vivid green in the darkness.

"We've finally got the evidence," said Polowski. "All we need to hang 'em. They'll be desperate. Ready to try anything. From here on out, folks, it's going to be a game of cat and mouse."

As if it wasn't already, thought Cathy as she huddled closer to Victor. She longed for a chance to be alone with him. There had been no time for tearful reunions, no time for any confessions of love. They'd spent the last two hours on a harrowing journey down backroads, always avoiding the police. By now the break-in at Viratek would have been reported to the authorities. The state police would be on the lookout for a van with frontal damage.

Polowski was right. Things were only getting more dangerous.

"Soon as we hit the city," said Polowski, "we'll get those vials off to separate labs. Independent confirmation.

That should wipe any doubts away. You know names we can trust, Holland?''

"Fellow alum back in New Haven. Runs the hospital lab. I can trust him.''

"Yale? Great. That'll have clout.''

"Ollie has a pal at UCSF. They'll take care of the second vial.''

"And when those reports get back, I know a certain journalist who loves to have a little birdie chirp in his ear.'' Polowski gave the steering wheel a satisfied slap. "Viratek, you are dead meat.''

"You enjoy this, don't you?'' said Cathy.

"Workin' the right side of the law? I say it's good for the soul. It keeps your mind sharp and your feet on their toes. It helps you stay young.''

"Or die young,'' said Cathy.

Polowski laughed. "Women. They just never understand the game.''

"I don't understand it, at all.''

"I bet Holland here does. He just had the adrenaline high of his life. Didn't you?''

Victor didn't answer. He was gazing ahead at the black-top stretching before their headlights.

"Well, wasn't it a high?'' asked Polowski. "To claw your way to hell and back again? To know you made it through on nothing much more than your wits?''

"No,'' said Victor quietly. "Because it's not over yet.''

Polowski's grin faded. He turned his attention back to the road. "Almost,'' he said. "It's almost over.''

They passed a sign: San Francisco: 12 Miles.

Four in the morning. The stars were mere pinpricks in a sky washed out by streetlights. In a North Beach doughnut shop, five weary souls had gathered around steaming coffee and cheese Danish. Only one other table was occupied, by a man with bloodshot eyes and shaking hands. The girl behind the counter sat with her nose buried in a paperback. Behind her, the coffee machine hissed out a fresh brew.

"To the Old Coots," said Milo, raising his cup. "Still the best ensemble around."

They all raised their cups. "To the Old Coots!"

"And to our newest and fairest member," said Milo. "The beautiful—the intrepid—"

"Oh, *please,*" said Cathy.

Victor wrapped his arm around her shoulder. "Relax and be honored. Not everyone gets into this highly selective group."

"The only requirement," said Ollie, "is that you have to play a musical instrument badly."

"But I don't play anything."

"No problem." Ollie fished out a piece of waxed paper from the pile of Danishes and wrapped it around his pocket comb. "Kazoo."

"Fitting," said Milo. "Since that was Lily's instrument."

"Oh." She took the comb. Lily's instrument. It always came back to *her,* the ghost who would forever be there. Suddenly the air of celebration was gone, as though swept away by the cold wind of dawn. She glanced at Victor. He was looking out the window, at the garishly lit streets. *What are you thinking? Are you wishing she was here? That it wasn't me being presented this silly kazoo, but her?*

She put the comb to her lips and hummed an appropriately out-of-tune version of "Yankee Doodle." Everyone laughed and clapped, even Victor. But when the applause was over, she saw the sad and weary look in his eyes. Quietly she set the kazoo down on the table.

Outside, a delivery truck roared past. It was 5:00 a.m.; the city was stirring.

"Well, folks," said Polowski, slapping down a dollar tip.

"We got a hotshot reporter to roust outta bed. And then you and I—" he looked at Victor "—have a few deliveries to make. When's United leave for New Haven?"

"At ten-fifteen," said Victor.

"Okay. I'll buy you the plane tickets. In the meantime, you see if you can't grow yourself a new mustache or something." Polowski glanced at Cathy. "You're going with him, right?"

"No," she said, looking at Victor.

She was hoping for a reaction, any reaction. What she saw was a look of relief. And, strangely, resignation.

He didn't try to change her mind. He simply asked, "Where will you be going?"

She shrugged. "Maybe I should stick to our original plan. You know, head south. Hang out with Jack for a while. What do you think?"

It was his chance to stop her. His chance to say, *No, I want you around. I won't let you leave, not now, not ever.* If he really loved her, that's exactly what he would say.

Her heart sank when he simply nodded and said, "I think it's a good idea."

She blinked back the tears before anyone could see them. With an indifferent smile she looked at Ollie. "So I guess I'll need a ride. When are you and Milo heading home?"

"Right now, I guess," said Ollie, looking bewildered. "Seeing as our job's pretty much done."

"Can I hitch along? I'll catch the bus at Palo Alto."

"No problem. In fact, you can sit in the honored front seat."

"Long as you don't let her behind the wheel," grumbled Milo. "I want a nice, quiet drive home if you don't mind."

Polowski rose to his feet. "Then we're all set. Everyone's got a place to go. Let's do it."

Outside, on a street rumbling with early-morning traffic, with their friends standing only a few yards away, Cathy and Victor said their goodbyes. It wasn't the place for sentimental farewells. Perhaps that was all for the best. At least she could leave with some trace of dignity. At least she could avoid hearing, from his lips, the brutal truth. She would simply walk away and hold on to the fantasy that he loved her. That in their brief time together she'd managed to work her way, just a little, into his heart.

"You'll be all right?" he asked.

"I'll be fine. And you?"

"I'll manage." He thrust his hands in his pockets and looked off at a bus idling near the corner. "I'll miss you," he said. "But I know it doesn't make sense for us to be together. Not under the circumstances."

I would stay with you, she thought. *Under any circumstances. If I only knew you wanted me.*

"Anyway," he said with a sigh, "I'll let you know when things are safe again. When you can come home."

"And then?"

"And then we'll take it from there," he said softly.

They kissed, a clumsy, polite kiss, all the more hurried because they knew their friends were watching. There was no passion here, only the cool, dry lips of a man saying goodbye. As they pulled apart, she saw his face blur away through the tears.

"Take care of yourself, Victor," she said. Then, shoulders squared, she turned and walked toward Ollie and Milo.

"Is that it?" asked Ollie.

"That's it." Brusquely she rubbed her hand across her eyes. "I'm ready to go."

"Tell me about Lily," she said.

The first light of dawn was already streaking the sky as they drove past the boxy row homes of Pacifica, past the cliffs where sea waves crashed and gulls swooped and dove.

Ollie, his gaze on the road, asked: "What do you want to know?"

"What kind of woman was she?"

"She was a nice person," said Ollie. "And brainy. Though she never went out of her way to impress people, she was probably the smartest one of all of us. Definitely brighter than Milo."

"And a lot better-looking than Ollie," piped a voice from the backseat.

"A real kind, real decent woman. When she and Gersh got married, I remember thinking, 'he's got himself a saint.'" He glanced at Cathy, suddenly noticing her silence. "Of course," he added quickly, "not every man *wants* a saint. I know I'd be happier with a lady who can be a little goofy." He flashed Cathy a grin. "Someone who might, say, crash a van through an electrified fence, just for kicks."

It was a sweet thing to say, a comment designed to lift her spirits. It couldn't take the edge off her pain.

She settled back and watched dawn lighten the sky. How she needed to get away! She thought about Mexico, about warm water and hot sand and the tang of fresh fish and lime. She would throw herself into working on that new film. Of course, Jack would be on the set, Jack with his latest sweetie pie in tow, but she could handle that now. Jack would never be able to hurt her again. She was beyond that now, beyond being hurt by any man.

The drive to Milo's house seemed endless.

When at last they pulled up in the driveway, the dawn had already blossomed into a bright, cold morning. Milo climbed out and stood blinking in the sunshine.

"So, guys," he said through the car window. "Guess here's where we go our separate ways." He looked at Cathy. "Mexico, right?"

She nodded. "Puerto Vallarta. What about you?"

"I'm gonna catch up with Ma in Florida. Maybe get a load of Disney World. Wanna come, Ollie?"

"Some other time. I'm going to go get some sleep."

"Don't know what you're missing. Well, it's been some adventure. I'm almost sorry it's over." Milo turned and headed up the walk to his house. On the front porch he waved and yelled, "See you around!" Then he vanished through the front door.

Ollie laughed. "Milo and his ma, together? Disney World'll never be the same." He reached for the ignition. "Next stop, the bus station. I've got just enough gas to get us there and—"

He didn't get a chance to turn the key.

A gun barrel was thrust in the open car window. It came to rest squarely against Ollie's temple.

"Get out, Dr. Wozniak," said a voice.

Ollie's reply came out in a bare croak. "What—what do you want?"

"Do it now." The click of the hammer being cocked was all the coaxing Ollie needed.

"Okay, okay! I'm getting out!" Ollie scrambled out and backed away, his hands raised in surrender.

Cathy, too, started to climb out, but the gunman snapped, "Not you! You stay inside."

"Look," said Ollie, "You can have the damn car! You don't need her—"

"But I do. Tell Mr. Holland I'll be in contact. Regarding Ms. Weaver's future." He went around and opened the passenger door. "You, into the driver's seat!" he commanded her.

"No. Please—"

The gun barrel dug into her neck. "Need I ask again?"

Trembling, she moved behind the wheel. Her knee brushed the car keys, still dangling from the ignition. The man slid in beside her. Though the gun barrel was still thrust against her neck, it was the man's eyes she focused on. They were black, fathomless. If any spark of humanity lurked in those depths, she couldn't see it.

"Start the engine," he said.

"Where—where are we going?"

"For a drive. Somewhere scenic."

Her thoughts were racing, seeking some means of escape, but she came up with nothing. That gun was insurmountable.

She turned on the ignition.

"Hey!" yelled Ollie, grabbing at the door. "You can't do this!"

Cathy screamed, "Ollie, no!"

The gunman had already shifted his aim out the window.

"Let her go!" yelled Ollie. "Let her—"

The gun went off.

Ollie staggered backward, his face a mask of astonishment.

Cathy lunged at the gunman. Pure animal rage, fueled by the instinct to survive, sent her clawing first for his eyes. At the last split second he flinched away. Her nails scraped down his cheek, drawing blood. Before he could shift his aim, she grabbed his wrist, wrenching desperately for control of the gun. He held fast. Not with all her strength could she keep the gun at bay, keep the barrel from turning toward her.

It was the last image she registered: that black hole, slowly turning until it was pointed straight at her face.

Something lashed at her from the side. Pain exploded in her head, shattering the world into a thousand slivers of light.

They faded, one by one, into darkness.

12

"Victor's here," said Milo.

It seemed to take Ollie forever to register their presence. Victor fought the urge to shake him to consciousness, to drag the words out of his friend's throat. He was forced to wait, the silence broken only by the hiss of oxygen, the gurgle of the suction tube. At last Ollie stirred and squinted through pain-glazed eyes at the three men standing beside his bed. "Gersh. I didn't—couldn't—" He stopped, exhausted by the effort just to talk.

"Easy, Ollie," said Milo. "Take it slow."

"Tried to stop him. Had a gun..." Ollie paused, gathering the strength to continue.

Victor listened fearfully for the next terrible words to come out. He was still in a state of disbelief, still hoping that what Milo had told him was one giant mistake, that Cathy was, at this very moment, on a bus somewhere to safety. Only two hours ago he'd been ready to board a plane for New Haven. Then he'd been handed a message at the United gate. It was addressed to passenger Sam Polowski, the name on his ticket. It had consisted of only three words: *Call Milo immediately.*

Passenger "Sam Polowski" never did board the plane.

Two hours, he thought in anguish. What have they done to her in those two long hours?

"This man—what did he look like?" asked Polowski.

"Didn't see him very well. Dark hair. Face sort of... thin."

"Tall? Short?"

"Tall."

"He drove off in your car?"

Ollie nodded.

"What about Cathy?" Victor blurted out, his control shattered. "He—didn't hurt her? She's all right?"

There was a pause that, to Victor, seemed like an eternity in hell. Ollie's gaze settled mournfully on Victor. "I don't know."

It was the best Victor could hope for. *I don't know.* It left open the possibility that she was still alive.

Suddenly agitated, he began to pace the floor. "I know what he wants," he said. "I know what I have to give him—"

"You can't be serious," said Polowski. "That's our evidence! You can't just hand it over—"

"That's exactly what I'm going to do."

"You don't even know how to contact him!"

"He'll contact *me.*" He spun around and looked at Milo. "He must've been watching your house all this time. Waiting for one of us to turn up. That's where he'll call."

"If he calls," said Polowski.

"He will." Victor touched his jacket pocket, where the two vials from Viratek still rested. "I have what he wants. He has what I want. I think we're both ready to make a trade."

The sun, glaring and relentless, was shining in her eyes. She tried to escape it, tried to close her lids tighter, to stop those rays from piercing through to her brain, but the light followed her.

"Wake up. *Wake up!*"

Icy water slapped her face. Cathy gasped awake, coughing, rivulets of water trickling from her hair. She struggled to make out the face hovering above her. At first all she saw was a dark oval against the blinding circle of light. Then the man moved away and she saw eyes like black agate, a slash of a mouth. A scream formed in her throat, to be instantly frozen by the cold barrel of a gun against her check.

"Not a sound," he said. "Got that?"

In silent terror she nodded.

"Good." The gun slid away from her cheek and was tucked under his jacket. "Sit up."

She obeyed. Instantly the room began to spin. She sat clutching her aching head, the fear temporarily overshadowed by waves of pain and nausea. The spell lasted for only a few moments. Then, as the nausea faded, she became aware of a second man in the room, a large, broad-shouldered man she'd never before seen. He sat off in a corner, saying nothing, but watching her every move. The room itself was small and windowless. She couldn't tell if it was day or night. The only furniture was a chair, a card table and the cot she was sitting on. The floor was a bare slab of concrete. *We're in a basement,* she thought. She heard no other sounds, either outside or in the building. Were they still in Palo Alto? Or were they a hundred miles away?

The man in the chair crossed his arms and smiled. Under different circumstances, she might have considered that smile a charming one. Now it struck her as frighteningly inhuman. "She seems awake enough," he said. "Why don't you proceed, Mr. Savitch?"

The man called Savitch loomed over her. "Where is he?"

"Who?" she said.

Her answer was met by a ringing slap to her cheek. She sprawled backwards on the cot.

"Try again," he said, dragging her back up to a sitting position. "Where is Victor Holland?"

"I don't know."

"You were with him."

"We—we split up."

"Why?"

She touched her mouth. The sight of blood on her fingers shocked her temporarily into silence.

"Why?"

"He—" She bowed her head. Softly she said, "He didn't want me around."

Savitch let out a snort. "Got tired of you pretty quick, did he?"

"Yes," she whispered. "I guess he did."

"I don't know why."

She shuddered as the man ran his finger down her cheek, her throat. He stopped at the top button of her blouse. *No,* she thought. *Not that.*

To her relief, the man in the chair suddenly cut in. "This is getting us nowhere."

Savitch turned to the other man. "You have another suggestion, Mr. Tyrone?"

"Yes. Let's try using her in a different way." Fearfully Cathy watched as Tyrone moved to the card table and opened a satchel. "Since we can't go to him," he said, "we'll have Holland come to us." He turned and smiled at her. "With your help, of course."

She stared at the cellular telephone he was holding. "I told you. I don't know where he is."

"I'm sure one of his friends will track him down."

"He's not stupid. He wouldn't come for me—"

"You're right. He's not stupid." Tyrone began to punch in a phone number. "But he's a man of conscience. And that's a flaw that's every bit as fatal." He paused, then said into the telephone, "Hello? Mr. Milo Lum? I want you to pass this message to Victor Holland for me. Tell him I have something of his. Something that won't be around much longer..."

"It's him!" hissed Milo. "He wants to make a deal."

Victor shot to his feet. "Let me talk to him—"

"Wait!" Polowski grabbed his arm. "We have to take this slow. Think about what we're—"

Victor pulled his arm free and snatched the receiver from Milo. "This is Holland," he barked into the phone. "Where is she?"

The voice on the other end paused, a silence designed to emphasize just who held the upper hand. "She's with me. She's alive."

"How do I know that?"

"You'll have to take my word for it."

"Word, hell! I want proof!"

Again there was a silence. Then, through the crackle of the line, came another voice, so tremulous, so afraid, it almost broke his heart. "Victor, it's me."

"Cathy?" He almost shouted with relief. "Cathy, are you all right?"

"I'm...fine."

"Where are you?"

"I don't know—I think—" She stopped. The silence was agonizing. "I can't be sure."

"He hasn't hurt you?"

A pause. "No."

She's not telling me the truth, he thought. *He's done something to her...*

"Cathy, I promise. You'll be all right. I swear to you I'll—"

"Let's talk business." The man was back on the line.

Victor gripped the receiver in fury. "If you hurt her, if you just touch her, I swear I'll—"

"You're hardly in a position to bargain."

Victor felt a hand grasp his arm. He turned and met Polowski's gaze. *Keep your head* was the message he saw. *Go along with him. Make a bargain. It's the only way to buy time.*

Nodding, Victor fought to regain control. When he spoke again, his voice was calm. "Okay. You want the vials, they're yours."

"Not good enough."

"Then I'll throw myself into the bargain. A trade. Is that acceptable?"

"Acceptable. You and the vials in exchange for her life."

An anguished cry of *"No!"* pierced the dialogue. It was Cathy, somewhere in the background, shouting, "Don't, Victor! They're going to—"

Through the receiver, Victor heard the thud of a blow, followed by soft moans of pain. All his control shattered. He was screaming now, cursing, begging, anything to make the man stop hurting her. The words ran together, making no sense. He couldn't see straight, couldn't think straight.

Again, Polowski took his arm, gave it a shake. Victor, breathing hard, stared at him through a gaze blurred by tears. Polowski's eyes advised: *Make the deal. Go on.*

Victor swallowed and closed his eyes. *Give me strength,* he thought. He managed to ask, "When do we make the exchange?"

"Tonight. At 2:00 a.m."

"Where?"

"East Palo Alto. The old Saracen Theater."

"But it's closed. It's been closed for—"

"It'll be open. Just you, Holland. I spot anyone else and the first bullet has her name on it. Clear?"

"I want a guarantee! I want to know she'll be—"

He was answered by silence. And then, seconds later, he heard a dial tone.

Slowly he hung up.

"Well? What's the deal?" demanded Polowski.

"At 2:00 a.m. Saracen Theater."

"Half an hour. That barely gives us time to set up a—"

"I'm going alone."

Milo and Polowski stared at him. "Like hell," said Polowski.

Victor grabbed his jacket from out of the closet. He gave the pocket a quick pat; the cigarette case was right where he'd left it. He turned and reached for the door.

"But Gersh!" said Milo. "He's gonna kill you!"

Victor paused in the doorway. "Probably," he said softly. "But it's Cathy's only chance. And it's a chance I have to take."

"He won't come," said Cathy.

"Shut up," Matt Tyrone snapped and shoved her forward.

As they moved down the glass-strewn alley behind the Saracen Theater, Cathy frantically searched her mind for some way to sabotage this fatal meeting. It *would* be fatal, not just for Victor, but for her, as well. The two men now escorting her through the darkness had no intention of letting her live. The best she could hope for was that Victor would survive. She had to do what she could to better his chances.

"He's already got his evidence," she said. "You think he'd give that up just for me?"

Tyrone glanced at Savitch. "What if she's right?"

"Holland's coming," said Savitch. "I know how he thinks. He's not going to leave the little woman behind." Savitch gave Cathy's cheek a deceptively gentle caress. "Not when he knows exactly what we'll do to her."

Cathy flinched away, repelled by his touch. *What if he*

really doesn't come? she thought. *What if he does the sensible thing and leaves me to die?*

She wouldn't blame him.

Tyrone gave her a push up the steps and into the building. "Inside. Move."

"I can't see," she protested, feeling her way along a pitch-black passage. She stumbled over boxes, brushed past what felt like heavy drapes. "It's too dark—"

"Then let there be light," said a new voice.

The lights suddenly sprang on, so bright she was temporarily blinded. She raised her hand to shield her eyes. Through the glare she could make out a third man, looming before her. Beyond him, the floor seemed to drop away into a vast blackness.

They were standing on a theater stage. It was obvious no performer had trod these boards in years. Ragged curtains hung like cobwebs from the rafters. Panels of an old set, the ivy-hung battlements of a medieval castle, still leaned at a crazy tilt against the back wall, framed by a pair of mops.

Tyrone said, "Any problems, Dafoe?"

"None," said the new man. "I've reconned the building. One door at the front, one backstage. The emergency side doors are padlocked. If we block both exits, he's trapped."

"I see the FBI deserves its fine reputation."

Dafoe grinned and dipped his head. "I knew the Cowboy would want the very best."

"Okay, Ms. Weaver." Tyrone shoved Cathy forward, toward a chair placed directly under the spotlight. "Let's put you right where he can see you. Center stage."

It was Savitch who tied her to the chair. He knew exactly what he was doing. She had no hope of working her hands free from such tight, professional knots.

He stepped back, satisfied with his job. "She's not going anywhere," he said. Then, as an afterthought, he ripped off a strip of cloth tape and slapped it over her mouth. "So we don't have any surprises," he said.

Tyrone glanced at his watch. "Zero minus fifteen. Positions, gentlemen."

The three men slipped away into the shadows, leaving Cathy alone on the empty stage. The spotlight beating down on her face was hot as the midday sun. Already she could feel beads of sweat forming on her forehead. Though she couldn't see them, by their voices she could guess the positions of the three men. Tyrone was close by. Savitch was at the back of the theater, near the building's front entrance. And the man named Dafoe had stationed himself somewhere above, in one of the box seats. Three different lines of fire. No route of escape.

Victor, don't be a fool, she thought. *Stay away...*

And if he doesn't come? She couldn't bear to consider that possibility, either, for it meant he was abandoning her. It meant he didn't care enough even to make the effort to save her.

She closed her eyes against the spotlight, against the tears. *I love you. I could take anything, even this, if I only knew you loved me.*

Her hands were numb from the ropes. She tried to wriggle the bonds looser, but only succeeded in rubbing her wrists raw. She fought to remain calm, but with every minute that passed, her heart seemed to pound harder. A drop of sweat trickled down her temple.

Somewhere in the shadows ahead, a door squealed open and closed. Footsteps approached, their pace slow and deliberate. She strained to see against the spotlight's glare, but could make out only the hint of shadow moving through shadow.

The stage floorboards creaked behind her as Tyrone strolled out from the wings. "Stop right where you are, Mr. Holland," he said.

13

Another spotlight suddenly sprang on, catching Victor in its glare. He stood halfway up the aisle, a lone figure trapped in a circle of brilliance.

You came for me! she thought. *I knew, somehow I knew, that you would....*

If only she could shout to him, warn him about the other two men. But the tape had been applied so tightly that the only sound she could produce was a whimper.

"Let her go," said Victor.

"You have something we want first."

"I said, *let her go!*"

"You're hardly in a position to bargain." Tyrone strolled out of the wings, onto the stage. Cathy flinched as the icy barrel of a gun pressed against her temple. "Let's see it Holland," said Tyrone.

"Untie her first."

"I could shoot you both and be done with it."

"Is this what it's come to?" yelled Victor. "Federal dollars for the murder of civilians?"

"It's all a matter of cost and benefit. A few civilians may have to die now. But if this country goes to war, think of all the millions of Americans who'll be saved!"

"I'm thinking of the Americans you've already killed."

"Necessary deaths. But you don't understand that. You've never seen a fellow soldier die, have you, Holland. You don't know what a helpless feeling it is, to watch good boys from good American towns get cut to pieces. With this weapon, they won't have to. It'll be the enemy dying, not us."

"Who gave you the authority?"

"I gave myself the authority."

"And who the hell are *you?*"

"A patriot, Mr. Holland! I do the jobs no one else in the Administration'll touch. Someone says, 'Too bad our weapons don't have a higher kill ratio.' That's my cue to get one developed. They don't even have to ask me. They can claim total ignorance."

"So you're the fall guy."

Tyrone shrugged. "It's part of being a good soldier. The willingness to fall on one's sword. But I'm not ready to do that yet."

Cathy tensed as Tyrone clicked back the gun hammer. The barrel was still poised against her skull.

"As you can see," said Tyrone, "the cards aren't exactly stacked in her favor."

"On the other hand," Victor said calmly, "how do you know I've brought the vials? What if they're stashed somewhere, a publicity time bomb ticking away? Kill her now and you'll never find out."

Deadlock. Tyrone lowered the pistol. He and Victor faced each other for a moment. Then Tyrone reached into his pocket, and Cathy heard the click of a switchblade. "This round goes to you, Holland," he said as he cut the bindings. The sudden rush of circulation back into Cathy's hands was almost painful. Tyrone ripped the tape off her mouth and yanked her out of the chair. "She's all yours!"

Cathy scrambled off the stage. On unsteady legs, she moved up the aisle, toward the circle of the spotlight, toward Victor. He pulled her into his arms. Only by the thud of his racing heart did she know how close he was to panic.

"Your turn, Holland," called Tyrone.

"Go," Victor whispered to her. "Get out of here."

"Victor, he has two other men—"

"Let's have it!" yelled Tyrone.

Victor hesitated. Then he reached into his jacket and pulled out a cigarette case. "They'll be watching me," he whispered. "You move for the door. Go on. *Do it.*"

She stood paralyzed by indecision. She couldn't leave him to die. And she knew the other two gunmen were somewhere in the darkness, watching their every move.

"She stays where she is!" said Tyrone. "Come on, Holland. The vials!"

Victor took a step further, then another.

"No further!" commanded Tyrone.

Victor halted. "You want it, don't you?"

"Put it down on the floor."

Slowly Victor set the cigarette case down by his feet.

"Now slide it to me."

Victor gave the case a shove. It skimmed down the aisle and came to a rest in the orchestra pit.

Tyrone dropped from the stage.

Victor began to back away. Taking Cathy's hand, he edged her slowly up the aisle, toward the exit.

As if on cue, the click of pistol hammers being snapped back echoed through the theater. Reflexively, Victor spun around, trying to sight the other gunmen. It was impossible to see anything clearly against the glare of the spotlight.

"You're not leaving yet," said Tyrone, reaching down for the case. Gingerly he removed the lid. In silence he stared at the contents.

This is it, thought Cathy. *He has no reason to keep us alive, now that he has what he wants....*

Tyrone's head shot up. "Double cross," he said. Then, in a roar, *"Double cross! Kill them!"*

His voice was still reverberating through the far reaches of the theater when, all at once, the lights went out. Blackness fell, so impenetrable that Cathy had to reach out to get her bearings.

That's when Victor pulled her sideways, down a row of theater seats.

"Stop them!" screamed Tyrone in the darkness.

Gunfire seemed to erupt from everywhere at once. As Cathy and Victor scurried on hands and knees along the floor, they could hear bullets thudding into the velvet-backed seats. The gunfire quickly became random, a blind spraying of the theater.

"Hold your fire!" yelled Tyrone. "Listen for them!"

The gunfire stopped. Cathy and Victor froze in the darkness, afraid to give away their position. Except for the pounding of her own pulse, Cathy heard absolute silence. *We're trapped. We make a single move and they'll know where we are.*

Scarcely daring to breathe, she reached back and pulled off her shoe. With a mighty heave, she threw it blindly across the theater. The clatter of the shoe's landing instantly drew a new round of gunfire. In the din of ricocheting bullets, Victor and Cathy scurried along the remainder of the row and emerged in the side aisle.

Again, the gunfire stopped.

"No way out, Holland!" yelled Tyrone. "Both doors are covered! It's just a matter of time...."

Somewhere above, in a theater balcony, a light suddenly flickered on. It was Dafoe, holding aloft a cigarette lighter. As the flame leapt brightly, casting its terrible light against the shadows, Victor shoved Cathy to the floor behind a seat.

"I know they're here!" shouted Tyrone. "See 'em, Dafoe?"

As Dafoe moved the flame, the shadows shifted, revealing new forms, new secrets. "I'll spot 'em any second. Wait. I think I see—"

Dafoe suddenly jerked sideways as a shot rang out. The

flame's light danced crazily on his face as he wobbled for a moment on the edge of the balcony. He reached out for the railing, but the rotten wood gave way under his weight. He pitched forward, his body tumbling into a row of seats.

"Dafoe!" screamed Tyrone. "Who the hell—"

A tongue of flame suddenly slithered up from the floor. Dafoe's lighter had set fire to the drapes! The flames spread quickly, dancing their way along the heavy velvet fabric, toward the rafters. As the first flames touched wood, the fire whooshed into a roar.

By the light of the inferno, all was revealed: Victor and Cathy, cowering in the aisle. Savitch, standing near the entrance, semiautomatic at the ready. And onstage, Tyrone, his expression demonic in the fire's glow.

"They're yours, Savitch!" ordered Tyrone.

Savitch aimed. This time there was no place for them to hide, no shadows to scurry off to. Cathy felt Victor's arm encircle her in a last protective embrace.

The gun's explosion made them both flinch. Another shot; still she felt no pain. She glanced at Victor. He was staring at her, as though unable to believe they were both alive.

They looked up to see Savitch, his shirt stained in a spreading abstract of blood, drop to his knees.

"Now's your chance!" yelled a voice. *"Move, Holland!"*

They whirled around to see a familiar figure silhouetted against the flames. Somehow, Sam Polowski had magically appeared from behind the drapes. Now he pivoted, pistol clutched in both hands, and aimed at Tyrone.

He never got a chance to squeeze off the shot.

Tyrone fired first. The bullet knocked Polowski backward and sent him sprawling against the smoldering velvet seats.

"Get out of here!" barked Victor, giving Cathy a push toward the exit. "I'm going back for him—"

"Victor, you can't!"

But he was on his way. Through the swirling smoke she could see him moving at a half crouch between rows of seats. *He needs help. And time's running out....*

Already the air was so hot it seemed to sear its way into her throat. Coughing, she dropped to the floor and took in a few breaths of relatively smoke-free air. She still had time to escape. All she had to do was crawl up the aisle and out the theater door. Every instinct told her to flee now, while she had the chance.

Instead, she turned from the exit and followed Victor into the maelstrom.

She could just make out his figure, scrambling before a solid wall of fire. She raised her arm to shield her face against the heat. Squinting into the smoke, she crawled forward, moving ever closer to the flames. "Victor!" she screamed.

She was answered only by the fire's roar, and by a sound even more ominous: the creak of wood. She glanced up. To her horror she saw that the rafters were sagging and on the verge of collapse.

Panicked, she scurried blindly forward, toward where she'd last spotted Victor. He was no longer visible. In his place was a whirlwind of smoke and flame. Had he already escaped? Was she alone, trapped in this blazing tinderbox?

Something slapped against her cheek. She stared, at first uncomprehending, at the human hand dangling before her face. Slowly she followed it up, along the bloodied arm, to the lifeless eyes of Dafoe. Her cry of terror seemed to funnel into the fiery cyclone.

"Cathy?"

She turned at the sound of Victor's shout. That's when she saw him, crouching in the aisle just a few feet away.

He had Polowski under the arms and was struggling to drag him toward the exit. But the heat and smoke had taken its toll; he was on the verge of collapse.

"The roof's about to fall!" she screamed.

"Get out!"

"Not without you!" She scrambled forward and grabbed Polowski's feet. Together they hauled their burden up the aisle, across carpet that was already alight with sparks. Step by step they neared the top of the aisle. Only a few yards to go!

"I've got him," gasped Victor. "Go—open the door—"

She rose to a half crouch and turned.

Matt Tyrone stood before her.

"Victor!" she sobbed.

Victor, his face a mask of soot and sweat, turned to meet Tyrone's gaze. Neither man said a word. They both knew the game had been played out. Now the time had come to finish it.

Tyrone raised his gun.

Just as he did, they heard the loud crack of splintering wood. Tyrone glanced up as one of the rafters sagged, spilling a shower of burning tinder.

That brief distraction was all the time Cathy needed. In an act of sheer desperation she lunged at Tyrone's legs, knocking him backward. The gun flew from his grasp and slid off beneath a row of seats.

At once Tyrone was back on his feet. He aimed a savage kick at her. The blow hit her in the ribs, an impact so agonizing she hadn't the breath to cry out. She simply sprawled in the aisle, stunned and utterly helpless to ward off any other blows.

Through the darkness gathering before her eyes, she saw two figures struggling. Victor and Tyrone. Framed against a sea of fire, they grappled for each other's throats. Tyrone threw a punch; Victor staggered back a few paces. Tyrone charged him like a bull. At the last instant Victor side-stepped him and Tyrone met only empty air. He stumbled and sprawled forward, onto the smoldering carpet. Enraged, he rose to his knees, ready to charge again.

The crack of collapsing timber made him glance sky-ward.

He was still staring up in astonishment as the beam crashed down on his head.

Cathy tried to cry out Victor's name but no sound escaped. The smoke had left her throat too parched and swollen. She struggled to her knees. Polowski was lying beside her, groaning. Flames were everywhere, shooting up from the floor, clambering up the last untouched drapes.

Then she saw him, stumbling toward her through that vision of hellfire. He grabbed her arm and shoved her toward the exit.

Somehow, they managed to tumble out the door, dragging Polowski behind them. Coughing, choking, they pulled him across the street to the far sidewalk. There they collapsed.

The night sky suddenly lit up as an explosion ripped through the theater. The roof collapsed, sending up a whoosh of flames so brilliant they seemed to reach to the very heavens. Victor threw his body over Cathy's as the windows in the building above shattered, raining splinters onto the sidewalk.

For a moment there was only the sound of the flames, crackling across the street. Then, somewhere in the distance, a siren wailed.

Polowski stirred and groaned.

"Sam!" Victor turned his attention to the wounded man. "How you doing, buddy?"

"Got...got one helluva stitch in my side...."

"You'll be fine." Victor flashed him a tense grin. "Listen! Hear those sirens? Help's on the way."

"Yeah." Polowski, eyes narrowed in pain, stared up at the flame-washed sky.

"Thanks, Sam," said Victor softly.

"Had to. You...too damn stupid to listen..."

"We got her back, didn't we?"

Polowski's gaze shifted to Cathy. "We—we did okay."

Victor rubbed a hand across his smudged and weary face. "But we're back to square one. I've lost the evidence—"

"Milo..."

"It's all in there." Victor stared across at the flames now engulfing the old theater.

"Milo has it," whispered Sam.

"What?"

"You weren't looking. Gave it to Milo."

Victor sat back in bewilderment. "You mean you *took* them? You took the vials?"

Polowski nodded.

"You—you stupid son of a—"

"Victor!" said Cathy.

"He stole my bargaining chip!"

"He saved our lives!"

Victor stared down at Polowski.

Polowski returned a pained grin. "Dame's got a head on her shoulders," he murmured. "Listen to her."

The sirens, which had risen to a scream, suddenly cut off. Men's shouts at once sliced through the hiss and roar of the flames. A burly fireman loped over from the truck and knelt beside Polowski.

"What've we got here?"

"Gunshot wound," said Victor. "And a wise-ass patient."

The fireman nodded. "No problem, sir. We can handle both."

By the time they'd loaded Polowski into an ambulance the Saracen Theater had been reduced to little more than dying bonfire. Victor and Cathy watched the taillights of the ambulance vanish, heard the fading wail of the siren, the hiss of water on the flames.

He turned to her. Without a word he pulled her into his arms and held her long and hard, two silent figures framed against a sea of smoldering flames and chaos. They were both so weary neither knew which was holding the other up. Yet even through her exhaustion, Cathy felt the magic of that moment. It was eerily beautiful, that last sputtering glow, the reflections dancing off the nearby buildings. Beautiful and frightening and final.

"You came for me," she murmured. "Oh, Victor, I was so afraid you wouldn't...."

"Cathy, you knew I would!"

"I *didn't* know. You had your evidence. You could have left me—"

"No, I couldn't." He buried a kiss in her singed hair. "Thank God I wasn't already on that plane. They'd have had you, and I'd have been two thousand miles away."

Footsteps crunched toward them across the glass-littered pavement. "Excuse me," a voice said. "Are you Victor Holland?"

They turned to see a man in a rumpled parka, a camera slung over his shoulder, watching them.

"Who are you?" asked Victor.

The man held out his hand. "Jay Wallace. *San Francisco Chronicle.* Sam Polowski called me, said there'd be some fireworks in case I wanted to check it out." He gazed at the last remains of the Saracen Theater and shook his head. "Looks like I got here a little too late."

"Wait. *Sam* called you? When?"

"Maybe two hours ago. If he wasn't my ex-brother-in-law, I'd a hung up on him. For days he's been dropping hints he had a story to spill. Never followed through, not once. I almost didn't come tonight. You know, it's a helluva long drive down here from the city."

"He told you about me?"

"He said you had a story to tell."

"Don't we all?"

"Some stories are better than others." The reporter glanced around, searching. "So where is Sam, anyway? Or didn't the Bozo show up?"

"That Bozo," said Victor, his voice tight with anger, "is a goddamn hero. Stick *that* in your article."

More footsteps approached. This time it was two police officers. Cathy felt Victor's muscles go taut as he turned to face them.

The senior officer spoke. "We've just been informed that a gunshot victim was taken to the ER. And that you were found on the scene."

Victor nodded. His look of tension suddenly gave way to one of overwhelming exhaustion. And resignation. He said, quietly, "I was present. And if you search that building, you'll find three more bodies."

"Three?" The two cops glanced at each other.

"Musta been some fireworks," muttered the reporter.

The senior officer said, "Maybe you'd better give us your name, sir."

"My name..." Victor looked at Cathy. She read the message in those weary eyes: *We've reached the end. I have to tell them. Now they'll take me away from you, and God knows when we'll see each other again....*

She felt his hand tighten around hers. She held on, knowing with every second that passed that he would soon be wrenched from her grasp.

His gaze still focused on her face, he said, "My name is Victor Holland."

"Holland... Victor Holland?" said the officer. "Isn't that..."

And still Victor was looking at her. Until they'd clapped on the handcuffs, until he'd been pulled away, toward a waiting squad car, his gaze was locked on her.

She was left anchorless, shivering among the dying embers.

"Ma'am, you'll have to come with us."

She looked up, dazed, at the policeman. "What?"

"Hey, she doesn't have to!" cut in Jay Wallace. "You haven't charged her with anything!"

"Shut up, Wallace."

"I've had the court beat. I know her rights!"

Quietly Cathy said, "It doesn't matter. I'll come with you, officer."

"Wait!" said Wallace. "I wanna talk to you first! I got just a few questions—"

"She can talk to you later," snapped the policeman, taking Cathy by the arm. "*After* she talks to us."

The policemen were polite, even kind. Perhaps it was her docile acceptance of the situation, perhaps they could sense she was operating on her last meager reserves of strength. She answered all their questions. She let them examine the rope burns on her wrists. She told them about Ollie and Sarah and the other Catherine Weavers. And the whole time, as she sat in that room in the Palo Alto police station, she kept hoping she'd catch a glimpse of Victor. She knew he had to be close by. Were they, at that very moment, asking him these same questions?

At dawn, they released her.

Jay Wallace was waiting outside near the front steps. "I have to talk to you," he said as she walked out.

"Please. Not now. I'm tired...."

"Just a few questions."

"I can't. I need to—to—" She stopped. And there standing on that cold and empty street, she burst into tears

"I don't know what to do," she sobbed. "I don't know
how to help him. How to reach him."

"You mean Holland? They've already taken him to San
Francisco."

"What?" She raised her startled gaze to Wallace.

"An hour ago. The big boys from the Justice Department
came down as an escort. I hear tell they're flying him
straight to Washington. First-class treatment all the way."

She shook her head in bewilderment. "Then he's all
right—he's not under arrest—"

"Hell, lady," said Wallace, laughing. "The man is now
a genuine hero."

A hero. But she didn't care what they called him, as long
as he was safe.

She took a deep breath of bitingly chill air. "Do you
have a car, Mr. Wallace?" she asked.

"It's parked right around the corner."

"Then you can give me a ride."

"Where to?"

"To…" She paused, wondering where to go, where Victor would look for her. Of course. Milo's. "To a friend'
house," she said. "I want to be there when Victor calls."

Wallace pointed the way to the car. "I hope it's a long
drive," he said. "I got a lot of gaps to fill in before the
story goes to press."

Victor didn't call.

For four days she sat waiting near the phone, expecting
to hear his voice. For four days, Milo and his mother
brought her tea and cookies, smiles and sympathy. On the
fifth day, when she still hadn't heard from him, those terrible doubts began to haunt her. She remembered that day
by the lake bed, when he'd tried to send her away with
Ollie. She thought of all the words he could have said, but
never had. True, he'd come back for her. He'd knowingly

walked straight into a trap at the Saracen Theater. But wouldn't he have done that for any of his friends? That was the kind of man he was. She'd saved his life once. He remembered his debts, and he paid them back. It had to do with honor.

It might have nothing to do with love.

She stopped waiting by the phone. She returned to her flat in San Francisco, cleaned up the glass, had the windows replaced, the walls replastered. She took long walks and paid frequent visits to Ollie and Polowski in the hospital. Anything to stay away from that silent telephone.

She got a call from Jack. "We're shooting next week," he whined. "And the monster's in terrible shape. All this humidity! Its face keeps melting into green goo. Get down here and do something about it, will you?"

She told him she'd think about it.

A week later she decided. Work was what she needed. Green goo and cranky actors—it was better than waiting for a call that would never come.

She reserved a one-way flight from San José to Puerto Vallarta. Then she packed, throwing in her entire wardrobe. A long stay, that's what she planned, a long vacation.

But before she left, she would drive down to Palo Alto. She had promised to pay Sam Polowski one last visit.

14

(AP) Washington.

Administration spokesman Richard Jungkuntz repeated today that neither the President nor any of his staff had any knowledge of biological weapons research being conducted at Viratek Industries in California. Viratek's Project Cerberus, which involved development of genetically altered viruses, was clearly in violation of international law. Recent evidence, gathered by reporter Jay Wallace of the *San Francisco Chronicle*, has revealed that the project received funds directly authorized by the late Matthew Tyrone, a senior aide to the Secretary of Defense.

In today's Justice Department hearings, delayed four hours because of heavy snowstorms, Viratek president Archibald Black testified for the first time, promising to reveal, to the best of his knowledge, the direct links between the Administration and Project Cerberus. Yesterday's testimony, by former Viratek employee Dr. Victor Holland, has already outlined a disturbing tale of deception, cover-ups and possibly murder.

The Attorney General's office continues to resist demands by Congressman Leo D. Fanelli that a special prosecutor be appointed...

Cathy put down the newspaper and smiled across the hospital solarium at her three friends. "Well, guys. Aren't you lucky to be here in sunny California and not freezing your you-know-what's off in Washington.''

''Are you kidding?'' groused Polowski. ''I'd give anything to be in on those hearings right now. Instead of hooked up to all these—these *doohickeys*.'' He gave his intravenous line a tug, clanging a bottle against the pole.

''Patience, Sam,'' said Milo. ''You'll get to Washington.''

''Ha! Holland's already told 'em the good stuff. By the time they get around to hearing my testimony, it'll be back-page news.''

''I don't think so,'' said Cathy. ''I think it'll be front-page news for a long time to come.'' She turned and looked out the window at the sunshine glistening on the grass. *A long time to come.* That's how long it would be before she'd see Victor again. If ever. Three weeks had already passed since she'd last laid eyes on him. Via Jay Wallace in Washington, she'd heard that it was like a shark-feeding whenever Victor appeared in public, mobs of reporters and federal attorneys and Justice Department officials. No one could get near him.

Not even me, she thought.

It had been a comfort, having these three new friends to talk to. Ollie had bounced back quickly and was discharged—or kicked out, as Milo put it—a mere eight days after being shot. Polowski had had a rougher time of it. Post-operative infections, plus a bad case of smoke inhalation, had prolonged his stay to the point that every day was another trial of frustration for him. He wanted out. He wanted back on the beat.

He wanted a real, honest-to-God cheeseburger and a cigarette.

One more week, the doctors said.

At least there's an end to his waiting in sight, Cathy

thought. *I don't know when I'll see or hear from Victor again.*

The silence was to be expected, Polowski had told her. Sequestration of witnesses. Protective custody. The Justice Department wanted an airtight case, and for that it would keep its star witness incommunicado. For the rest of them, depositions had been sufficient. Cathy had given her testimony two weeks before. Afterward, they'd told her she was free to leave town any time she wished.

Now she had a plane ticket to Mexico in her purse.

She was through with waiting for telephone calls, through with wondering whether he loved her or missed her. She'd been through this before with Jack, the doubts, the fears, the slow but inevitable realization that something was wrong. She knew enough not to be hurt again, not this way.

At least, out of all this pain, I've discovered three new friends. Ollie and Polowski and Milo, the most unlikely trio on the face of the earth.

"Look, Sam," said Milo, reaching into his backpack. "We brought ya something."

"No more hula-girl boxer shorts, okay? Caught hell from the nurses for that one."

"Naw. It's something for your lungs. To remind you to breathe deep."

"Cigarettes?" Polowski asked hopefully.

Milo grinned and held up his gift. "A kazoo!"

"I really needed one."

"You really do need it," said Ollie, opening up his clarinet case. "Seeing as we brought our instruments today and we weren't about to leave you out of this particular gig."

"You're not serious."

"What better place to perform?" said Milo, giving his piccolo a quick and loving rubdown. "All these sick, depressed patients lying around, in need of a bit of cheering up. Some good music."

"Some peace and quiet!" Polowski turned pleading eyes to Cathy. "They're not serious."

She looked him in the eye and took out her kazoo. "Dead serious."

"Okay, guys," said Ollie. "Hit it!"

Never before had the world heard such a rendering of "California, Here I Come!" And, if the world was lucky, never again. By the time they'd played the last note, nurses and patients had spilled into the solarium to check on the source of that terrible screeching.

"Mr. Polowski!" said the head nurse. "If your visitors can't behave—"

"You'll throw 'em out?" asked Polowski hopefully.

"No need," said Ollie. "We're packing up the pipes. By the way, folks, we're available for private parties, birthdays, cocktail hours. Just get in touch with our business manager—" at this, Milo smiled and waved "—to set up your own special performance."

Polowski groaned, "I want to go back to bed."

"Not yet," said the nurse. "You need the extra stimulation." Then, with a sly wink at Ollie, she turned and whisked out of the room.

"Well," said Cathy. "I think I've done my part to cheer you up. Now it's time I hit the road."

Polowski looked at her in astonishment. "You're leaving me with these lunatics?"

"Have to. I have a plane to catch."

"Where you going?"

"Mexico. Jack called to say they're shooting already. So I thought I'd get on down there and whip up a few monsters."

"What about Victor?"

"What about him?"

"I thought—that is—" Polowski looked at Ollie and Milo. Both men merely shrugged. "He's going to miss you."

"I don't think so." She turned once again to gaze out the window. Below, in the walkway, an old woman sat in a wheelchair, her wan face turned gratefully to the sun. Soon Cathy would be enjoying that very sunshine, somewhere on a Mexican beach.

By their silence, she knew the three men didn't know what to say. After all, Victor was their friend, as well. They couldn't defend or condemn him. Neither could she. She simply loved him, in ways that made her decision to leave all the more right. She'd been in love before, she knew that the very worst thing a woman can sense in a man is indifference.

She didn't want to be around to see it in Victor's eyes.

Gathering up her purse, she said, "Guys, I guess this is it."

Ollie shook his head. "I really wish you'd hang around. He'll be back any day. Besides, you can't break up our great little quartet."

"Sam can take my place on the kazoo."

"No way," said Polowski.

She planted a kiss on his balding head. "Get better. The country needs you."

Polowski sighed. "I'm glad somebody does."

"I'll write you from Mexico!" She slung her purse over her shoulder and turned. One step was all she managed before she halted in astonishment.

Victor was standing in the doorway, a suitcase in hand. He cocked his head. "What's this about Mexico?"

She couldn't answer. She just kept staring at him, thinking how unfair it was that the man she was trying so hard to escape should look so heartbreakingly wonderful.

"You got back just in time," said Ollie. "She's leaving."

"What?" Victor dropped his suitcase and stared at her in dismay. Only then did she notice his wrinkled clothes, the day-old growth of beard shadowing his face. The toe of a sock poked out from a corner of the closed suitcase.

"You can't be leaving," he said.

She cleared her throat. "It was unexpected. Jack needs me."

"Did something happen? Is there some emergency?"

"No, it's just that they're filming and, oh, things are a royal mess on the set...." She glanced at her watch, a gesture designed to speed her escape. "Look, I'll miss my plane. I promise I'll give you a call when I get to—"

"You're not his only makeup artist."

"No, but—"

"He can do the movie without you."

"Yes, but—"

"Do you *want* to leave? Is that it?"

She didn't answer. She could only look at him mutely, the anguish showing plainly in her eyes.

Gently, firmly, he took her hand. "Excuse us, guys," he said to the others. "The lady and I are going for a walk."

Outside, leaves blew across the brown winter lawn. They walked beneath a row of oak trees, through patches of sun and shadow. Suddenly he stopped and pulled her around to face him.

"Tell me now," he said. "What gave you this crazy idea of leaving?"

She looked down. "I didn't think it made much difference to you."

"Wouldn't make a *difference?* Cathy, I was climbing the walls! Thinking of ways to get out of that hotel room and back to you! You have no idea how I worried. I wondered if you were safe—if this whole crazy mess was really over.

The lawyers wouldn't let me call out, not until the hearings were finished. I did manage to sneak out and call Milo's house. No one answered.''

"We were probably here, visiting Sam."

"And I was going crazy. They had me answering the same damn questions over and over again. And all I could think of was how much I missed you." He shook his head. "First chance I got, I flew the coop. And got snowed in for hours in Chicago. But I made it. I'm here. Just in time, it seems." Gently he took her by the shoulders. "Now. Tell me. Are you still flying off to Jack?"

"I'm not leaving for Jack. I'm leaving for *myself*. Because I know this won't work."

"Cathy, after what we've been through together, we can make *anything* work."

"Not—not this."

Slowly he let his hands drop, but his gaze remained on her face. "That night we made love," he said softly. "That didn't tell you something?"

"But it wasn't *me* you were making love to! You were thinking of Lily—"

"*Lily?*" He shook his head in bewilderment. "Where does she come in?"

"You loved her so much—"

"And you loved Jack once. Remember?"

"I fell out of love. You never did. No matter how much I try, I'll never measure up to her. I won't be smart enough or kind enough—"

"Cathy, stop."

"I won't be *her*."

"I don't want you to be her! I want the woman who'll hang off fire escapes with me and—and drag me off the side of the road. I want the woman who saved my life. The woman who calls herself average. The woman who doesn't know just how extraordinary she really is." He took her face in his hands and tilted it up to his. "Yes, Lily was a wonderful woman. She was wise and kind and caring. But she wasn't you. And she and I—we weren't the perfect couple. I used to think it was my fault, that if I were just a better lover—"

"You're a wonderful lover, Victor."

"No. Don't you see, it's *you*. You bring it out in me. All the want and need." He pulled her face close to his and his voice dropped to a whisper. "When you and I made love that night, it was like the very first time for me. No, it was even better. Because I loved you."

"And I loved you," she whispered.

He pulled her into his arms and kissed her, his fingers burrowing deep into her hair. "Cathy, Cathy," he murmured. "We've been so busy trying to stay alive we haven't had time to say all the things we should have...."

His arms suddenly stiffened as a startling round of applause erupted above them. They looked up. Three grinning faces peered down at them from a hospital balcony.

"Hit it, boys!" yelled Ollie.

A clarinet, piccolo and kazoo screeched into concert. The melody was doubtful. Still, Cathy thought she recognized the familiar strains of George Gershwin. "Someone to Watch Over Me."

Victor groaned. "I say we try this again, but with a different band. And no audience."

She laughed. "Mexico?"

"Definitely." He grabbed her hand and pulled her toward a taxi idling at the curb.

"But, Victor!" she protested. "What about our luggage? All my clothes—"

He cut her off with another kiss, one that left her dizzy and breathless and starved for more.

"Forget the luggage," she whispered. "Forget everything. "Let's just go...."

They climbed into the taxi. That's when the band on the hospital balcony abruptly switched to a new melody, one Cathy didn't at first recognize. Then, out of the muddy strains, the kazoo screeched out a solo that, for a few notes, was perfectly in tune. They were playing *Tannhäuser*. Wedding music!

"What the hell's that terrible noise?" asked the taxi driver.

"Music," said Victor, grinning down at Cathy. "The most beautiful music in the world."

She fell into his arms, and he held her there.

The taxi pulled away from the curb. But even as they drove away, even as they left the hospital far behind them, they thought they could hear it in the distance: the sound of Sam Polowski's kazoo, playing one last fading note of farewell.

Take 2 of "The Best of the Best™" Novels FREE

Plus get a FREE surprise gift!

Special Limited-Time Offer

Mail to The Best of the Best™

3010 Walden Avenue
P.O. Box 1867
Buffalo, N.Y. 14240-1867

YES! Please send me 2 free novels and my free surprise gift. Then send me 3 of "The Best of the Best™" novels each month. I'll receive the best books by the world's hottest romance authors. Bill me at the low price of $4.24 each plus 25¢ delivery per book and applicable sales tax, if any.* That's the complete price, and a saving of over 20% off the cover prices—quite a bargain! I understand that accepting the books and gift places me under no obligation ever to buy any books. I can always return a shipment and cancel at any time. Even if I never buy another book, the 2 free books and the surprise gift are mine to keep forever.

183 MEN CH74

Name	(PLEASE PRINT)
Address	Apt. No.
City	State Zip

This offer is limited to one order per household and not valid to current subscribers.
*Terms and prices are subject to change without notice. Sales tax applicable in N.Y.
All orders subject to approval.

UBOB-98   ©1996 MIRA BOOKS